Terrance wasn't sure it was Rachel

The woman's back was turned toward him, so he was unable to see if she possessed the expressive eyes that lingered in his memory. Finally she turned and he saw that it was indeed her. His throat felt tight, almost dry as he watched her smile. There was something beguilingly sexy about her smile.

Defying his better judgment, he moved slowly toward her. Rachel spotted him before he could speak, and that wide sexy mouth of hers broke into a welcoming grin. His muscles tightened, his dark suit suddenly felt too warm for the pleasant summer evening. Then Terrance knew he was in trouble—just as he had known it when he'd first learned she was divorced. The discovery had thrown him off balance.

Now, as Rachel held out her hand to greet him, Terrance felt as if he was treading the fine line between his usually reliable common sense— and what?

ABOUT THE AUTHOR

Judith Yoder decided at age thirty that she wasn't going to deny herself anymore her lifelong secret desire to write professionally. With that decision made, and with the help of an encouraging husband, Judy had her first romance novel published in 1984. And she hasn't stopped writing since. Judy makes her home in Virginia with her husband and two children.

September Glow
Judith Yoder

Harlequin Books

TORONTO • NEW YORK • LONDON
AMSTERDAM • PARIS • SYDNEY • HAMBURG
STOCKHOLM • ATHENS • TOKYO • MILAN

To Mary, Sara and Tommye:
For your help, encouragement and friendship

Published December 1987

First printing October 1987

ISBN 0-373-16228-6

Chapter One

Rachel Bonner sometimes had to wonder how it became her lot in life to ask men like Gordon Nelson for money. As the somber executive sitting behind the solid cherry desk droned on in a monologue riddled with if onlys, and a few too many unfavorable economic climates, Rachel struggled to hide her growing dismay behind a poised mask of rapt attention.

Were cushy profit margins all these Harvard M.B.A. types lived for? What about truth, beauty, art? The answer to her own question was too exasperating to dwell on.

For Rachel, soliciting large contributions from local corporations was the most difficult part of her job as assistant curator of the Wrentham Museum. She considered it a necessary evil, and much preferred to leave such work to the museum's professional fund-raisers whenever possible.

But now, face-to-face with the surprisingly young president of Nelson Business Machines, Rachel refused to allow even the slightest glimmer of retreat to shadow her determined green eyes. She desperately needed last-minute additional funding for an extensive exhibit of Hudson River school paintings scheduled at the Wrentham's picture gallery—a project that had been her baby from the start. She'd be damned if she would allow a visionless microchip vendor to keep her from making this exhibit as complete as she knew it could be.

"Mr. Nelson, need I remind you of how devoted this city is to the heritage of American art? The Hudson River school artists were the first group in this country to establish a uniquely American style of landscape painting," she explained, trying to maintain her professional dignity. "This visiting exhibit will be the most comprehensive collection of these landscapes to be shown in the Boston area."

Her argument was met by an ice-blue stare, which felt as chilly to Rachel as the office's air-conditioning. She knew it was time to try another tactic, albeit one she was sure Nelson had heard before. Still, it was known to be effective.

"This exhibit will probably garner a great deal of publicity in the New England press. Just think of the goodwill Nelson Business Machines will derive—not to mention the tax benefits if you help underwrite the costs."

Rachel's stomach turned with distaste as she spoke. Fund-raising was a thorny business, she contemplated warily as all the lovely paintings she was so eager to present to the public paraded in her mind.

"Of course, all that has been taken into consideration, Mrs. Bonner," Gordon Nelson finally said.

Of course. Rachel wanted to pack it in right then and there, escape Nelson's office, stop off at the Brighams on the corner for the solace of a chocolate frappe and then drive home to be both mommy and daddy to her young son. But as always had been the case in the course of her thirty-one years, Rachel Bonner knew her only choice was to tough it out. Time was just too short; the exhibit was scheduled to open in less than a month.

"Considering your company's well-known support of the arts in this community, I'm puzzled as to why—"

"That reputation belongs to my father's regime as Nelson's president, Mrs. Bonner. When he was running the company on a day-to-day basis, Terrance Nelson rightfully earned the reputation as benefactor to many different causes. But six months ago he turned the business over to me. And quite honestly, I'm not as inclined to give away company money as freely as my father did. As our PR department would have been happy to explain to you, Mrs. Bonner, we now have a set budget for charitable contributions." Nelson paused, clasping his hands together on his desk in a practiced gesture of conclusion. "In the case of your exhibit, the numbers just don't fit."

Too bad this wasn't a case of like father like son, she thought dismally. In fact, the father's reputation for generously supporting the arts was what initially had drawn her to Nelson Business Machines. The word among her network of professional contacts was that Terrance Nelson was a genuine knight in shining armor when it came to rescuing financially troubled arts projects.

At least, that was the advice she had received. And it was why she used every contact her boss, John Hollings, could muster in order to sidestep Nelson's PR people and speak to the president of the company directly. Although she was aware that Gordon had been made company president, who could have known that Terrance Nelson's son would turn out to be a numbers cruncher?

"Let's see if we can make the numbers work for you, Mr. Nelson," Rachel suggested, refusing to give up just yet. As she dug inside her brown leather satchel for a hand calculator, Gordon Nelson's telephone rang out in bubbly high-tech tones.

"Can't you handle that?" she overheard him impatiently query his caller. "All right, all right. I'll be right down."

Rachel's heart sank. He was going to get away from her.

"A matter down in R & D needs my immediate attention, Mrs. Bonner. You'll have to excuse me." Nelson strode quickly toward the office door. "I shouldn't be more than a few minutes, if you'd care to wait. Then we can take a look at your numbers." He cracked a polite, sliver-thin smile—his first since Rachel had arrived.

"I'll wait," she replied as the young man departed, leaving his office door wide open. She was just relieved that he hadn't altogether dismissed her.

Still, Rachel wasn't very optimistic about her chances of winning over Gordon Nelson. She tapped the small keys of her calculator while jotting down some pertinent figures on a large pad of yellow paper. She studied the numbers for several minutes before shifting her attention to the comfortable elegance of Nelson's sizable wood-paneled office.

It just didn't seem to suit the guarded and aloof young executive with whom she had just been haggling. The room was conservatively furnished with traditional but quite handsome cherry pieces. A huge floor-to-ceiling window provided a sense of open airiness with its panoramic view of the glistening Boston Harbor. Deep burgundy and navy upholstery and fine old Persian rugs lent the office a warm, welcoming character—a personality that certainly didn't reflect its inhabitant. Some interior designer must have used a lot of creative imagination in decorating this room for Gordon Nelson.

Rachel found herself attracted to the enlarged framed photographs hanging so prominently on the walls. She thought photographs were a refreshing change from the usual uninspired office prints, and these were particularly gorgeous. Drawn by the rich, luscious color of the photo landscapes, she walked over to inspect them closer.

The pictures of mountains and valleys all had an ethereal quality that captured, quite romantically, the essence of what she thought she recognized as the Berkshire area of western Massachusetts. She wondered who took these pictures. He or she certainly had a distinctive style.

After gazing at the photographs for a while, Rachel casually glanced at her wristwatch. Good Lord! Gordon Nelson had been gone for almost thirty minutes. Renewed anxiety about losing Nelson's ear rushed over her, and she nervously returned to the reality of her calculator and the yellow paper scribbled with numbers.

Still a bit tense after her difficult first meeting with the man, she sat stiffly in front of his desk. She just stared at that yellow paper hoping the jumble of numbers would jell into an irrefutable reason for Nelson to donate thousands of dollars to the Wrentham's Picture Gallery. She stared at the numbers until they blurred before her eyes.

Feeling restless, Rachel leaned her elbows on Nelson's desk and bent her head lazily. She wondered if the air-conditioning was malfunctioning. The once chilly blast, which had previously produced goose bumps on her bare arms, seemed now to have had wilted into a tepid breeze. Rachel's fingers reached to lift the heavy weight of her dark auburn hair off her neck. A wisp of cool air grazed her damp skin.

Maybe her nerves were just getting the better of her. Rachel knew that only her skills of persuasion, not a compilation of figures, would convince Gordon Nelson to give the museum money. She would just have to keep trying, she told herself, scarcely hearing her own weary sigh.

"It can't be all that bad."

Rachel spun her head around at once, jolted by the masculine voice's sudden intrusion into her private thoughts. "What?" her voice cracked with surprise at seeing the mature dark-haired man standing in the office doorway.

"Sorry I startled you. I should have knocked, but up until six months ago this was my office," the man explained with a refined, Harvard-laced enunciation that bespoke of New England old money. "I usually forget and just come breezing in here, much to my son's consternation, I'm afraid."

Rachel stood up at once. "Son's office? You're Terrance Nelson?"

"Yes. And you?" he asked kindly, his light blue eyes regarding her carefully.

"Rachel Bonner. I'm—"

"A friend of Gordon's?" he inserted promptly, his eyes still focused squarely on her. "I'm sure we haven't met before; I wouldn't forget meeting such a lovely young woman."

The father certainly made up for all the charm and finesse his son lacked, Rachel noted wryly. The uneasiness she immediately had felt in Gordon's presence was remarkably absent now. Although Terrance's gaze was still intently upon her, she didn't feel uncomfortable at all. In fact, the gracious glint in his grayish blue eyes seemed to calm her edginess.

Intrigued, Rachel desperately tried to recall what her boss had told her about Terrance Nelson. But all she could remember was that his computer company, one of the largest in the country, was at the peak of success when his wife died rather suddenly several years ago.

Before Rachel had a chance to explain why she was waiting in his son's office, Gordon's secretary entered the room carrying a stack of mail in her hands.

"Mrs. Bonner, I'm afraid Mr. Nelson has been held up at Research and Development," the secretary announced without looking up. "And then he has an important luncheon meeting. He asked if you could come back later this afternoon, or perhaps another—oh! Mr. Nelson. I didn't see you come in," the graying woman sputtered with embarrassment.

"My fault, entirely, Mrs. Payne. I snuck by you."

Realizing she was being teased, the secretary smiled with relief. "Oh, Mr. Nelson, we have missed you while you were away. Your son was suddenly called down to R & D. He wasn't expecting you, was he?"

"No, I just arrived back from London yesterday. I wanted to discuss our presentation at the trade show there with him. And Mrs. Payne, why is my son so rudely deserting Mrs. Bonner, here?"

"Oh, Mr. Nelson, I forgot my manners," the older woman gushed. "Have you met Mrs. Bonner from the Wrentham Museum? She's here to discuss *business* with Mr. Gordon Nelson, but as I mentioned before he was called away."

Terrance turned to Rachel. "Just here on business? My son's loss, I assure you."

The sentiment behind the man's richly intoned compliment was so genuine, Rachel couldn't suppress a slight smile of pleasure. "I'm afraid your son would be just as happy to be rid of me. You see, I've come asking for money for an upcoming exhibit at the Wrentham Picture Gallery."

"Hmm. And Gordon's being difficult."

"I'm afraid so."

"That's my boy," Terrance said with noticeable exasperation.

At that moment, Mrs. Payne pointedly coughed as a tactful reminder of her presence. "Mrs. Bonner, shall I set aside an afternoon appointment for you with Mr. Nelson?"

"Well . . . yes, I suppose." How long was this agony going to be dragged out? Rachel wondered.

"Good for you," Terrance cheered. "Don't give up on Gordon yet."

Rachel shrugged. "I can't afford to give up."

"Mrs. Payne, what time is Gordon expected back?"

"Two-thirty, sir."

"An appointment at two-thirty?" he asked Rachel. At her nod of agreement, Terrance turned to the secretary. "Please put Mrs. Bonner down for two-thirty, Mrs. Payne."

Once the secretary had left, Terrance again turned to Rachel. "Are you requesting funding for a specific exhibit at the museum, Mrs. Bonner?"

Rachel nodded. "A Hudson River school showing that's scheduled to open at the end of the month. Some additional paintings are now available to us, but we need extra funds for transporting, insurance, security."

Terrance's eyes lit up. "Ah, the Hudson River school. Lovely. You better not give up on Gordon."

"I'll do my best."

Leaning his tall, slim frame against the edge of the desk, Terrance took a long, careful look at Rachel, much as if he were making an accounting of her mettle. "I'm sure you will."

He then took a deep breath. "Some would hold me responsible for my son's shoddy manners, so the least I can do is to take you to lunch to make up for Gordon's behavior. Besides, I'd love to discuss this exhibit with you further."

Rachel glanced at her watch, telling herself she didn't really want to go all the way back to the museum in Brookline just to turn around again to come back. As if that mattered at all. There was no question that lunch with Terrance Nelson would be immensely enjoyable: a reviving antidote for the tense morning she had just turned in. "I'd love to join you for lunch."

"Wonderful," Terrance said. Then he glanced at the calculator, papers and pens she had scattered on top of Gordon's desk. "Why don't you gather your paraphernalia here, while I go out to have a brief word with Mrs. Payne. Then I'll be right back for you."

Watching him stroll smoothly toward the door, Rachel realized that even with his hands stuck carelessly in his pants pockets, Terrance Nelson moved with an unstudied grace.

"Mrs. Payne," Terrance began before he was out the office door, "I thought Gordon was going to have this office redecorated. It looks exactly the same as the day I left it."

Hearing that, Rachel again looked around the office that once had been Terrance's. And suddenly, the elegance, the warmth and the welcoming of the room all seemed to make sense.

ALTHOUGH THE TEMPERATURE outdoors was rising to unseasonable highs for the early Boston summer, Rachel was feeling cool and relaxed as she sat across a round table from Terrance. The small Italian restaurant he had taken her to in the city's North End was surprisingly quiet and unhurried during the height of the lunch hour. She was still nursing the single glass of pale crisp wine she had limited herself to when the waiter inquired about dessert.

"Rachel? They make some marvelous pastries right here in the kitchen," Terrance informed her.

"Sounds awfully tempting, but dessert is one thing my body can't afford after this huge lunch."

"You shouldn't worry. You have a lovely figure."

"And you're a lovely man for saying that," she said lightly, believing—just for a moment—those eight pounds she had so stupidly gained over the past winter had miraculously dissolved. "I'll just have coffee, thanks."

After sending the waiter off with an order for two coffees, Terrance returned the full friendly force of his blue eyes to Rachel. "So now that we've discussed your museum's exhibit and my recent business trip to London, why don't you tell me a little more about yourself?"

"Well, I've already told you something about my job—"

"Yes, yes. But tell me about your family. Let's see, you're married. Any children?"

Married? She'd never said anything about being married. Yet she did recall Mrs. Payne addressing her as Mrs. Bonner. She hurried to explain. "I have a son who'll turn eight next week, but I've been divorced for about seven years now."

His eyes flashed with awkward surprise. Then his gaze held hers for a confusing moment, as if he felt uncomfortable with her single status. He glanced down at her ringless left hand, which was playing with the stem of her wineglass.

"I'm sorry," Terrance said with a slight trace of embarrassment. "I should have realized."

"It was a natural mistake," she offered kindly, feeling vaguely disappointed with his uneasy reaction. "I kept the 'Mrs. Bonner' for Danny's sake. I think it helps for mother and son to have the same last name."

"I think you're quite right about that," he said with a seemingly distracted air.

The apparent ambivalence in his eyes was unnerving to say the least. The lighthearted mood had suddenly evaporated, and Rachel wasn't sure why. Not a word was spoken between them while the waiter served the coffee in colorful handmade earthen cups. For Rachel, this silence only emphasized the sudden shift of mood.

She watched Terrance closely as he discussed the lunch check with the waiter. The gentle crinkles near his crystal blue-gray eyes and the laugh lines at the corners of his lips lit his tanned face with appealing character. Clearly, Terrance Nelson was a man who lived life fully. Fun and laughter were probably not strangers to him, Rachel surmised.

Then she noticed how the gradually silvering sideburns of his trim, almost black hair framed his handsome patrician Yankee features. His face was angular without being overly sharp. His straight nose fit his face perfectly, adding to the man's already dignified air. The expression in his eyes when they'd first met had been straightforward, yet warm. But it was the easy, even smile of his that had appealed to her.

As Terrance sipped his hot coffee, his gaze seemed to recover from its brief bit of confusion. It was once again forthright and friendly, and Rachel felt comfortable again. She appreciated the seemingly effortless way he made her feel at ease.

"For you to have an eight-year-old, you must have married rather young," he said.

"Yes, I was still in college. Greg and I were high school sweethearts."

"So were Eleanor and I. We married at nineteen and had both our sons by the time we were twenty-six. Those were crazy, hectic years," Terrance observed with a wistful tone. "My wife passed away five years ago."

"You still miss her."

Terrance smiled gently. "I've just gotten used to living alone this past year or so. Until then I buried myself in my work. I'm okay now, and I want to make up for all the things I missed when I was working eighteen-hour days. That's why I turned the day-to-day business over to Gordon."

"That's quite an expression of faith in your son."

"Although we differ on many things, Gordon and I are in solid agreement about the direction and goals of the company. Having built that business with my own two hands, I find his enthusiasm for it gratifying," Terrance explained. "Yes, Gordon will do just fine with the company. He has ideas and he's motivated. He knows what he wants to do. I wish I could say the same for Kerry."

"Your younger son?"

Terrance nodded. "His mother's death hit him particularly hard. He's sort of been drifting these past few years and I just couldn't find a way to help him. I tried to get him interested in the business—to give him something to focus his energies on."

Rachel could sense Terrance's deep concern for his son as well as his frustration over his inability to help Kerry.

"Sounds as if you both were having a tough time," she offered kindly.

"We were. But things are better now. For both of us," he added with a shrug and a quick smile. "In fact, Kerry finally graduated from college in May. He's even following in his old man's steps in one respect. He's just become engaged to his childhood sweetheart. Now Kerry will join the company soon. I'm sure of it."

Yet Rachel thought she caught a glimmer of uncertainty in Terrance's eyes. Maybe he wasn't as sure of his son's plans as he sounded.

Terrance shifted his long, lean body in his chair and quickly changed the subject. "But what about you?" he asked. "Raising a young boy all by yourself can't be easy."

"It's crazy and hectic, as you put it. But we manage. And Danny has lots of contact with his father what with holidays and weekend visits. They're very close, and he gets along well with his stepmother. That means so much."

It sounded so smoothly efficient and simple, but Rachel could never forget the difficult, lonely years when she had been both studying for her M.F.A. and interning at the Smithsonian. Newly divorced, she had left her family and friends behind in Boston. Except for her baby, Rachel was completely alone and on her own for the first time in her life. Looking back, Rachel now believed that she had survived the more desolate days of those years in Washington through sheer strength of will. But survive she did.

"So your son will be eight soon," Terrance commented, pulling Rachel back to the present. "What have you planned for his birthday?"

Her talk with Terrance brightened considerably when Rachel began comparing the increasingly elaborate state of affairs regarding eight-year-olds' birthday parties with Terrance's memories of the simple pin the tail on the donkey and musical chairs variety of his sons' childhoods. Before they knew it, another hour had passed, and Rachel had to hurry back to keep her appointment with Gordon Nelson.

As they wove their way through the winding narrow streets of Boston's financial district, Rachel was very much aware of the man walking beside her. He looked so straight and tall in his exquisite gray suit. He was almost protective in the way he guided her along the sidewalk with gentle touches on her elbow and back. These were the rather courtly manners that men of Terrance's generation took for granted. All Rachel knew was that he was making her feel special. And for a woman who had been fighting the jungle of daily life on her own for almost seven years, feeling special was a pleasant change of pace.

Terrance escorted her into the Nelson Building, and while they rode an elevator up to the penthouse offices, Rachel couldn't help but speculate about him. His personality was so different from his son's. She and Gordon had clashed immediately while she and Terrance had seemed to take to each other right away. Terrance was the type of person she'd like to get to know better, a man she'd like to have for a friend. As the elevator zoomed upward, Rachel stole another glance at the man standing beside her. Small chance of that, she thought regretfully. She doubted she'd ever see Terrance Nelson again after today.

"Now, Rachel," Terrance said, stopping a few feet short of his son's office door, "don't let Gordon intimidate you. He's a shrewd, bright fellow and very stubborn."

"I'll say. He's sure making me work hard for this money."

"Maybe he's overcompensating because he's so new to the job. Just give back what he dishes out. He'll see the light eventually."

Rachel shook her head. "I'm of the you get more with honey than with vinegar school. But somehow that tact doesn't seem to be working on your son."

"Hmm—I don't know why not. Honey always makes giving away money so much sweeter for me," Terrance claimed with exaggerated innocence. Then he answered her appreciative grin with a sly smile.

"Just remember one thing," he continued as he nudged her toward the office door. "I'm still chairman of the board, and I can always gently twist the president's arm." He opened the door and edged her inside the office. "But frankly, I don't think you'll need my help."

Chapter Two

Rachel returned to her office at four o'clock, tired but victorious from her campaign to win a contribution from Nelson Business Machines. She leaned back against her desk chair, grateful that the caretaker had finally turned on the central air-conditioning because it was sticky hot outside and the Green Line streetcar she had taken from downtown back to Brookline had been crowded with pre-rush hour commuters.

Thank God this was the end of her commuting for the day, for home was not more than a few hundred yards away. Her two-bedroom bungalow was one of three former guest houses that dotted the grounds of the old Wrentham estate, now known as the Wrentham Museum. Miss Elsie Wrentham, the last survivor of the old New England family's line, established a trust for a museum bearing the Wrentham name. When she died just before World War II, she willed her fabulous collection of American art and artifacts, the family mansion and grounds to the Wrentham Museum Trust.

Almost fifty years later the Wrentham Museum, although small, had one of the most extensive and prestigious collections of nineteenth and twentieth century American art. Rachel felt lucky to have her job as assistant curator. She loved her work, the museum staff, the lovely, well tended grounds and the cozy little house that she received rent free as part of her salary compensation package. After three years of working and living quite happily at the Wrentham Museum, those tough years of juggling school, job and child seemed worth it.

Most importantly, however, Danny seemed to be thriving in the close-knit atmosphere where the staff were like family, and where he had lots of room in which to run and play. And even though Danny cherished every moment he spent with his father, he seemed to have accepted Greg's part-time involvement in his life. Considering the imperfect world of the single parent household, Rachel knew that her son was a relatively well adjusted, happy boy.

Danny's eighth birthday was approaching fast, and Rachel hadn't done much planning for his party the Sunday after next. The guests had been invited, but that was as far as she had gotten before she had learned about the additional paintings for the exhibit. Well, she couldn't afford the troupe of juggling clowns that had entertained at the Lawton boy's party, she mused wearily as she closed her eyes for just a moment or two.

Rachel heard her office door creak open and a familiar lilac scent filled the room. "Hello, Ilsa," she greeted, slowly opening her eyes.

"Lovey, you're back." The six-foot tall blonde wearing a red-and-white print sundress loomed over Rachel's desk. "Was it a success?" Ilsa asked in her light German accent.

"A success—finally. I left Gordon Nelson's office at three-thirty with exactly the amount of money I asked for and with the condescending warning that I was lucky to get it."

"But you got it. That is great." Then Ilsa dropped a pile of magazines in front of Rachel. "Here are two months' worth of *People*. Jimmy threatened to throw them out because of fire hazards. When I told him I had promised them to you, he said he did not understand how two educated women could read such lowbrow stuff."

"Did he really?"

"Ya. But I told him we like our juicy gossip as much as the next guy, and that I'd divorce him before I'd give up my *People*."

Rachel laughed and shook her head. "You'd better be careful, Ilsa. One of these days, Jim might take you up on it."

"Na. He is crazy about me."

Rachel knew this to be true. James Baird, youngest son of a well-known Boston Brahmin family and partner in one of the finest law firms on Beacon Hill, had met Ilsa during a tour of army duty in West Germany, and ten years and three children later, he was still very devoted to his rather unconventional and gregarious wife.

Ilsa plopped her statuesque body into the chair beside Rachel's desk. "How wonderful to be downtown all day with real grown-ups. Did you happen to meet a gorgeous hunk who threw himself at your feet?"

"No one, I assure you, threw himself at my feet today," Rachel replied dryly, wondering about Ilsa's habitual preoccupation with attractive men.

"Bad luck, lovey. Maybe tomorrow."

"Maybe." Rachel glanced through a pile of magazines. "Hey, don't we have a tennis lesson tomorrow afternoon?" she asked, more to change the subject than anything else.

"Yes, and don't you try to back out of it again."

"I won't, I won't," insisted Rachel. "Though why I'm allowing you to teach me something I have absolutely no talent for is beyond me."

"You said you needed the exercise."

"I should have joined an aerobics class."

"Tennis is more fun than jumping around in a leotard. Besides, you have never had a tennis instructor like Ilsa. Ya?"

"Ilsa, in all honesty I have to admit you're right," Rachel acknowledged, trying to keep a straight face.

Ilsa tossed her head back with a haughty air. "Go ahead, make fun. But I will not fail you like those others did. I will not let you quit like you did before. You wait and see. Just be at the court tomorrow at four. We will work on your serve."

"Yes, sir."

"Oh, and I told Danny already he is having supper with us tomorrow night while you are at the reception for that new gallery on Charles Street."

"Thanks for taking him. I owe you one."

"No problem. Johanna is thrilled about it. She has a mad crush on Danny. You know, his love life is more exciting than yours."

"No doubt," Rachel answered dully.

"Do not ignore me, Rachel. You are in a rut. Ruts are for married people," Ilsa insisted, her usually mild German accent becoming more pronounced as her voice lilted with excitement.

"I'm sorry if you find my life boring, Ilsa," Rachel replied with amused indulgence. "But as I told you, there wasn't one spare hunk roaming loose around town this afternoon."

"Ah. You were not paying attention. I know you. What about this Gordon Nelson you met with?" Ilsa persisted. "Jimmy says he is considered the most eligible bachelor in town. And rich, ya?"

The thought of her and Gordon Nelson was enough to make Rachel shudder. "Forget that one. He and I mix like oil and water." At her secretary's crestfallen expression she took pity and added, "But I did meet a nice gentleman today—Terrance Nelson."

"Terrance Nelson? He is divine."

"You've met him?"

"Once or twice at parties. Another partner at Jimmy's firm handles his personal business."

Rachel scarcely had time to digest Ilsa's startling news that she had met Terrance when two little whirlwinds dashed into the office.

Rachel crouched down to hug her sandy-haired son, while Ilsa's seven-year-old Johanna climbed up into her mother's ample lap.

"Guess what Mom?" Danny asked happily.

"What?"

"Ilsa is making her famous spaghetti and meatballs for supper tomorrow night, and I'm the guest of honor."

"That's wonderful, honey," Rachel acknowledged, although Ilsa's dinner menu reminded her of the sadly empty state of their own refrigerator. She was running so behind schedule today that she had forgotten to stop off at the supermarket on her way back from Nelson Business Machines. But Rachel knew Danny would love the solution to the there's-nothing-in-the-house-for-dinner dilemma.

"Hey, kiddo, why don't we eat at McDonald's tonight and then do some heavy-duty food shopping afterward?"

"Neat. Can we go to the one with the playground?"

"Sure."

"But we have to call Dad and Nancy when we get home and tell them what time to pick me up Saturday. They're taking me to Hampton Beach, remember?"

"I remember. We'll call them the minute we get home."

"All right," Danny declared, wasting no time bolting for the door as soon as Rachel had agreed to his requests. Rachel noticed little Johanna's envious eyes following her son's quickly disappearing back. Rachel cast an inquiring look at Ilsa.

"You want to go with Rachel and Danny?" Ilsa asked her daughter. With an exuberant yes, Johanna dashed out after Danny.

Later, as Rachel stood at the edge of the Ronald McDonald playground watching the two children play, she felt very much the single suburban parent. She couldn't help but compare this scene of boisterous kids and work-wearied parents with the quiet, urbane setting of her midday meal. Now that outing seemed light-years away. And so did her congenial lunch companion. Although she and Terrance had found so much to talk about during lunch and had seemed to share many common interests, Rachel just couldn't see how those interests could prevail against the major differences in their lives. How could a young working mother laden with guilt about feeding her eight-year-old fast-food for the second time in a week even entertain thoughts of a friendship with a sophisticated and successful businessman who also happened to be about twenty years her senior? A man with two adult sons? It was scarcely possible. But why on earth was she even worrying about all this anyway? After all, she and Terrance only had lunch. She'd never see him again.

Yet reminding herself of this couldn't keep Rachel from thinking about Terrance. Maybe, just maybe, she liked Terrance a bit more than she had first thought. After all, they did have such a nice time together at lunch. Rachel hadn't felt so immediately in tune with a man since the day she had met Tom French back in Washington. Yet that had been so different. She and Tom eventually had fallen in love—or so she had thought.

Rachel shook her head. She didn't want to think about that unmitigated disaster of a relationship. It was years ago. Now she was here, watching her son and his friend play. Their carefree joy was a pleasure to see, and it helped to clear all traces of Tom and Terrance from her mind.

AT FIRST, Terrance wasn't sure that the woman standing near the French doors across the crowded party room was actually Rachel Bonner. The woman's back was turned toward him, so he was unable to see if she possessed the expressive green eyes that had lingered in his memory. Yet this woman carried herself as Rachel had—like a woman who had listened well when her mother had reminded her to stand up straight, shoulders back, head high. And the way this woman's wavy reddish-brown hair just barely grazed her narrow shoulders reminded him very much of Mrs. Bonner.

Finally, the woman turned to greet two acquaintances, and Terrance saw that it was indeed Rachel. She was here at Franz Menzies' new gallery, standing not more than twenty feet away from him. His throat felt tight, almost dry, as he watched her smile warmly at the young couple. Terrance thought there was something beguilingly sexy about her smile. He had immediately noticed it when he met her in Gordon's office yesterday, and he'd been constantly aware of it during their luncheon at Felicia's.

Defying his own better judgment, he moved slowly toward her, nodding courteously to several acquaintances as he walked across the cocktail chatter-filled room. But Rachel spotted him before he could speak, and that wide sexy mouth of hers broke into a welcoming grin. His muscles tightened; his dark suit suddenly felt too warm for the pleasant summer evening. Then Terrance knew he was in trouble—just as he had known it yesterday at lunch when he'd first learned she was divorced. Single. Perhaps available. Terrance remembered how much that discovery had thrown him off balance.

Now, as Rachel held out her hand to greet him, Terrance felt as if he were treading the fine line between his usually reliable common sense and . . . and what?

"Nice to see you again, Terrance," she said, her voice sounding winsomely light.

He clasped her small hand gently and held it. "I understand congratulations are in order."

Her dark green eyes flickered with confusion. "Congratulations?"

"On persuading Gordon to underwrite your Hudson River school exhibit."

"I see, he's told you already."

"We played tennis together last night after work. I think he was still trying to figure out how you managed to break him down. He said it was impossible to say no to you."

Although a rush of color warmed her cheeks, Rachel answered gamely, "I find that hard to believe."

"You shouldn't underestimate yourself so."

"Well, after the pep talk you gave me, I felt I had no choice but to prevail and conquer." Then she added in a more serious tone. "I'm very grateful for the company's contribution. It really does save the day for the exhibit."

"I'm glad."

Terrance realized their conversation had reached the point where it could easily be ended with the superficial farewells of cocktail party banter before they shuffled along their separate ways. Or they could continue on together. Noticing the champagne glass in her hands was empty, Terrance made his choice and hoped Rachel's would be the same.

"May I get you a refill?"

Rachel glanced down at her glass, then slowly lifted her eyes to meet his. Terrance nodded in silent encouragement, knowing only that he didn't want them to part just yet.

"Maybe one more glass will be all right," she agreed, her voice hesitant.

Rachel's arm shook slightly as she handed him her glass, and Terrance reached out to steady it with his free hand. "I hope I'm not making you that nervous," he said lightly, yet very much aware of the smooth feel of her bare skin beneath his fingers.

"Of course not, Terrance." She shook her head with a smile. "I've been practicing my tennis serve all afternoon and I guess this arm is exhausted. My instructor is worse than a drill sergeant," she added disparagingly.

"Well, don't let that turn you off the game. Tennis has been a passion of mine since I was ten years old. I still play every chance I get."

"I'm afraid I'm just a neophyte. In fact, this is about the third time I've started up lessons. I'm hoping I'll get the hang of it this time around," she admitted sheepishly.

Terrance was about to offer to practice with her, but then decided against it. She probably already had someone else with whom to practice her game. "I'm sure you'll do well," he said instead as he took her empty glass.

Returning moments later with more champagne, Terrance was reminded, once again, of how attractive he found her. The creamy white dress she was wearing seemed to envelop her soft round curves like a silken cloud. Her pretty green eyes seemed especially luminous and bright. Her face looked fresh and glowing under a light touch of makeup. Yes, Rachel Bonner was one good-looking woman. And despite what his two sons might think, he wasn't too over-the-hill to appreciate feminine beauty, or to respond to it. Hell, he was still a few months shy of his forty-ninth birthday.

Yet yesterday, he had allowed himself to enjoy the company of this very personable and intelligent woman while managing—with mixed results—to brush aside any attraction he felt for Rachel. Tonight, however, he found himself responding to her in a much more sexual way. He couldn't push away this response as easily as he had yesterday, for now it was pulling him under like the dangerously insistent tug of an unsuspected undertow.

"I think it was wonderful of Franz to open his new gallery with a show of Boston's promising unknowns," Rachel said when Terrance rejoined her. "He's done so much for new talent in this town."

Terrance gazed at several of the starkly brilliant canvases mounted on the wall. "Yes, Franz is quite the fairy godmother," he said casually while wondering if Rachel had even given him a second thought after their lunch yesterday. Why would she? he asked himself as he

thought of all the younger professional men Boston had
to offer a woman like Rachel.

"Ter? Terrance Nelson! It is you."

Terrance recognized the gravelly voice at once. "Max
Windom, how are you?" he greeted as the large hulk of
a man pumped his hand briskly. Terrance wasn't surprised to find Max's massive arm entwined with the
slender arm of a very striking and very young blonde.
Although Terrance hadn't met Max's new bride yet, he'd
heard plenty about the second Mrs. Maxwell Windom.

The shocking news that Max had left his wife of
twenty-five years and had married a woman young
enough to be his own daughter had been hotly discussed
and joked about among their circle of mutual friends.
Terrance hadn't much cared for the snide remarks, yet
Max's recent remarriage had disturbed him nonetheless.
After all, Max's ex-wife, Blaine, had been Eleanor's
closest friend. Now Blaine was living in Manhattan with
her adult daughter, Max was married to someone else,
and Eleanor was gone.

"How long has it been since we've seen each other, old
man? Two years?" Max asked in a voice roughened by
years of compulsive cigarette smoking. "You haven't met
Laurie, have you?"

"No, I haven't had the pleasure."

This entire encounter with the Windoms felt so odd to
Terrance. It seemed even stranger when he politely introduced Rachel to the couple. The conclusion they'd
reached concerning Rachel's presence by his side was
tactlessly obvious when Max gave Terrance a quick
thumbs-up sign of approval. Terrance's grip tightened
around his champagne glass.

"Max, you look terrific," he commented, appealing to the man's vanity in order to keep the Windoms from embarrassing Rachel further.

"Let me tell you, Ter, I feel terrific, too. Laurie put me on a diet—lost thirty pounds. She's also got me seeing a hypnotist to help me quit smoking. Can you believe it? Me quitting cigarettes?"

"Fantastic."

"You never did smoke, did you, Ter?" Max rasped on. "Smart guy. But then you were always the fittest guy in our old crowd. Hell, you're still in great shape." Max suddenly turned to Rachel. "It's great to see this fella back in circulation, Rachel, just great. He kept to himself way too long."

Rachel responded in the only way possible—with a polite, noncommittal nod of her head. Terrance hoped she wasn't too upset by Max's presumptuous remarks. She did seem to be taking it all in stride. Her eyes were unrevealing, calm; her lips were set in a warm, but discreet smile. He absentmindedly gazed at her intriguing mouth. She was beautiful.

"Perhaps the four of us could get together sometime," Laurie Windom suggested out of the blue. "We're sailing at Marblehead next Saturday—we'd love it if you two could join us."

Terrance stared blankly at Laurie, realizing the situation had gotten slightly out of hand. He felt obliged to set matters straight once and for all. Taking up with a younger woman was all well and good for Max, but Terrance resented the Windoms' misconception that he had done likewise. He'd never want a fine woman like Rachel to be the butt of tactless remarks and snide jokes.

"I'm afraid you two have completely misunderstood the relationship between Mrs. Bonner and myself,"

Terrance began to explain in a tone effusing control and tact—a tone he usually saved for the most sensitive of business dealings. "Rachel and I are simply business acquaintances. In fact, we met for the first time only yesterday, and our running into each other here tonight was mere coincidence."

While the Windoms fell over themselves apologizing, Terrance glanced over at Rachel. Her flushed, hurt expression made it clear that he had just embarrassed her much more than the Windoms ever could. Damn! he cursed at himself silently as the confusing ambivalence of yesterday descended upon him once again. What was the matter with him?

"Rachel . . ." he murmured beseechingly, not caring what the Windoms thought.

She held out her hand to stop him from speaking further. "Terrance, I really must be running along, now. It was good to see you," she declared with an admirable composure that belied the distress Terrance could read in her eyes. "Mr. and Mrs. Windom, it's been a pleasure meeting you. Good night."

Stunned, Terrance watched her drift away from him as she wove a steady path through the congested room toward the gallery's front entrance. He knew he couldn't let her leave like that.

He caught up with her on Charles Street where she was standing beside the doorman Franz had hired specifically for his gallery's grand opening. "Rachel, please wait," he called as he ambled down the low front steps.

"I really can't stay any longer, Terrance," she said, her voice steady but distant. "I took a cab here because I hate driving downtown at night. The doorman is trying to hail me another cab to take me back to Brookline. You know how difficult it is to find cabs at this time of night."

"Forget the taxi. I'll drive you home."

"Oh no, I couldn't let—"

"Rachel, please. We have to talk."

Her eyes flared with anger. "Whatever do two mere business acquaintances have to talk about?"

Terrance glanced awkwardly down at the sidewalk. "I deserve that, I know. But at least allow me to explain. To apologize."

"It's not that important."

"It is to me. Please, stay."

"I'd rather not go back inside."

Sensing that she was waging a battle with herself over what to do, Terrance urged gently, "Let's walk around the block. It'll be quieter."

With a belligerent sigh, Rachel agreed.

Terrance then lightly cupped her elbow. Walking close beside her, he became aware of her sweet, light perfume. "I hadn't meant what I said inside to be so callous. And I'm very sorry that's how it sounded. What I wanted was for them to leave you alone, to stop embarrassing you."

"Embarrassing whom?" she interrupted curtly. "Look, if it bothered you because they assumed I was with you, just say so."

"All right. I may have been slightly embarrassed, too. But not for that reason." He looked down at her lovely eyes, which were unashamedly revealing her bewilderment and hurt. Feeling badly that he had caused it, his voice softened. "How could I be embarrassed at being thought your escort?"

Rachel shook her head. "Then I don't understand."

"Join the club." At the street corner, Terrance paused, trying to grapple with the reasons for his behavior. "All I know is that I felt awkward standing there with the Windoms. I've known Max and his ex-wife for over twenty years. Eleanor and I used to play bridge with Blaine and Max twice a month. We shared a beach house on the Cape every August. Our kids played together. Now the kids are grown; Max and Blaine have split up; Eleanor's dead. And tonight, there Max and I were in the company of two very young women instead of with Eleanor and Blaine."

Feeling awkward, he shrugged his shoulders as he continued. "Besides, Max obviously concluded that you and I were romantically involved. Rachel, I've been a widower for five years, but I have to admit it's still disconcerting when friends link me with a woman. I guess there are times when I still think of myself as Eleanor's husband. We were married for such a long time." He gave her a hesitant look. "Sound silly?"

Rachel's face softened with compassion. "Not at all. Especially with Max stirring up all those memories for you."

Terrance was glad she understood. "That's part of it," he agreed, resuming their leisurely walk along the brightly lit sidewalk. "I also didn't think you appreciated being linked with an old coot like me."

"Terrance! I hardly put you in the 'old coot' category. Besides, if truth be known, I was rather flattered that they thought we were together."

"Were you now?" He wanted to believe she meant it— that she hadn't said it just to be kind. "Does this all mean that I'm forgiven?"

"Yes, forgiven."

Terrance grinned, feeling genuinely relieved and happy to see Rachel's smile again. "Good, I'm glad. But forgiven or not, my offer of a ride back to Brookline still stands. I promise a smoother drive than any taxi in this city can provide. I'll even let you sit up in the front seat with me."

"How can I turn down an offer like that?"

THE DRIVE ALONG BEACON STREET in Terrance's luxury car was indeed smooth and comfortable. Rachel couldn't get over how calm she felt now. Not more than an hour ago she had been delighted and excited when Terrance had first approached her at the Menzies Gallery. Half an hour ago she had been hurt and angry when he'd practically denied knowing her. But his apology—the sincerity of which she'd never doubted for a moment—had mollified her anger, and now she was glad to be with him.

Amazing how her emotions had been flip-flopping since she had first laid eyes on Terrance Nelson yesterday afternoon, Rachel mused. Leaning back comfortably into the car's lush bucket seat, she glanced at the man beside her. As Terrance steered his car through the relatively light evening traffic, the garish lights of Kenmore Square couldn't mar his dark handsome features. Rather, they illuminated his refined, angular face with an exciting warmth that enticed Rachel to draw closer to him. Of course she held back, too reticent and unsure. Yet, at that one precise moment, getting to know Terrance Nelson better didn't seem as unimaginable as it had yesterday.

Her next words tumbled out of her mouth without hesitation. "Two paintings for the exhibit arrived from New York the other day: a Cole and a Durand. They've already been unpacked and mounted. Would you like to stop off and see them?"

"I'd like to very much." The gleam in Terrance's eyes verified the enthusiasm in his voice.

At the Wrentham's front gate, Rachel asked the guard to alert the museum's night watchman of their impending visit. When she and Terrance entered the mansion, the watchman had already turned on the lights in the special exhibit room on the second floor.

"There they are," she said, indicating the two sole paintings hanging on the oval room's muted gray walls. She quietly followed behind Terrance as he wordlessly approached the paintings.

"I've seen this Cole in New York," he said before turning to the second painting. "But I've never seen this Durand before." He regarded the large landscape carefully for several minutes, and Rachel enjoyed watching his fascinated gaze drift over the canvas.

"You know, Rachel," Terrance finally said in a low voice, his eyes still fixed on the painting, "I'm a trained engineer and a businessman. I know how to build state-of-the-art computers, and I know how to sell them. Yet I'm always amazed by how an artist can create such beauty with just paint and brush."

Then he turned to Rachel and added, "I'm sorry to say I've no artistic flair whatsoever."

"None at all?"

"Well, I am something of a weekend photographer." He glanced back at the huge paintings, his gray-blue eyes slyly twinkling. "Landscapes are my specialty."

Rachel immediately remembered the photographs she had admired the day before. "Did you take those pictures hanging in your son's office?"

"You noticed them?"

"Yes. I liked them very much. Berkshires, right?"

"Right. I have a summer place out there, and I putter around a lot with my camera on weekends. I took up photography to help fill my time after Eleanor's death."

"Well, those photographs are lovely."

"Thanks. It's nice to hear. Still, I can hardly qualify my photographs as art when I'm standing in front of paintings like these."

After discussing the two paintings for a few minutes longer, Terrance insisted on escorting her back to her bungalow. Walking along the dimly lit path from the rear of the museum to her home, Rachel felt the pull of an insistent yearning as her admiration for Terrance increased. She wasn't surprised to learn he had taken those photos hanging in Gordon's office. It made perfect sense, just as the emotions blossoming in her head and heart made sense. She was a normal, red-blooded woman who happened to think Terrance Nelson a very special man. Why shouldn't she be having such strong feelings for him?

Beneath the hazy sheen of the faint quarter moon and a starry sky, Terrance moved beside her with an evocative grace. The evening light sent shadows dancing across his face and highlighted the silver glints threaded sparsely through his dark hair. All this stirred Rachel to a heightened awareness of her new feelings.

For the second time that evening, she wanted to reach for him, to touch him. Again she held back. Except now she had to ask herself why. Was making such a move toward a dignified man like Terrance too bold, too obvious? Or was their age difference affecting her more than she was willing to admit? Was she wary of a kind, yet embarrassing rebuff?

When they reached the black wrought iron fence that enclosed the tiny yard of her bungalow, Rachel stopped at the gate. She searched his eyes.

"What is it?" he asked gently.

"I'm feeling very confused right now."

"About me?"

Her eyes widened in surprise. How did he know? "Yes," she murmured.

"I've been feeling the same way about you since yesterday."

"Then I haven't been imagining this—this—"

"Attraction? You know I thought I might be imagining it myself. Or wishing for it."

Her heart was pounding so fast it made her almost breathless. "Terrance," she rasped, reaching for his hand at last.

He enclosed her hand in an urgent grasp, powered by a desire she recognized as equal to her own. She gazed up at him, wanting to hold him close, wanting to feel his arms close tightly around her.

"Why don't we go sit on your porch for a while?" he said lowly, nodding over his shoulder at the wicker settee on her front porch.

Rachel's spirit soared happily as she swung open the gate, her other hand still tightly enclosed between Terrance's fingers. So lighthearted was she that, as she led him to the front steps, she didn't see Danny's bike lurking in their darkened path until she almost fell over it.

"Damn," she cried as Terrance prevented her from losing her balance by quickly pulling her against his chest.

"Are you all right?"

"Yes, yes." Rachel moved away from Terrance and began dragging the bicycle out of the way. "It's my son's bike—I've told him a hundred times to keep it away from the steps." She wheeled the squat two-wheeler across the yard and leaned it against the house, extremely annoyed by its abrupt intrusion into an important moment.

"Yes, your little boy," Terrance said, as if he were reminding himself of the boy's existence.

Rachel returned to his side and immediately sensed him slipping away from her along with the all too brief spell of intimacy. From the look on his face she could see whatever he was contemplating was not promising. But then he reached out for her, his hands gently kneading her shoulders. She was relieved to feel his touch and wanted more.

His clear eyes bore down on hers. "Rachel, it'd be foolish of me to pretend to you or to myself that I wasn't very attracted to you. But—"

"But what?"

Terrance took a deep breath, his eyes never wavering from hers. "But I think it would be both sensible and sane if we said good-night right now."

"Why?"

"Rachel, I've never been the type to be carried away by my feelings and I'm not about to start at this point in my life. I'm not sure I want to get involved in something that could be more than I'm willing to handle."

"More than you're willing to handle? What do you mean?"

His voice was as gentle as his gaze. "I mean you're someone I would want to give more to than—" Terrance paused, straightening his shoulders as he searched for exactly what he wanted to say. "You're the type of woman who needs and deserves more from a man than I'm willing or capable of giving now—or possibly ever. It wouldn't be fair to mislead you."

Speechless, Rachel stared back at Terrance, her heart pounding.

"I honestly think it's better this way." He lightly squeezed her shoulders before dropping his arms to his sides. "Good night Rachel."

"Good night," she responded, too bewildered to declare any protest.

As she heard Terrance's footsteps on the flagstone walk gradually fade away, her bewilderment turned into a restless anger. And disappointment.

"Better this way? Sensible and sane?" Rachel muttered to herself. Who was Terrance Nelson to decide what was sensible and sane for her? she wondered while wishing she had had the presence of mind to have asked him that to his face.

A few seconds passed before Rachel realized that her telephone was ringing. Pulling her keys from her purse, she quickly unlocked the front door and hurried to the kitchen phone. Short of breath when she finally answered, Rachel was somewhat surprised to hear her ex-husband's voice on the other end of the line.

"At last. I've been calling all night."

"I've been out. And hello to you, too, Greg."

"Sorry, Rachel," Greg replied. "I wanted to talk to Danny before he goes to bed. We're going to have to cancel out on this weekend at the beach. Nancy's sick."

"That's too bad. Nothing serious I hope."

"I doubt it. Probably some virus that's going around. But she isn't up to going anywhere. And she feels really badly about disappointing Danny."

Rachel believed this. During the three years of Greg's second marriage, his new wife had been very good to Danny. Rachel could see that Nancy genuinely cared for her stepson.

"Danny's spending the night at a friend's, Greg. But I'm sure he'll understand when I tell him," Rachel assured.

"Yeah, he's a good kid. Rachel, could we take him next week instead? I know it's not my weekend to have him, but I sure would like to make it up to him."

"Oh, Greg, normally I'd say fine, but I've planned a birthday party for him. He's already invited his friends." Feeling awkward, Rachel extended an invitation to the party to Greg. Of course, she didn't expect him to accept.

And he didn't. "Nancy and I are planning a little party for him when my folks visit us next month. Just tell Danny that we'll try for the beach the weekend after next."

Rachel promised to relay the message. After hanging up the phone, she wondered just how she would tell her son about the canceled beach weekend. He would understand why his father had to back out, but he'd be disappointed nonetheless.

She was reminded briefly of her own disappointment in Terrance Nelson. She could understand why he backed away from her, but it still made her angry. What did it matter now? she asked herself. He wouldn't be back. Besides, life went on, and right now, Danny was her main concern.

Chapter Three

Terrance shut the apartment door quietly behind him, dropped his briefcase on the hall table and draped his suit jacket over the back of the wing chair. Loosening his necktie, he sank down on the living room sofa, relieved that this particularly hectic workday was finally over. Not only had he still been attempting to catch up with the business he had missed during his trip to London, but today he'd been constantly attending to one crisis after another. God, he was tired. And hot. This current heat wave certainly didn't help any.

He glanced at his wristwatch. Six o'clock. Kerry and Martha wouldn't be arriving for at least another hour, and their dinner reservations were for eight. Plenty of time to shower and change, he thought wearily, his eyes drifting closed. But before Terrance could steal a moment's sleep, the doorbell beckoned.

At the door Terrance found his younger son and the boy's fiancée, smiling and holding hands.

"Hi Dad."

"Kerry, Martha. Aren't you a little early?" Terrance checked his watch to make sure he had the correct time.

"Well Dad, we are," Kerry said, leading Martha into

the living room. "I'm afraid we're going to have to cancel out of dinner."

"But why?" Terrance asked, disappointed. He had been looking forward to a relaxing get-together with Kerry and Martha all day. It had been the much anticipated bright spot in an otherwise grueling day.

Martha looked up at Terrance with earnest blue eyes. "You see, Mr. Nelson, my former roommate from college just flew into town for the day, and we have to see her before she leaves in the morning." She nervously tucked a silky blond strand of hair behind her ear, adding shyly, "I want to ask her to be maid of honor at our wedding this fall."

"That is important," Terrance acknowledged and then smiled gently at Martha's pretty, well scrubbed face.

"Then you understand?" Kerry asked. "I know you went to a lot of trouble to get reservations at Maison Robert."

"Don't worry about it. We'll make it some other time," reassured Terrance, although he really didn't want to stay home alone this evening. Sometimes the apartment seemed so quiet. "Can you stay for a drink at least?"

Kerry cast a questioning glance at Martha.

"Sure. I don't see why not," the young woman said sweetly.

"A round of gin and tonics?" Terrance asked over his shoulder as he headed for the bar setup in the corner of his living room.

Kerry offered to fill the ice bucket and slice up some limes for his father. After he stepped into the kitchen, Martha joined Terrance at the mahogany liquor cabinet. "Kerry and I picked out my engagement ring yesterday, Mr. Nelson. Would you like to see it?"

"I certainly would," he replied graciously, taking her tanned hand in his and gazing at the diamond ring with proper admiration. The gem was sizable, yet the setting was tastefully simple—appropriate for a young woman of Martha's affluent upbringing. "It's lovely, Martha."

"Thank you. I'm very happy with it."

The excitement shimmering in her voice struck a chord of tenderness in Terrance. He had known Martha all of her life. She had been a sweet, gentle child, and she had grown into a loving, unpretentious young woman. She was perfect for his son, and he couldn't have asked for a nicer daughter-in-law.

Still, Kerry and Martha were only twenty-three. Terrance hoped they were doing the right thing by marrying soon after graduating from college. Although they had grown up together and knew each other very well, Terrance still felt it necessary to discuss with Kerry, when he had announced the engagement, if he was ready for marriage.

Kerry had assured him he was, his voice intense with sincerity. At that moment, with his curly sandy brown hair, serious blue eyes and sharp, proud chin, Kerry had resembled his mother a great deal. When he insisted he knew exactly what he was doing, he even sounded a bit like Eleanor.

At the time, Terrance found little to contradict in Kerry's argument. Besides, Terrance felt it would be hypocritical of him to harp on the kids' ages when he and Eleanor had married at nineteen. And Kerry claimed he was happy. In fact, for the first time since Eleanor's death his younger son seemed centered, calm.

"How do you like the ring, Dad?" Kerry asked as he plunged through the kitchen door with ice bucket and limes in tow.

"It's a beauty," replied Terrance. An expensive beauty at that, he thought to himself. Most likely money from the large trust fund he and Eleanor had set up for Kerry paid for the ring. Kerry had been living comfortably off the trust fund's interest since his twenty-first birthday. But Terrance wondered if Kerry realized he'd need more income than that to support a wife and eventually a family. Yes, Kerry would inherit a great deal of money someday. But Terrance didn't want Kerry thinking he had a free ride for the rest of his life. He wanted his son to have goals and achievements of his own. Nelson Business Machines would offer him limitless opportunities to do just that.

Terrance eyed his son thoughtfully. Kerry seemed so young—too unsure of himself. Maybe he needed his old man to nudge him in the right direction. "Now that the engagement's official, can your brother and I expect you to join us at the office soon?"

"Where else would I go?" Kerry answered flatly, yet without looking directly at Terrance.

Kerry's offhand tone made Terrance uncomfortable. "Well you haven't talked much about it. I thought there might be some other line of work that interested you more."

"Can't think of a thing, Dad." An odd smile crossed Kerry's lips when he finally met his father's gaze. "But first things first. Martha and I still haven't set a date."

"Oh, but it will definitely be this fall," Martha hastened to add.

"It's already June now. Not much time left," Terrance commented, directing a meaningful glance at Kerry.

But Kerry had already turned his back to Terrance as he reached for the glassware on the shelf above the liquor cabinet. "Dad," he continued nonchalantly, "did

Martha tell you her godmother is throwing an engagement party for us next month?''

Martha shook her head. "I haven't had a chance yet, honey."

Kerry winked at Terrance. "It's going to be one big shindig."

"Oh, Kerry," Martha chastised, and then turned her attention back to Terrance. "It's going to be on the last Saturday in July, so keep that evening open. You'll be receiving an invitation in the mail. You're welcomed to bring a guest, too, of course."

Kerry placed three tall glasses on the cabinet top, and then he curved a fatherly arm around Terrance's shoulder. "Who are you dating these days?"

Realizing Kerry was attempting to keep the conversation from returning to his plans for the future, Terrance decided to let the matter drop.

"I'm not seeing anyone in particular," he answered indifferently as he began mixing the drinks. Yet the memory of Rachel Bonner immediately trespassed into his thoughts for the umpteenth time since he had left her at her doorstep the night before last.

"What about the lady you brought to Aunt Liz's Christmas party? She was nice."

"Helen Richards. I haven't seen her in months. In fact, I heard that she recently remarried."

Martha accepted a gin and tonic from Terrance, and, thankfully, intercepted Kerry's line of questioning. "We want you at the party, date or no date. I just wanted you to feel free to invite someone."

"We'll see." Terrance lowered his eyes to his glass. He could just imagine the splash he'd make arriving at Kerry and Martha's engagement party with Rachel Bonner on his arm. His sister Liz would be dumbfounded, Gordon would be stunned speechless for once, and the rest of his family and friends would be wondering what he was doing with a woman practically young enough to be his own daughter.

That scene was only likely to occur in his imagination, for Terrance doubted he'd invite Rachel to that family party. After being with her the other night, his reliable old Yankee common sense had convinced him that he should forget about her—for both their sakes.

But Rachel Bonner had been harder to shake from his mind than he'd expected. Even as Kerry and Martha said their farewells, leaving Terrance to face an empty evening, his thoughts homed in on Rachel. The vulnerability in her eyes when she had spoken of her confused emotions came back to him, as did the warmth of her hand and the enticing scent of her perfume. And just before her little boy's bicycle served as a stark reminder of the disparity in their ages, he had been close, so close, to taking her in his arms.

Now for the life of him he wished he had.

RACHEL LEANED BACK in her desk chair just as the antique clock on the fireplace mantel struck seven o'clock. "Thank God, that's done." She tossed her pen down on the much toiled-over revised budget for the upcoming exhibit that had to be on John Hollings' desk in the morning. She looked across the office to where Ilsa sat typing like a demon. "How are you managing with those insurance forms? Need help?"

Ilsa's long fingers flew across the keyboard with one last flourish. "All done," she announced, pulling the completed printed form from the typewriter. "I'll drop these at the post office on my way home."

"Great. Thanks for staying to help with the paper-work. Otherwise I'd be here until midnight."

"No problem. With Jimmy out of town tonight and the kids having dinner at his sister's, I am in no rush to go home."

"Speaking of dinner," Rachel said, peering through the doorway to the outer office where Danny sat on the floor immersed in an imaginary interplanetary game with his Transformer robots, "I better get a meal into that boy, pronto. Care to join us, Ilsa?"

A thoughtful expression crossed Ilsa's face. "What are you serving?"

Rachel groaned, exasperated. "Simple macaroni and cheese. But it's my mother's recipe and it's wonderful. And it's rude of you to ask."

"I'm sorry, but you don't want an unhappy dinner guest, do you?" Ilsa implored with her usual drama. "Never mind, anyway. I love macaroni and cheese. How long will it take to cook? I'm starving."

"It's all made, I just have to heat it up. I'll crack open a bottle of Chablis while we're waiting."

The telephone rang just as Ilsa was accepting Rachel's dinner invitation. Because of the late hour, the two women exchanged puzzled glances. "Probably my sister-in-law," Ilsa concluded, her long arm reaching for the phone.

"Or my mother. I left my home phone on call forwarding," Rachel added quickly.

"Wrentham Museum, Mrs. Baird speaking." Ilsa greeted with automatic efficiency.

But then Rachel saw Ilsa's mouth drop open in astonishment—a rare occurrence indeed. "Terrance Nelson?" she croaked weakly.

Rachel swallowed hard when she heard his name. After the other night, she wasn't sure she'd hear from him again. She wasn't sure she wanted to. It wasn't that she was still angry with him; she rarely stayed mad at anyone for long. She had even come to understand his qualms about getting involved, for she had nagging doubts of her own. Still, Rachel had decided her life would be a whole lot easier if she forgot about Terrance Nelson.

Ilsa's finger hit the hold button hard, her eyes flashing. "Terrance Nelson! What is going on? Have you been holding out on me?"

Rachel shot a reproving eye at Ilsa, knowing her friend would shamelessly listen to every word on her side of the conversation. Nervously picking up the receiver of her own phone, Rachel concentrated on taming the excitement she felt rising in her voice. She took a deep breath. "Hello, Terrance."

"Rachel. I was afraid you wouldn't accept my call."

She paused for a moment, contemplating the disarming resonance of his voice. "If you had called yesterday, I probably wouldn't have," she finally admitted.

"I wouldn't blame you. I'm sorry."

"It's past now. Let's forget about it."

Terrance sighed deeply. "My problem is I can't forget about it, or you. Now I know the sanest thing I can do is to see you again."

Rachel hesitated. "What about sensible?"

"The jury's still out on that, but I'm not sure it even matters. The bottom line for me is that I want to see you. I want to get to know you."

"Are you sure?" Rachel had to ask, uncertain that she could contend with his ambivalence again.

"Yes," he claimed flatly. "Rachel, you may be eighteen years younger than I, but you are a grown woman nevertheless. If you choose to spend time with me, I have to trust that you know what you want."

"Now that sounds more like it, Terrance. I can take care of myself."

"And very well, I'm sure." She could hear the tone of his voice easing. "So, will you have dinner with me tonight?" he asked. "I know it's a last-minute invitation—"

"Dinner tonight?" she repeated, and suddenly Ilsa came to life. Rachel ignored her friend's silent, yet very animated nods urging her to accept. "Terrance, I can't, I have my son at home."

"I imagine it is too late to get a baby-sitter," he commented, disappointment lacing his words.

Ilsa, in the meantime, was flailing her arms frantically. "I will take care of Danny," she whispered loudly. "Go. Go."

Rachel excused herself and put Terrance on hold in order to speak with Ilsa. "I can't let you baby-sit. You've already taken care of Danny once this week, and who will take care of your own kids when they get back from their aunt's?"

"Not to worry. My au pair girl will be there," Ilsa asserted. "You are a fool if you do not go, Rachel. You want to. I can see it in your eyes. Eh? Am I not right?"

Ilsa was right. Rachel returned to Terrance to accept his dinner invitation. When she hung up the phone, she glanced affectionately at the blonde now towering over her desk. "Thank you, honey."

Ilsa waved Rachel's thanks off. "I still want my macaroni and cheese. When you come home tonight I want to hear all about it. And I mean details!"

"Okay, but you've got to help me pick out something suitable to wear to Maison Robert that still fits. Most of my good things are too tight," Rachel declared, mentally kicking herself for not losing those blasted eight pounds.

"So Ilsa waltzed into my office three years ago claiming she was bored with staying at home and tired of lunching with the ladies from the Junior League every week," Rachel explained to Terrance as the busboy cleared their table. "She said she typed seventy-five words a minute—in English—and that she wanted to work part-time so that she only had to worry about a job when she was actually doing it. At first I thought she was a little nutty, but I was desperate for help, so I hired her. She worked out just great."

"And that's how James Baird's wife became your secretary?" Terrance smiled and shook his head. "She sounds like a character."

"She is. She's also become my best friend. In fact, I have her to thank for being here with you tonight."

"I'm glad you came." Terrance's gray eyes held her gaze.

"So am I. Even if I was second choice after your son and his fiancée," she added mischievously.

Yet with her blood warmed by the dinner wine and her heart lifted by Terrance's presence, Rachel couldn't have cared if she was third or fourth choice. So long as she was his choice. Although they had talked of many things—except themselves—throughout dinner, she felt the same immediate kinship with him that she had experienced the first time they had met. It was almost scary how happy and secure she felt when she was alone with him.

Telling herself she was lucky that her forest-green silk dress with the elasticized waistband still fit, Rachel forced herself to wave away the delectable concoctions on the pastry cart. But she did say yes to an after-dinner brandy. As she took her first sip, she was aware that Terrance was watching her thoughtfully, leaving his own drink untouched. She put her snifter down and waited, knowing the small talk was over at last.

"We've managed to skirt the major issue so far, haven't we?" he said, his long graceful fingers toying with the stem of his glass.

"You mean our ages?"

"Our age difference," Terrance corrected. "Rachel, I'm almost forty-nine years old. I've been a widower for five years. I've managed a social life of sorts since my wife's death, but this is the first time I've been so attracted to a much younger woman."

"That bothers you?"

"In a way. But that hasn't prevented me from being with you now. What I want you to know is that pursuing younger women is not a game to me. I don't need your youth to gratify my ego."

Touched by his apparent need to tell her this, Rachel reached for his hand. "I think I've known that since that incident with the Windoms," she said, giving his hand a firm squeeze. "You should know that I have never dated an older man. I don't want or need a father figure."

Terrance grimaced. "The thought had crossed my mind, I must admit."

"Well don't worry. My father is alive and well and living in Cambridge. He's there when I need him."

"What would he think of your seeing a man who's closer to his age than to yours?"

"My father is seventy years old, Terrance," she revealed, hoping it would help put this father-daughter business to rest. "Besides, at this stage of the game the fact that I'm seeing a man would thrill him. I'm sure he's convinced I've taken a vow of celibacy since my divorce."

Terrance's gray eyes glimmered with amusement. "From where I sit, you look like you could have your pick of men. And I can't believe that in the—what? seven, eight years?—you've been single there hasn't been a special man in your life."

Terrance's last statement thrummed uncomfortably in her ears, reminding her of the one unhappy, inescapable fact of her life. "Oh, I had one close call. It just didn't work out," she said with a shrug.

Rachel disliked being evasive. But she didn't want to ruin a pleasant evening by discussing the major contributing factor to her breakup with Tom all those years ago, and the main reason why she hadn't allowed any man to get too close since. That reason cut to the quick of her existence, and as much as she was drawn to Terrance, she wasn't ready yet to share such personal information with him. She might never be.

Rachel was grateful when the waiter interrupted them by presenting Terrance with the credit card receipt to sign. "This has been a lovely evening," she blurted hastily as the waiter departed. She was anxious to avoid continuing with their previous line of conversation.

"It doesn't have to end now, does it?" he inquired hopefully. "We could take a walk, or go somewhere else for a nightcap."

"I think I've had enough to drink for one night," Rachel replied, realizing that the liquor she had consumed was just beginning to make her feel a little floaty.

She glanced around the dining room, its ultra-refined elegance seeming, all of a sudden, to close in on her. "Let's go dancing," she suggested, impetuously reacting to her body's restless urge to move freely.

"Dancing? That's what you want to do?" Terrance sounded surprised, yet Rachel could see the idea appealed to him. "I should warn you that my wildly gyrating days had their last gasp with Chubby Checker and the twist. And I don't believe the jitterbug is au courant in Boston these days."

"Perhaps we can find a happy medium."

Terrance thought for a moment. "Off the top of my head I know of an evening harbor cruise where they have dancing to Big Band music. Something like that wouldn't interest you would it? It might be too touristy."

"Who cares? It sounds like fun."

Twenty minutes later they hurriedly boarded the *Bayliner* just before it shoved off on its late cruise. The upper open-air deck was festively decorated with strings of lights in Christmas tree colors. A large sign welcoming aboard delegates to the New England Association of Dentists' Convention loomed over the bandstand.

The band started playing almost immediately. People streamed onto the dance floor without hesitation, apparently more than ready to party. Despite the passengers' spirited exuberance, it didn't take Rachel long to notice that she was probably the youngest person in this crowd of middle-to-golden-agers. She had to admit it felt a bit odd. But that sensation lasted only until Terrance led her onto the dance floor.

"I might be a little rusty," she warned self-consciously when Terrance took her hands to lead her through the first upbeat trumpet-and-trombone-filled dance. He smoothly guided her along, making Rachel forget her initial awkwardness. Soon she was following his lead easily and enjoying herself immensely.

After several brisk swing numbers, a slender silver-haired woman approached the microphone at the front edge of the stage, and the band broke into the opening bar of a romantic ballad. The lights dimmed as the crowd shifted gears to the slower pace.

Rachel greeted this dance with more self-assurance. "Waltzing is one thing I know how to do," she murmured when Terrance pulled her closer to him, wrapping one long arm gently around her. She nestled against him, lightly resting her head on his muscular shoulder. His subtle sandalwood scent, mixed with the salty tang of the sea air, was arousing in its power to alert every nerve in her body to the confident solidity of Terrance's embrace.

With the refreshing ocean breeze caressing her skirted legs and tossing about her thick length of hair, a sense of freedom and lightness came over her. Terrance was indeed a skillful dancer; he didn't shuffle from foot to foot as a contemporary of hers might. He was surefooted, graceful as he guided her across the dance floor. She closed her eyes and drifted easily in his arms, feeling much like a figure skater gliding across the ice on silver blades.

The soloist continued with several more tunes, familiar sounding love songs that Rachel had heard before yet never knew the names of. Now, dancing in Terrance's arms on a boat skimming across the bay under a violet-blue sky, those love songs became more memorable than any others she had ever heard.

This was one time Rachel was grateful to her mother for sending her and Greg to ballroom dance lessons before their wedding nine years ago. In spite of the hushed-up circumstances surrounding her rather sudden marriage to her long-time boyfriend after her junior year of college, her parents had insisted she have at least some sort of party to celebrate the big day. Rachel was their only daughter and they had had their dreams for her. Their need to give her a wedding, no matter how pared down, still struck Rachel as sweet, but absurd—just as it had when she was younger. An ironic chuckle vibrated unsounded through her body.

Terrance peered down at her as they swayed in time to the music. "Are you laughing or shivering?"

"Oh, I was just thinking about my wedding." Rachel tried to explain about the dance class. "Ballroom dancing wasn't exactly in fashion when we were adolescents, so Greg and I had never learned. When it came to our wedding, however, my mother was adamant. She wouldn't have us disgracing ourselves with four left feet at our own reception. She had been planning this wedding since the day I was born, and she wanted everything to be perfect. At that point, I just wanted everything to be perfect for her." She cast a guarded eye up at Terrance. "You see, the bride was just a little bit pregnant."

Terrance's dark brows lifted in surprise. "I see," was all he said.

"The wedding was small of course, just family and a few very close friends. I think we justified having a wedding reception at all by the fact that Greg and I had planned to get married as soon as we completed college. We just happened to get a few years ahead of our game plan."

"And you didn't want to disappoint your parents," Terrance said kindly.

"That's right." She was glad he understood—not everyone did. Tom, in a moment of rare, flagrant insensitivity, had said he couldn't believe that she had agreed to such "a tacky exhibition;" and why hadn't she gone to Planned Parenthood for birth control in the first place?

Reminiscing about her wedding to Greg had overshadowed her enjoyment of the dancing, leaving her feeling somewhat glum. How much in love she had been on that day. How full of hope. Yet that was before she had to drop out of school when Danny was born, before the money got tight; before the barriers between her and Greg became insurmountable, and before the complications during the birth of her son, which changed her forever. With nine years' worth of bittersweet hindsight she could see how her life had set sail on a course she had never ever dreamed of when she was an idealistic young girl.

Perhaps sensing her wistfulness, Terrance drew her even closer to him in comforting, tender rhythm with the music. Although Rachel wasn't exactly sure why she had revealed the circumstances of her marriage and pregnancy, she was glad she did. It felt right, and his response felt even better. She allowed herself to be enveloped in his warmth, taking pleasure in the reassuring power of his arms and finding excitement in the alluring pressure of her breasts against his chest.

Tossing her head back, she chanced to look up at Terrance. He grinned happily, the boyish crinkles around his eyes delighting Rachel. "You're lucky you didn't have to take dance lessons when you were a child," he told her. "I did—every Wednesday afternoon at four o'clock for two years. The offspring of the old Lowell-Lawrence textile mill gentry were expected to attend Miss God-

win's School of Etiquette and Dance. She was an old ty-
rant of a woman, a real stickler for propriety. Years later
she came to our wedding, and I swear she was watching
every step Eleanor and I took on that dance floor.''

The music stopped then, and the singer announced a
fifteen minute break for the band. When Terrance released her from his arms, Rachel attempted to smooth
her auburn hair with her fingers. The sea breeze was
having its own way about the matter, convincing Rachel
that her efforts were useless. Maybe, impeccable, scarcely
ruffled Terrance liked a wild, windblown look in a
woman, Rachel mused wryly.

''I'm glad we came,'' she said as they strolled toward
the refreshment stand. ''How did you know about this
cruise?'' She didn't expect it was the type of thing he pa-
tronized regularly.

''My condominium is in one of those new high rises
overlooking the harbor.'' Terrance nodded back toward
the brightly lit buildings lining the waterfront. ''I can see
the cruiser, and depending on which way the wind is
blowing, I can sometimes hear the band from my bal-
cony.''

Following the break, the band picked up the tempo
considerably. Rachel and Terrance sat at one of the small
circular tables set up on the sidelines, drinking cold soda
while they watched others dance. The crowd grew nois-
ier and livelier as the music blared louder and faster.
People clapped and cheered on the dancers. Rachel realized age made no difference on this dance floor, as a
few couples who she was certain would never see sixty
again were noticeably outdoing their younger counter-
parts. The *Bayliner* was swinging gaily as it headed back
to the pier.

A man obviously caught up in the spirit of things called for yet another swing number, and the crowd enthusiastically applauded his request.

Terrance sat still for about thirty seconds after the dance began. "I don't suppose you can jitterbug?" he asked, straight-faced.

Rachel thought he was kidding. "Of course, can't everyone?"

"Great! Let's go." In an instant, Terrance was tossing off his jacket and tugging her onto the dance floor.

"Miss Godwin taught you how to jitterbug?" she called out over the loud music.

"Hell no. I learned this at prep school," he yelled back as he pulled her through the crowd to find an open spot. "I was the champ at Phillips Academy."

That piece of information petrified her. "Terrance, wait, I lied. I can't jitterbug," she hollered as loud as she could. Now she remembered that Terrance had mentioned the jitterbug at the restaurant.

"It doesn't matter. Just follow me."

With that he swung her around and his feet took flight. At first she followed lamely as Terrance two-stepped in and out without a miss, twirling her to and fro, round and round. Thankfully, he stopped short of the acrobatics that a few of the other dancers were performing. Before long she got the hang of it, though, managing to almost keep up with him while having a whale of a good time.

They collapsed into each others arms at the dance's end, out of breath yet somehow laughing.

"You're a natural," Terrance declared, his chest heaving rapidly. His hair, damp with perspiration, fell over his eyes in complete disarray, and his silk tie had become twisted around his collar and now dangled limply over his right shoulder. Disheveled as he was though, Rachel couldn't tear her eyes off him.

"And you," Rachel struggled to say between deep gasps of air, "I never suspected you harbored such a talent."

"Ah, you should have seen me in my prime."

"What prime? You were magnificent out there," she cried, appreciating what good physical shape he had to be in to be able to dance like that. "You sure looked like you knew what you were doing."

Terrance curved an arm around her narrow shoulders and grinned. "Sweetheart, there are some things a man never forgets."

Chapter Four

Rachel's subtle fragrance taunted Terrance as he drove her home from the pier. It brought back the memory of how she had felt in his arms when they danced. Her body had warmed his against the blustery sea air. The skin of her bare arms had been supple and smooth to his touch. And when she spoke, her breath had felt lush and soft against his neck. Lord, he'd forgotten how wonderful holding a woman close could make him feel. It had been a long time since he had felt the edge of excitement that keenly.

Terrance looked away from the road to steal a quick glimpse of Rachel. She caught his passing glance and answered it with a silent rich smile. Somehow that irresistible smile of hers fanned the memory of the pleasure of holding her into a strong desire. He had a sudden urge to pull off the road and hold her warm soft body close again. It was a tempting thought, but Terrance managed to convince himself that it was not the sensible thing to do.

Rachel was more than just a desirable woman. The perceptive depth of her lovely green eyes revealed an inner strength. She had more to offer than just lovemaking. That's why he couldn't stop thinking about her after they'd met. Sexual attraction had been the allure, but Rachel herself was the essence that kindled the scintillator of interest. She could understand the reasons behind his behavior in front of the Windoms; she could forgive him for walking away from her in a fit of unconscionable ambivalence; she could find beauty in his photographs; she could join him when he kicked up his heels to dance like a carefree old fool.

He wanted to make love with her, yes. But he wanted her in other ways too—ways that would take time. He only knew that he wanted very much to be with her. This desire was impulsive, crazy and so unlike him. It was dangerous. Yet this woman had touched something in him that had been resting dormant for five long years. Before Rachel, he'd begun wondering if he would ever be so attracted to a woman again.

He had not, however, been celibate in the five years following Eleanor's death. But those rare and significantly unenduring encounters were more to ease moments of unbearable loneliness and to dull the quiet ache of his sexual needs. His partners in these liaisons were chasing their own ghosts and salving their own physical desires. The needs of both parties were mutual; the emotions were compassion and gratitude.

But those emotions were far different from the mélange of feelings Rachel Bonner seemed to stir up in his mind and body.

Terrance briefly stopped the car at the gate to the Wrentham Museum grounds so Rachel could identify herself to the guard. Within seconds he was steering his car along the winding drive toward Rachel's small house while speculating if she'd be willing to see him tomorrow.

Then Rachel broke the silence. "Terrance, we're having a preview reception for the Hudson River school exhibit the evening before its official opening. I'll be sending you an invitation. I hope you'll come," she said, her voice sounding tentative, as if she didn't quite know what kind of response to expect from him.

They had just reached her house. Terrance switched off the car's engine and turned to her. The uncertainty in her spoken invitation was echoed in her liquid green eyes. He knew it was his fault that after having spent such an enjoyable evening together, Rachel might still fear he would reject her company. He'd given her cause.

Her vulnerable gaze stirred him to brush back the stray wave of auburn hair that shadowed her forehead. He caressed the thick strand between his fingers; it felt lustrous, buoyant.

"I wouldn't miss it for the world," he reassured, his eyes never leaving hers. "But surely we can get together again before that?" She smiled then, the tense indecision in her eyes dissolving. The delight shining in her face was completely disarming. Terrance found he could no longer restrain the desire to take her in his arms.

As he lifted his hand to her face her eyes followed its languorous movement. His thumb traced her smooth cheek in gentle circles. He closed his eyes and felt her silky *skin* shift against his fingers as she kissed the palm of his hand. His eyes opened as her full soft lips electrified his desire. He cupped her face between both his hands, his lips tenderly caressing her soft mouth. He snuggled closer. There was no shadow of doubt in her wide clear eyes, just a crystal clear mirror of his desire.

His lips grazed her mouth ever so lightly. Rachel answered his kiss with a tender urgency, which fueled his own fervor. His tongue explored the velvety texture of her lips. Rachel's lips parted, welcoming his deep searching kiss.

Terrance held Rachel fast to his chest, one arm around her back. His free hand slid down along her neck and shoulders, stopping finally at her breasts. His palms teased her nipples in slow circles, his fingers stroking and caressing. Terrance was lost in the sensations of her body, her kiss. Every nerve in his body ached for her.

He felt Rachel's body move slightly. Although Terrance instinctively held her closer, Rachel pulled her mouth away from his.

"Terrance, wait," she gasped. "This is happening way too fast. Besides, Ilsa might see us." She nodded over her shoulder toward her cottage.

Looking past Rachel and through the car window, Terrance saw right away what she meant. Inside the large front picture window he could clearly see Ilsa Baird sitting in Rachel's living room watching TV. Ilsa only had to glance over her right shoulder to get an equally clear view of their intimate embrace.

"If she sees us, I'll never hear the end of it," Rachel added reluctantly. "I think the world of Ilsa, but she's not the most tactful person I know."

Loosening his hold on her without releasing her completely, Terrance rested his forehead against her dark auburn hair. Regardless of Ilsa, he hadn't meant to get so carried away. "I'm sorry, Rachel."

She looked surprised. "For what? Kissing me? I'm not, not really. It's just all rather scary."

"It's the suddenness of it all, isn't it?"

"Exactly four days ago we were strangers, and tonight I feel very close to you."

"Tonight's been wonderful."

Rachel nodded. "I haven't felt this way in a long time."

"Neither have I. Not for a very long time."

His words seemed to have struck a chord in her; the emotion in her eyes deepened as her face slowly leaned closer. Her fingers grazed his hair as she kissed him fully, soundly on the lips. Brief though it was, her kiss was full of promise.

"Tomorrow?" Terrance asked, his voice sounding disembodied and far away to his own ear.

"Yes."

WHEN TERRANCE had first suggested they arrange an outing with Danny, Rachel had been slightly apprehensive. She couldn't help but wonder how Terrance and Danny would get along. What if they just didn't hit it off? Terrance, by his own admission, hadn't been around young children in years. And since her social life hadn't been terribly active of late, Danny was not used to socializing with his mom's men friends. The situation could be awkward.

Terrance believed they shouldn't put off the inevitable any longer. "This past week I've swept into your house three times, said, 'Hello, how are you?' to Danny, and then swept you out for the evening. He must be wondering what's going on."

"He hasn't said anything about it."

"As I recall, little boys don't always say what's on their minds. Besides, Rachel, I don't want Danny to think I'm shutting him out. He'd resent it."

Rachel knew he was right. She and Terrance had been seeing each other almost daily; she agreed it was time for Terrance and Danny to get together. And since a scheduled teachers' meeting at the school gave her son a day off during the middle of the week, the three of them had a perfect opportunity to spend an afternoon together. Terrance went ahead and made arrangements to meet Rachel and Danny downtown for lunch.

As soon as they arrived at The European, a large family restaurant in the North End, Terrance took the situation well in hand. "Your mother told me pizza is your favorite food," Terrance noted as he led Danny to a corner booth. "It's one of my favorites, too. And this place has the best in town. Ever been here before?"

"No sir," Danny replied with some reticence.

"Mind if I go over the menu with you? They have so many different varieties of pizza. I imagine I've sampled them all at one time or another."

"You have?"

"Sure have." Terrance spread out the menu on the table. "Here, let me tell you which ones I think are good, and which ones are not so hot."

As she watched Terrance and her son study the restaurant menu, Rachel felt her apprehensions slip away. By the time the three of them had finished devouring a huge sausage and green pepper pizza, they were all getting along famously.

"What about dessert?" Danny asked when the waitress whisked away the pizza pan and plates.

Both Rachel and Terrance gaped at Danny with disbelief. "Young man, after all that pizza, you still want dessert?" Rachel cried.

"Yeah. I was thinking of a great big hot fudge sundae."

Rachel groaned. "No way. You'll be as sick as a dog later on."

"Ah, Mom, you always say that."

"Your mother has a point. We've just eaten an awful lot of pizza," Terrance calmly interceded. "But maybe we can reconsider your suggestion in a couple of hours—after we've had a chance to digest this meal."

Danny wasn't sure he liked the idea. "Well what'll we do until then?"

"We could go over to the Museum of Science," Rachel suggested. "You always enjoy it there."

Terrance nodded agreeably before adding, "Or since it's such a beautiful day outside, we could go for a sail on the river."

Danny's face lit up immediately. "The river? I've never been sailing on the river before. Can we really do it?"

Terrance glanced over at Rachel. "The weather's perfect for a nice, leisurely sail. You and Danny are dressed casually enough to be comfortable. You both have jackets to protect you against the wind. All I have to do is stop by the office to change my shoes, get rid of this coat and tie and pull on a sweater. What do you say, Rachel?"

Looking from her son's pleading stare to Terrance's encouraging gaze, Rachel knew she could only say yes.

She was glad that she had. During the taxi ride from Terrance's office to the public boat house off Storrow Drive, Danny bombarded Terrance with excited questions about sailing on the Charles River. It pleased her to hear Terrance answer each and every question plainly and precisely, without dampening her son's enthusiasm. Clearly Terrance was looking forward to this sail as much as Danny was. She liked him immensely for that.

As Terrance had called ahead to reserve a boat, they didn't have to wait long for a dinghy to become available. Before they boarded the craft, Terrance made sure both Danny and Rachel had put on their life jackets properly. From that point on, Terrance became very much captain of the ship, which was just fine with Rachel. She didn't know the first thing about sailing. As long as they didn't capsize, she was perfectly willing to sit back and enjoy a sunny hour or two drifting along the Charles. Of course, Danny was wide-eyed, watching Terrance's every move, eagerly waiting to do whatever the skipper asked.

"Now before we get under way, Danny. We have to determine the direction of the wind."

"How do we do that, Terrance?"

"You can always wet a finger and hold it up. But you can also watch the movement of the waves. And the signs on the shore—like the flags over there on the boat house, or the smoke from the smokestack, or from the way the branches and leaves of trees are blowing in the wind."

Rachel smiled as the two of them put their heads together to figure out the wind's direction. She was sure Terrance could have performed that task by simply feeling the wind on his face, but he patiently worked with Danny step-by-step until the boy figured it correctly. Danny beamed with pride when Terrance gave him a triumphant pat on the back. Why had she been concerned that they wouldn't get along? Rachel wondered with relief.

She sat in the middle of the small sailboat as Terrance led Danny through the profusion of steps necessary to raise the sail. The terms Terrance used, such as halyard and cleat, were foreign to her, yet Danny seemed to be picking up their meanings easily. Soon Terrance and Danny were hoisting the sail, and one of the workers gave the boat a strong, straight push backward until it was clear of the mooring. With his hand on the tiller, Terrance steered the boat in a westward direction and soon they were smoothly under way.

Rachel felt exhilarated as the sailboat skimmed briskly along the river, the sun shining warmly as the gentle breezes washed over her. Although they were sailing closer to the Boston side of the river, Rachel had a wonderful view of the Cambridge shore with the distinctive MIT buildings along Memorial Drive gleaming in the sunshine. It was wonderful. After a lifetime of seeing sailboats dot the Charles on sparkling afternoons, she was excited to be finally sailing on the river herself.

Managing to drag her attention away from the dazzling view, Rachel turned to Danny. His face was stone still; his eyes were bright and attentive. His silence couldn't belie his enthusiasm and enjoyment. Gazing over Danny's sandy head, Rachel caught Terrance's eye and shot him a happy smile. After a quick glance at Danny, Terrance gave her a knowing wink. Then she looked away. An overwhelming sense of togetherness and belonging brought a smile to her face. This is what it would be like to be a family, she couldn't help thinking. She and Danny had been on their own for so long.

As she closed her eyes and let the sun warm her face, Danny called her attention to the Hatch Shell as they sailed past it. "Remember we went to the concert there, Mom, and then saw the fireworks afterward?"

Rachel nodded, turning to Terrance. "Last Fourth of July, we had a picnic during the Boston Pops concert and then watched the fireworks over the river," she explained. "Danny was enthralled by the *1812 Overture*."

"Yeah, it was neat. They set off real cannons during the music," Danny added.

Danny's enthusiasm made Terrance grin. "My boys always enjoyed that part."

"Do you take your boys sailing, too, Terrance?" he asked.

"Not in years. My sons are both grown-up and living on their own now."

"They are?" Danny said, looking slightly confused. "You mean your sons aren't little like me?"

"Danny, I told you about Terrance's two sons," Rachel reminded, "Gordon and Kerry. Remember?"

"Oh. Yeah, I think so." Combing his windblown hair away from his eyes, Danny looked back at Terrance. "Do they know how to sail, too?"

Terrance nodded. "I taught them when they were younger, and then they had lessons every summer we spent on the Cape."

"Boy, they were lucky." Danny then gave Rachel a beseeching stare. "Mom . . . ?"

"We'll talk about it later," she answered, knowing full well he was about to ask for sailing lessons.

Thankfully, Terrance diverted Danny's attention by announcing it was time to turn back. As Terrance explained to Danny how he was changing the sailboat's direction, Rachel glanced at her wristwatch. They had been out an hour and a half. How quickly the time had passed. And how enjoyable it had been—for all three of them. But especially for Danny. Although he saw his father regularly, her little boy still craved male attention. That's why he was so attached to Edgar, the museum's caretaker, as well as to her father and brothers. Even after spending a day with Ilsa and Jim Baird and their kids, Danny would often speak wistfully about how "neat" it would be to have his dad around all the time. It was enough to make her heart ache for him.

As her son seemed to genuinely like Terrance, Rachel knew Danny would enjoy seeing him often. And from the way Terrance was interacting with Danny, the feeling was probably mutual. Yet, her relationship with Terrance was really just beginning. Who knew how long it might last or where it would lead them? Rachel shrugged off those thoughts, realizing it was pure folly to try to predict or second-guess the future. Over the years she had learned that one could exert only so much control over one's future. She could only try to do her best by Danny, and pray that she'd make the right decisions.

Rachel realized Terrance had headed the sail into the wind to make a landing at the boat house dock. Another party was already waiting there to take over the boat. As they left the dock and walked toward the street, Danny skipped happily in front of Rachel and Terrance. Curling her arm through his, Rachel smiled up at Terrance. "This was a wonderful idea. We both had a great time."

"So did I. Better than I had expected." He squeezed her hand. "I guess I'd forgotten how eager and enthusiastic children can be. I always enjoyed being with my kids when they were little. Unfortunately I was so caught up with the business that I didn't spend as much time with them as I should have. I never took an afternoon off to take the boys sailing. Sundays and vacations were the designated family times. But expectations were different back then. Fathers were the breadwinners and mothers raised the kids. That's how it was."

"Your sons turned out just fine. And you seem to be close to them."

"I'm lucky."

"I suspect it was more than just luck, Terrance."

"Maybe so. Ah, but if I knew then what I know now," he mused wistfully. "These days, fathers are more involved with their kids. They're even in the delivery room when their babies are born, for God's sake. That must be wonderful. You know it's almost enough to make a man want a second chance."

A second chance? The words made Rachel flinch. What did he mean by that? she wondered uneasily. But before she could ponder the idea further, Rachel noticed that Danny had run quite a distance ahead of them and was getting dangerously close to the curb. "Danny Bonner, stop right there and wait for us," she called out.

When they caught up with him, Rachel gently reprimanded Danny for wandering off. Then they resumed walking along the sidewalk with Danny skipping beside them now. She glanced down at her son. "I was just telling Terrance what a good time we had sailing this afternoon. Didn't we, Danny?" she added, hoping he would remember his manners.

Danny stopped skipping long enough to grab hold of Terrance's free hand. "Yeah, it was neat," he declared. "Thanks for taking us, Terrance. Can we do it again sometime?"

Gently slipping his arm away from Rachel, Terrance stooped down until his eyes were level with Danny's. "Sure we can," he assured. "You know, Danny, I hope to be seeing a lot of your mother, and of you, too. Would that be all right with you?"

"Yeah," Danny answered quickly. Then he added a bit hesitantly, "If it's okay with my mom, I mean."

Still kneeling by her son, Terrance cocked his head to the side to gaze up at Rachel. "Is it okay with you?"

The look in Terrance's eyes made her heart melt. A profusion of emotions took control of her voice. "It's okay with me," she could barely whisper.

"Good. Then that's settled." Terrance returned his gaze to Danny. "I don't know about you, son, but all this fresh air has made me hungry again."

"Me, too," Danny echoed.

Standing again, Terrance turned to Rachel. "How do you feel about a trip to the ice-cream parlor?"

"I guess it would be all right."

"All right!" Danny exclaimed as he gleefully skipped ahead of them.

Terrance reached for Rachel's hand. "A nice big hot fudge sundae really would hit the spot right about now, don't you think?"

Without saying a word, Rachel playfully patted Terrance's flat stomach. He was as bad as Danny, she thought affectionately. As for herself, though, a hot fudge sundae was beginning to sound very tempting indeed.

RACHEL QUIETLY CLOSED the door to Danny's bedroom. Now that he was finally able to sleep, she wanted her son to get as much rest as possible. She could use a nap herself. But she had several phone calls to make before she could rest.

In her small sunny kitchen, she poured herself a cup of coffee before calling Terrance to break their date for that evening—their fifth in as many days.

"There's no doubt about it, Terrance," Rachel said, twirling the long phone cord between her fingers as she leaned lazily against the yellow kitchen wall. "The pediatrician has confirmed your diagnosis."

"Chicken pox?"

"Chicken pox. And the poor baby is miserable."

"Ah, how well I remember the trials and tribulations of childhood diseases," Terrance mused wryly. "Did the doctor say he'll be better soon?"

"Oh, yes, Danny will be able to start day camp right on schedule. I'll have to cancel his birthday party on Saturday, though. He should be feeling better, but it'll be too soon to expose him to other kids. I've already called his father to postpone their trip to the beach—again."

"What rotten luck. Poor kid."

"I think canceling the party and missing the beach bother him much more than the itchy blisters. He's so disappointed."

"Is there something I can do for Danny to help make up for the party?" Terrance asked. "Anything he needs? Wants?"

Rachel appreciated Terrance's generosity. "He might like a visit from you. He really enjoyed himself when you took us sailing on the Charles the other day. He was quite impressed with your boating skills."

"Was he?"

"Oh yes. Sailing is now on his list of things to learn— along with playing the guitar and riding a horse."

Terrance chuckled. "Maybe I should give him a sail-boat for his birthday, or how about a horse?"

"Absolutely not, Terrance. Just yourself will do." Although Rachel assumed he was joking, she also knew Terrance could well afford to give Danny such gifts.

"Okay, okay. But I'll come up with something to help get his mind off the canceled party," Terrance said.

"I have one more cancellation to discuss with you."

"Our dinner tonight?"

"Afraid so. I don't want to leave Danny with a sitter when he's sick. And I think I'm going to have to stick pretty close to him for the next few days," Rachel explained. "I'd invite you over here, but I know I'm going to be running myself ragged. Between caring for Danny and getting the exhibit ready for the opening next week, my time will be very tight. Thank God I live on the museum grounds."

"Well, I'm sorry about our date, but I understand."

"Are you sure?" she asked uneasily.

"Rachel, of course I understand. Don't forget, I raised two sons of my own. I've lived through chicken pox, measles, mumps—you name it."

Terrance sounded very reassuring, a little too reassuring. "Wait a minute Terrance, you don't sound that disappointed about canceling our date," she accused, trying to sound playful.

Terrance's reply was to the point; his tone clearly meant business. "I think you know I'll miss seeing you."

Rachel supposed she did know that, and she was just teasing him. Or was she? When she hung up the phone, she had to admit that a slim thread of uncertainty had motivated her prompting of Terrance. The past few days with Terrance had been exciting. He was witty, gallant, kind, fun. Yet Rachel sensed an undefinable distance in his attitude toward her—a distance that certainly hadn't been evident during their first date.

It wasn't as though he was keeping her at arm's length. Rachel welcomed Terrance's affectionate embraces and tender kisses. But never did those kisses match the passionate intensity of their first kiss. It seemed to her that in holding back physically, Terrance was really withholding a part of himself from her.

Perhaps he regretted that sudden burst of intimacy that first night, or he found himself getting more involved than he had planned. Perhaps Danny's illness would give Terrance an excuse to back off completely. "And perhaps you should just stop analyzing this to death," Rachel scolded herself quietly.

Overanalyzing her relationships with men was a wretched habit that had snuck up on her around the time of her divorce from Greg, and it had gotten much worse during her breakup with Tom French. She supposed the rejections she'd suffered and the feelings of loss she always experienced when a relationship soured were at the root of this problem. She sometimes believed that if she could foresee any trouble spots on the horizon, or smooth over any rocky patches before they became divisive cracks, she might save herself a lot of grief. Of course, it never worked out that way. Yet as unproductive and pointless as she knew this habit to be, she couldn't shake it.

She swallowed the last of her now lukewarm coffee and then set about preparing soup for Danny's lunch. Better to keep busy than to dwell on matters over which she had no control, she reminded herself. For wasn't that exactly how she had survived the last few years?

Between taking care of Danny and finalizing innumerable details for the Hudson River school exhibit, Rachel kept herself very busy. Although Terrance was never far from her thoughts, Rachel had many more pressing matters to concern herself with. Preopening interest in the exhibit was at its peak and she had to give several interviews to reporters from local newspapers and TV stations—something she'd never done before. She also had to oversee all the arrangements for the opening reception that was only a few days off. Back at the home front, Rachel not only had to keep Danny from scratching his chicken pox scabs, she also had to make a concerted effort to keep his spirits up.

Rachel was in the midst of her Saturday morning housecleaning when Terrance called to inquire if Danny was well enough for a surprise visit. Rachel's heart soared with excitement. Wonderful as Terrance's nightly phone calls had been, they couldn't match the warmth and fun of his actual presence. It had been only eight days since she'd last seen him, but it felt more like eight weeks.

On the phone, Terrance said he was at a friend's home in Concord and that he would get to Rachel's within a half hour. Then he asked for Edgar's telephone number. But when she questioned him about wanting the caretaker's number, Terrance was curiously closemouthed. He would only say it was part of the surprise.

Unfortunately her house was in utter chaos at the moment. The beds had been stripped of their linen; a week's worth of dirty laundry was piled in the hallway between the two bedrooms; she hadn't yet attacked the dustballs floating under the living room furniture; and Danny was at the kitchen table, still in his pajamas, playing games with his bowl of cornflakes.

Rachel grimaced as she dragged the vacuum cleaner out of the hall closet. She couldn't stand having anyone see her home in such a messy state, whether it be her better-than-perfect-housewife mother or just Ilsa—who genuinely didn't care. Rachel had long ago accepted that her need to display a neat, orderly home was some sort of compulsive personality quirk. She just couldn't help it.

So she plowed through the house like a demon, vacuuming, dusting, making the beds, bagging the dirty laundry for her next trip to the laundromat. She had just scooted Danny off to his room to change into playclothes when she heard a very noisy vehicle pull up in front of the cottage. Rachel stole a quick glance at herself in the full-length mirror hanging inside the hallway closet door. She straightened her turquoise T-shirt and blue jeans and tried to neaten the loose tendrils of her thick French braid. No time to change clothes now, but at least the house is clean, Rachel thought wryly.

Stepping onto the front porch as Terrance and Edgar climbed out of the cab of a green truck, Rachel's mouth fell open in amazement. HORSES was emblazoned in bold white letters on the trailer linked to the truck. Before she knew it, the two men had opened the trailer's rear gate and were gently urging a golden palomino pony down a sloping ramp.

"What on earth is all this?" she cried out.

"It's Mr. Nelson's birthday present for little Danny," Edgar replied, obviously relishing the excitement.

No, it couldn't be. She really believed Terrance had been kidding about giving Danny a horse. "Terrance," she croaked nervously, "what have you done?"

While stroking the skittish pony to calm him, Terrance glanced up at Rachel with a bright, playful smile. "Relax, Rachel, I've only borrowed Goldenrod for the morning. I thought Danny might enjoy riding him now that he's feeling better."

Relieved, yet pleased by Terrance's thoughtfulness, Rachel walked around the truck and trailer to join him. "So this is why you wanted Edgar's telephone number," she said.

"I figured I'd better get his permission before I brought Goldenrod tramping all over the grounds. He insisted on helping."

"Didn't wanna miss the look on the kid's face when he takes a gander at this," Edgar added with grandfatherly affection.

"He's going to go crazy over this pony," Rachel said when she reached the two men. "But I hope you've already had the chicken pox, Edgar."

The caretaker let out a mirthful hoot. "Not to worry. I had them long before you were even born, Mrs. Bonner." Edgar's head bobbed around impatiently. "Where is that little rascal of yours, anyway?"

"Getting dressed. And taking his sweet time about it. Would you like to go hurry him up, Edgar?"

"I sure would, Mrs. Bonner. But don't you worry, I won't ruin the surprise."

Rachel watched the white-haired man hobble lamely up the porch steps. "I don't know who's going to get the bigger kick out of this, Danny or Edgar," she said turning to Terrance.

He kissed her lightly on the forehead and handed her the reins. "Here, you hold these while I saddle up Goldenrod."

"Whoa, steady," Rachel murmured in the pony's ear as it shifted nervously when Terrance went inside the trailer. She gently stroked the pony's golden mane until Terrance returned with the leather saddle. "Are you sure he's been exposed to chicken pox before? We wouldn't want to start an epidemic back at the stables."

"Not to worry, Mrs. Bonner." Terrance replied with a wink and a grin.

She watched him carefully as he tossed the saddle onto Goldenrod's back. It was her first chance to take a really good look at Terrance since his arrival. He looked slightly different to her, younger, more relaxed. Right away, she knew it was because of his clothes. Before this morning, she had only seen him wearing conservative business suits or crisp blazers and slacks. Even when he had taken Rachel and Danny sailing after lunch that day, Terrance had simply donned a cotton knit sweater over his shirt and tie, and he had replaced his black wingtips with a pair of canvas shoes he kept in his office. Today, however, he was wearing casual tan slacks that hugged his slim hips in a most unconservative manner. And the short-sleeved navy blue polo shirt exposed two tanned, muscular arms that those crisp blazers unfortunately had hidden.

From his boyishly wind-tossed hair down to the well-worn tennis shoes on his feet, Rachel eyed Terrance with pleasure as he finished saddling the pony. She had always thought Terrance handsome. But today he seemed more ruggedly appealing and even sexier than before.

When her gaze finally settled on his eyes, she realized that Terrance was studying her just as intently, yet differently. His gray eyes, their hue made bluer by the color of his shirt, seemed slightly distressed—as if something about her were not quite right. Rachel was about to ask if she had her T-shirt on inside out when Danny came barreling down the front steps, whooping with joy.

"Take it easy, Danny," Rachel admonished. "You're frightening Goldenrod."

Danny calmed down at once. "Is he here for me?" he asked, trying very hard to keep his voice low.

Terrance smiled down at the boy. "You don't have to whisper around Goldenrod, Danny. Just don't shout or make any quick, startling moves. And he's here for you—for the morning anyway. Happy Birthday."

"This is so incredibly neat! Thanks a lot, Terrance."

Terrance gave Danny a boost up onto the pony. Rachel watched as her son settled himself proudly in the saddle. "Mom, Edgar, look at me." He beamed as Terrance led pony and rider away from the house. With his sandy hair awash with glistening highlights from the morning sun and a smile a mile wide, Danny looked happy and healthy. Rachel was certain that Terrance's surprise would help Danny get over his disappointment about his canceled birthday celebrations. And for that she was truly grateful.

Terrance slowly guided Danny and Goldenrod back to Rachel and Edgar. "Hey Edgar, what do you think?" Danny cried.

"I think you're doin' just fine, Sonny. But I wanna have a chance at leadin' you around. How about it, Mr. Nelson?"

"All yours." Terrance turned the reins over to Edgar.

Rachel gazed happily at her son as he trotted away with Edgar and Goldenrod. "I think your birthday surprise is a success, Terrance."

"I thought Danny would like it. I remembered how much my boys enjoyed visiting the horses on my friend Ted's farm when they were about Danny's age. They couldn't wait to learn to ride. I was the same myself when I was a boy."

Rachel glanced up at Terrance, trying to imagine what he'd been like as a child. "I suppose as an 'offspring of the Lowell-Lawrence textile mill gentry,'" she began thoughtfully, recalling the terminology Terrance had used himself, "you had horses of your own when you were growing up?"

He shook his head. "By that time, my father's business had already started its downward slide. The stable was one of the first things to go. Then went the summer house on the Cape, the extra cars, the household help. Finally, my father sold the mills to a manufacturer from North Carolina the year I graduated from college. He took an enormous loss. All we had left after that was the house, my mother's small inheritance and a few empty factory buildings that we couldn't even give away."

"Terrance, I had no idea. It sounds as if things got pretty dismal for your family."

"My father never really got over the loss of a business that had been in the family for generations," Terrance replied with a sad shrug of his shoulders. Then he gently cupped her chin with his hand and the expression in his eyes brightened. "As you know, I made my own way. In fact, those empty buildings Dad had been unable to sell eventually became the first offices and factories for Nelson Business Machines. Many of our employees are descendents of people who used to work in the old textile mills."

"Yes, I'd heard your company brought a lot of jobs back to that area."

"You know, laying off so many workers from their jobs through the years really tore my father up. I just wish he'd lived to see those factories thriving once again. He felt he had nothing to leave me or my children and that haunted him until the day he died." Shaking his head, Terrance lifted his gaze toward the sun. "But out of the ruins of that business, we managed to build a new, stronger one for his grandsons. It's their heritage."

Touched by the wistfulness in Terrance's voice, Rachel tried to cheer him. "He would have been very proud of you, Terrance. In any case, you should be proud of what you've accomplished."

Terrance smiled warmly into her eyes. "Thank you. You're very sweet." He lowered his mouth to hers and kissed her lips with a warmth that matched the look in his eyes. "And you make me feel very good," he murmured lowly in her ear.

Excitement sparkled pleasurably up and down Rachel's spine. "Do I now?" she questioned in a tone she knew was a tad provocative. She sought his gaze and found its expression verified his claim. Yet she also found the contrast between his earlier, almost perturbed gaze and this look of unmasked longing a bit jarring. Jarring enough to make her pause.

She moved away from him. "Terrance, I have to ask you about something."

Despite her shift of mood Terrance replied evenly, "Certainly. Ask away."

Rachel took a deep breath before speaking. "You were looking at me rather strangely while you were saddling up Goldenrod. As if you'd never seen me before. To tell the truth, I was wondering if I had mysteriously grown a third eye or something like that."

Terrance pursed his lips into a wry, self-deprecating smirk and shook his head. "Was I that obvious?"

Rachel nodded.

"I suppose the way you're dressed this morning caught me by surprise. You look like a college kid—like my son's friends."

Looking down at her T-shirt and jeans, Rachel instantly surmised what Terrance was getting at. "Young enough to make you uneasy."

"Maybe a little, I admit, but it—"

"Terrance, this is how I dress for a Saturday morning at home. I'm comfortable. I like it." Rachel knew she sounded testy, but Terrance's sensitivity about their age difference always tended to make her feel edgy. College kid? Jeans and T-shirts had been staples of her casual wardrobe for years. She didn't like feeling defensive about it. "I don't deliberately try to appear older or younger. I just want to look and feel good," she continued. "Believe me Terrance, I want very much to be attractive to you, but you're going to have to accept me as I am."

"Well, I'm happy to do just that. And if you'd let me get a word in edgewise, I could tell you that after feeling uneasy for about thirty seconds I realized that you looked more alluring than any college girl I've seen since the day I graduated from Harvard.''

Terrance's claim, accompanied by that easy, devil-may-care smile of his, melted her edginess as well as her heart. "You don't know how relieved I am to hear you say that," she murmured, her voice deep and raw with excitement. "Because when you were staring at me as if I had three eyes, I was thinking that you looked absolutely gorgeous."

His gray eyes widened at her frankness, but he was clearly pleased. Circling her waist with his arms, Terrance pulled her to him. "Tell me more," he growled seductively in her ear.

Rachel responded by wrapping her arms around him in a fervent embrace. She held him close, loving the satisfying feel of his strong chest against her breasts and the way her skin tingled as he nuzzled her neck. His very touch told her all was well. Her uneasiness was quelled. In her relief, Rachel could bask in his tenderness and feel free to return it. "I've missed you this week," she told him.

Their embrace evolved into an emotional hug. For a few moments everything around them seemed to vanish as they held each other. Terrance's enfolding arms and the quiet evenness of his breathing was the focal point of her world. Her limbs felt like warm liquid, so at the mercy of the man holding her close. Yet, his very touch was reassuring, for she could feel the emotion behind it. He was letting himself care, letting himself show it. His mind and body was there—for her. United like this, Rachel could easily believe that nothing could touch them, nothing could harm them. Comforted by the thought, she rested her head on Terrance's shoulder.

Edgar, Danny and the palomino pony came into her line of vision immediately. Returning from their jaunt around the expansive grounds, Edgar led the pony and rider at a cautious, even pace. Gradually, Danny's face came into full focus, and Rachel realized he was staring at her with slowly comprehending eyes.

He was clearly surprised by what he saw.

Chapter Five

"Is Terrance your boyfriend, Mom?"

As she tucked the smooth bedsheet under Danny's arms, Rachel gave careful thought about how to phrase her reply. This was a new experience for her and Danny. He'd been just a toddler when she was involved with Tom, so he wouldn't remember that relationship. And there hadn't been anyone since, at least no one Danny would've seen her snuggling with.

"I guess he is, honey," she said, knowing that she couldn't be anything but completely honest with her son. She sat on the edge of Danny's single bed where he'd been resting since Terrance and Edgar had left with the pony. "How do you feel about that?"

Danny shrugged. "I dunno."

"Do you like Terrance?"

"Yeah, I guess so. He's okay." Danny paused to stifle a yawn. "Are you gonna get married?"

"Goodness, what a question." Rachel smiled as she smoothed his warm forehead. "It's much too soon to be thinking about that. Why do you ask?"

Danny yawned again and leaned back into the pillows. "Just wondering."

Standing up, Rachel straightened the top sheet and pulled the lightweight blanket over Danny. "Take a nap now, hon. You've had a big morning. We'll talk about this again, okay?"

Danny nodded sleepily. "Can I have some lemonade later on?"

"Sure thing. I'll go make it right now." She quickly bussed Danny's cheek. "Go to sleep, sweetie. Grandma and Grandpa are coming over later this afternoon, so you need to rest up."

She watched him punch his pillow once, before turning onto his sleeping side. As soon as he closed his eyes, she left for the kitchen. Was her involvement with Terrance going to be a problem for Danny? she wondered. He'd always seemed happy to see Terrance and happy to spend time with him. Was Danny having second thoughts now?

Rachel pulled a burning cold can of lemonade concentrate from the freezer. Then she thought how Danny never had to share her with anyone before. Not really. Her son had always been the center of her attention. He was everything to her. But her growing feelings for Terrance were compelling. He was becoming very important to another side of her life—the womanly side, which had been neglected far too long. She and Danny would both have to make room in their lives for this man. As always, Danny was still her main concern. Except now he wasn't her only one. She hoped he could adjust to that.

As she mixed the frozen lemonade and water in a glass pitcher, the telephone rang.

"Rachel, it's Greg. How's Danny doing?"

"Much better," she replied flatly, although she couldn't suppress a wry grin. Greg wasn't one to waste time on the simple formalities of polite telephone conversation. *Hello, how are you?* was just not in his vocabulary. At least it wasn't when he was speaking to her.

"That's good. Look, I'm afraid we have to change our plans about coming down there tomorrow."

"What? Don't tell me you're canceling out again. He hasn't seen you in weeks."

"Wait just a second, Rachel, you're getting ahead of me." Impatience edged Greg's voice. "I'm still coming tomorrow, but Nancy won't be able to make it."

"Oh, is she still ill?"

"No, not all, She's never been better. We just thought it best not to expose her to Danny even though he's getting better. We don't want to chance it."

His explanation sounded odd to Rachel. "You mean Nancy's never had the chicken pox?"

"She's had them, but we're still concerned about exposure. You see, Rachel..." Greg's voice broke off for a moment.

He was obviously uncomfortable about something, Rachel realized. She just couldn't fathom what it could be.

"Rachel, this is kind of awkward," he continued. "I hope it doesn't bother you, or hurt you or anything, but...Nancy's pregnant. We're expecting a baby."

For the briefest of seconds, Rachel could've sworn her heart stopped beating.

Rachel offered her congratulations to Greg at the end of their conversation. But when she hung up the phone she still felt like she'd just been hit with a sledgehammer. She was also bewildered by her strong reaction to Greg's news. Surely she knew he'd be starting a new family sooner or later. Greg had always said he wanted lots of kids. This very thought served as an unsettling reminder of past heartache, and Rachel closed her eyes tight as she shoved the painful memory from her mind. She'd learned long ago that it was useless to dwell on the past.

The telephone rang again almost right away, and she thought it was Greg calling back. Instead, it was Ilsa. "Lovey, I need to get away from my diseased children. I think I am getting chicken pox of the brain. Can you come out to lunch with me this afternoon?"

Getting away for lunch sounded wonderful. "I've really got to talk to you about something that's just come up," she told Ilsa. "I'm sure my parents won't mind coming over a little earlier this afternoon to baby-sit Danny."

A short while later, Rachel met Ilsa at a sidewalk café in Coolidge Corner in the heart of Brookline. As the Green Line streetcar clattered past them on the Beacon Street tracks, they each gave their luncheon order to the waitress.

"I cannot believe you ordered all that food," Ilsa exclaimed. "Reuben sandwich, onion rings, house salad and a beer? I thought you were dieting."

"Not today."

"Oh, oh, something really is on your mind. Tell Ilsa everything."

Rachel promptly told Ilsa about Greg's phone call and how it made her feel.

Ilsa leaned forward, cupping her fair-skinned face between her large hands. "Hit you hard?" she noted matter-of-factly. "Not because you still have feelings for your ex, I hope."

"Of course not," Rachel answered adamantly. "We're two completely different people now. The only thing Greg and I have in common is Danny." Rachel peered across the table at her friend. "But you know, I am worried about Danny. I'm not sure how he'll take this news."

"Hmm, could be tricky. Greg will tell him about the baby tomorrow?"

"No, not until next weekend when Danny goes up to New Hampshire. Greg says he and Nancy want to break the news to Danny together."

"Maybe that is good. I think Danny will get used to the idea." Ilsa took a swallow of cold beer.

"Maybe." Rachel stared down at her untouched sandwich for quite some time while she wrestled with her concerns. With a restless sigh, she finally lifted her eyes to Ilsa's patiently waiting gaze. "You know why Greg's announcement really got to me, don't you?"

Ilsa nodded her blond head knowingly. "You cannot have any more babies, and it hurts you to be reminded of it."

"Oh, I never ever forget that fact, Ilsa," Rachel said as her body tensed—as it always did—when she spoke of her own sterility. "And I learned to deal with it long ago. I know how lucky I am to have Danny. A lot of women would give anything to have just one baby...."

"Still, you feel sad about it."

"Sometimes," Rachel conceded, her fingers tightening around the handle of her beer mug. "Like when my ex-husband very self-consciously tells me his current wife is having a baby...the baby I could never have even if we'd stayed together. Or when it turns a promising relationship into a complete disaster—like what happened with Tom back in Washington. Things between us had been going so well until I told him."

"Ah that," Ilsa blurted out in disgust. "Everything you told me about that convinces me that Tom person was a jerk."

Rachel shook her head. "He wasn't. What he did was understandable."

"Cruel is more like it."

"He wanted children of his own...." Rachel shook her head again, unable to continue. It still hurt to think about it.

"Forget about Tom, anyway. What about Terrance?"

Perplexed, Rachel stared across the table at Ilsa. "What about Terrance?"

"Have you told him you cannot have babies?"

"For God's sake, Ilsa, I've only known the man a few weeks. That's not long enough."

"Much can happen between a man and a woman in a matter of weeks. Jimmy and I met and decided to marry within two weeks' time."

For the first time that afternoon, Rachel couldn't help smiling. "But Ilsa, you're an exception to every rule."

"Never mind that," Ilsa said sharply. "Whether you have known him long enough or not, you care for Terrance Nelson. I can see it. And you two are getting closer every day. Am I right?"

"Maybe."

"Maybe, maybe." Ilsa tossed her hands up in despair, but her voice softened. "Will you be afraid to tell him you can't have children because of what happened before? Surely you don't think that will make a difference to a man like Terrance?"

"All things considered, probably not. Yet that day he took us sailing he seemed to be enjoying Danny a great deal," she said almost wistfully, remembering Terrance's remark about wishing for a second chance with children.

Ilsa gave her a quizzical stare. "So?"

"Oh never mind." Rachel leaned back in her chair. "In any case, Terrance has a tendency to run hot and cold when it comes to us—he's concerned about our age difference. Why spill my heart out to him about something so—so—intimate about myself when he may be out of my life tomorrow?''

"I do not believe that," insisted Ilsa, her German accent sounding thicker. "I've seen the light in Terrance's eyes when he comes to pick you up for a date. And do you think he would bring that pony for Danny today if he did not think the world of you?''

"Ilsa—"

"And isn't he coming to our big exhibit opening tomorrow night? He's coming to be with you and for no other reason.''

Rachel sighed deeply, shaking her head wearily. "I wish I could be as sure of Terrance as you seem to be.'' She wished it from the bottom of her heart.

"Oh Rachel, why do you feel that way?''

"Self-preservation," Rachel replied dryly. "Tomorrow night is kind of a milestone, you know—at least it is in my mind.''

"How?''

"It's the first time we'll be together in front of friends and colleagues since we started seeing each other. Frankly, I don't know what to expect from him." Rachel couldn't help thinking about the night they ran into his friends at the gallery opening.

Ilsa frowned. "You think he will be distant... indifferent?''

"I don't know," Rachel answered. "But his son Gordon is accompanying him to the reception. Oh Ilsa, I'm sure Terrance hasn't told him we're involved. And that makes me real nervous.''

RACHEL WORKED in high gear all the next day attending to the final preparations for the opening of the museum's Hudson River school exhibit. She checked and rechecked everything from security details to how many bottles of champagne the caterer had on hand for the reception. Once satisfied with the food and liquor setups in the mansion's grand hallway, Rachel returned home to get herself ready.

She was grateful that Greg had taken Danny on an outing to his brother's house on the Cape to be followed by a late supper of pizza back at her place. After being sick for so long, Danny was finally well enough for a change of scene. Since Greg's brother lived alone, there was no chance of exposing anyone else to the chicken pox. The outing also gave Rachel the chance to bathe and dress for her big night without any distractions.

She felt she had her opening night jitters fairly well under control by the time she was making up her face. In a few hours the exhibit would be officially opened, the party would be over and she would be able to breathe easy at last. Everything would turn out just fine.

She experienced a brief resurgence of nervous butterflies when she looked again at the dress she'd specifically bought for this occasion. It was a gown of rich emerald silk, simple lines and beautiful cut. It was also strapless, and Rachel had never worn a strapless anything in her life. She didn't think herself overly modest or prudish—she just was a tad self-conscious about the amount of skin she'd be exposing. And what if, on the wildest of off chances, the bodice should slip an indelicate inch or so?

Of course, Rachel knew that was a ridiculously unjustifiable fear. Her figure filled the gown very nicely—and securely. Carefully slipping the silk over her head, she still worried that the gown was a bit much, a bit too sexy for tonight's reception. But Ilsa, who had gone shopping with her, had insisted it was perfect for the occasion. As Ilsa had attended many prominent social functions with her husband over the years, Rachel decided to rely on her friend's instincts. Besides, she did look pretty good in the dress. And it made her feel so wonderfully feminine and chic.

A look in the full-length mirror confirmed that impression again. Everything would be okay, she told herself again as she brushed her wavy auburn hair until its length neatly grazed her bare skin. Yet as she wrapped a matching silk stole around her shoulders and headed out her front door, Rachel still felt anxious. A well organized opening and looking her best would be of little help when she finally came face-to-face with Gordon Nelson again. She just didn't know what kind of reception to expect from Terrance's son.

When she arrived back at the mansion, she was too busy to dwell on her anxieties about Terrance and Gordon. The exhibit was officially opened and the party began. Rachel stood beside her boss, John Hollings, near the front of the hall to greet the arriving sponsors, patrons and friends of the Wrentham Museum.

During a lull in the stream of arrivals, John went off to speak with the mayor and Ilsa joined Rachel by the main entrance.

"Everyone is raving about the exhibit," Ilsa bubbled gleefully. "It is a hit!"

Rachel grinned widely. "I know. People keep coming back to congratulate us. John is pleased and I'm absolutely thrilled."

"You have a right to be. You masterminded this whole thing. Of course you had my expert help," Ilsa added lightly.

"I couldn't have done it without you," Rachel said, knowing it was the unvarnished truth.

"And was I not right about that dress?" Ilsa shamelessly reminded Rachel. "You are a knockout."

"You look pretty hot there yourself, Ilsa," Rachel offered, noting how nicely Ilsa's slim-fitting gold gown set off her Teutonic blond looks.

Glancing about the crowded room, Ilsa whispered to Rachel, "Have Terrance and his son arrived?"

"Not yet. But it's still on the early side."

"Hmm. This could be nerve-racking."

"You're telling me. By the way, where is that tall, handsome husband of yours?"

"Oh I lost Jimmy back at the shrimp bowl. He'll turn up," replied Ilsa, still carefully looking around her. "Speaking of the devil, though, looks like yours has shown up."

Rachel followed the direction of Ilsa's gaze. At the door stood Terrance and his son. Terrance spotted her at once and headed toward her, smiling. His eyes moved slowly down from her face and along the length of her dark green silk gown. She could tell he approved, and that knowledge added a girlish glow to her excitement at seeing him again.

Ilsa leaned down to murmur in Rachel's ear. "Apparently good looks run in that family. That Gordon is not bad himself."

Rachel's attention turned briefly to Gordon as he walked beside his father. He was as tall as Terrance, but had lighter coloring and curlier hair. He was as attractive as she'd remembered him. Yet he seemed to pale in comparison with his father. At least Rachel thought so. To her, the Terrance gradually approaching her now cut a marvelously romantic figure in his dark evening clothes.

"Rachel, I think it is time for me to leave before any fireworks begin," Ilsa informed her. "You are on your own. Bye."

"Coward," Rachel muttered in a low voice as Ilsa sauntered away. As the two Nelson men drew nearer, the butterflies in Rachel's stomach intensified. Everything will be all right, she kept telling herself over and over. And the welcoming light in Terrance's eyes gave her hope that he had told Gordon about her.

That hope, however, was quickly dashed when Terrance greeted her in a dispassionate manner. "You do remember Mrs. Bonner, don't you Gordon?" he continued in a startlingly neutral tone of voice.

Gordon squeezed her hand politely. "How could I forget the woman who wouldn't take no for an answer? I'm anxious to see how you put our money to use, Mrs. Bonner."

"I think you'll be pleased. And please, call me Rachel." She turned to Terrance, adding pointedly, "Both of you."

Rachel's mind was in a turmoil. She didn't know if she was more bitterly disappointed than angry. She supposed Terrance had a reason for keeping his involvement with her from his son. But she found it difficult to understand what it could be. Was it that same feeling of disloyalty to Eleanor that had overcome him when they had run into the Windoms at the gallery opening? she wondered with frustration. Or was he worried about Gordon's reaction to their relationship? Whatever was behind his behavior, she just knew that he wouldn't be intentionally demeaning. Besides, there was no rule set in stone that said Terrance's feelings for her was anyone else's business but their own.

Such rationale did not ease her mind at all. This charade Terrance evidently meant for them to play in front of his son made her tremendously uncomfortable. One would think he was ashamed of her, Rachel fumed.

She was glad that John Hollings chose that moment to return to her side. His effusive welcome to the exhibit's most important sponsors offered Rachel the opportunity to make a graceful exit. Under the pretense of needing to consult with the caterer, she promptly excused herself. She could sense Terrance's surprise at her sudden departure, and as she walked away she could feel his eyes following her.

She lost track of Terrance's whereabouts for some time after that. She'd last caught sight of her boss escorting Terrance and Gordon up the grand marble staircase leading to the special exhibit room. Then she threw herself into mingling with the reception guests. Terrance may have let her down, but professionally, this was her big night. She intended to enjoy every minute of it.

Yet after an hour of praise and congratulations about the exhibit, her success still felt incomplete. And that worried her—no—terrified her. For it reinforced what, subconsciously, she knew already: In a matter of a few short weeks, Terrance Nelson had become an almost essential ingredient in her happiness. How he looked at her, how he smiled, how he spoke, how he touched her, it had all come to mean much too much to her. Even her anger hadn't diminished those feelings.

She wanted him. Yet she still wasn't sure she could have him.

Clearly, she had to talk to him and get matters straightened out. This evening's masquerade in front of

Gordon had scared her badly. It made her realize that she couldn't live with the uncertainty of Terrance's ambivalence. She would not continue feigning indifference toward him for the benefit of his family and friends.

Searching the room, Rachel finally found Terrance speaking with two gentlemen from Hub Insurance Corporation. Gordon was nowhere in sight. Because Hub Insurance was a frequent museum sponsor, Rachel knew the two men with Terrance well enough to join them.

Terrance seemed more relaxed with her in front of these two men than he'd been in front of his own son. The four of them shared an easy, congenial conversation for several minutes until the Hub representatives excused themselves to leave. Terrance stayed by Rachel's side, however, smiling down at her with appreciative eyes.

"You look absolutely gorgeous," he whispered with a wink of his eye. "Ravishing. And I've been wanting to tell you that all evening."

Terrance's gaze made her pulse quicken, and she could feel her angry resolve softening. But just for a moment. "Terrance," she said quickly, "may I have a word with you outside please?" She nodded at the opened French doors leading to the terrace.

"My pleasure," he said, lightly cupping her elbow as they headed outside.

The huge stone-floored terrace was deserted—much to Rachel's relief. At the ornately carved stone railing, she stopped and turned to Terrance. The dim outdoor lighting and the overcast evening sky cast flickering half shadows across his face. They tended to shift and change with any slight movement he made. It was hard to focus on his face when it seemed so clouded and elusive.

But then Terrance bent his head down to brush her lips with a gentle kiss. "Rachel, the exhibit, the party, everything is wonderful," he said. "I'm so proud of you. You certainly should be proud." His eyes hovered over hers, and she could feel his warm breath against her cheek. Suddenly forgetting her grievances, Rachel wanted nothing more than to sink into his arms.

But she didn't. She wasn't about to permit her strong fascination with the man to overrule her common sense now. This hot and cold behavior of his would drive her crazy. Was Terrance aware of how it affected her? She didn't know. She did know she couldn't let it continue.

"Terrance, we have to sit down and talk," she finally blurted out. "Can you come by the house later to-night?"

His blue-gray eyes darkened with concern. "Rachel, what is it? What's the matter?"

"It can wait until we're alone."

"We are alone. And if something's troubling you, I want to know now. You know you can say anything to me," he urged.

With that, Rachel could no longer hold back. "I'm not so sure I can," she replied, resentment ringing strong in her voice. "Not when how you feel about me is as much a mystery to me as it is a secret to everyone else."

"Rachel, I—"

"You acted like you scarcely knew me in front of your son and everyone else," she continued briskly. "It hurt, Terrance, it hurt and—"

Shaking his head, he pulled her tight against his chest. "I should've realized. Rachel, hurting you is the last thing I want to do."

Rachel glanced up at his face. "Are you embarrassed about us?"

"No, I'm just an idiot," he answered sternly. "And I'm sure all the reasons I conjured up for not telling my sons aren't worth a damn. They certainly aren't worth upsetting you like this."

"Terrance, it's just that . . . I care for you," she haltingly began to explain, "and I never seem to know where I stand with you from one day to the next."

His eyes were filled with remorse. "Darling, I'm so sorry," he murmured as he tenderly stroked her hair.

A quick step resounded sharply against the stone floor. Startled, Terrance and Rachel glanced up at once. There at the door, shrouded by the evening shadows, stood Gordon. Rachel held her breath for several agonizing seconds. For even in the murky half-light, half-dark, Gordon's shocked expression was vivid proof that he'd seen his father embracing her.

"Gordon, what—?"

"Dad . . . No, look, I'm—sorry for intruding," Gordon stammered with much embarrassment. "I thought you might be ready to leave. But . . ." Turning abruptly around, Gordon muttered something about calling himself a cab. Then he was gone.

Rachel stared at the empty doorway, stunned. She knew something awful like this would happen. She just knew it. If Gordon didn't like her to begin with, Lord knows what he was thinking about her now. And at this point, Rachel wasn't even sure she cared.

"Damn! I should've known. . . ." Terrance's face looked grave as he turned to her.

"Yes, you should have."

"Rachel, I'm sorry this happened."

"Oh don't apologize to me," she said tersely while wondering if this relationship was more hassle than it was worth. She was pretty fed up with being the yo-yo on Terrance's string of ambivalence.

"Rachel, we have—"

She stopped him with an exasperated glare. She simply didn't want to hear it. "Terrance, why don't you just go talk to your son. I'm absolutely certain he'll be interested in what you have to say."

Chapter Six

He'd bungled things badly. Very badly. Terrance couldn't blame Rachel if she was furious with him. Driving back to her house several hours later, Terrance was determined to set matters right again. Somehow, someway.

Storrow Drive was almost deserted at this late hour. It was just as well. Although his eyes were riveted to the road ahead, his mind was not on his driving. He couldn't stop hearing the exasperation in Rachel's voice or seeing the shock on Gordon's face. It had all exploded in their faces tonight, and it was all his fault.

He had caught up with his son just as Gordon was unlocking the front door of his Beacon Hill town house. Once inside, Terrance had chosen his words carefully as he explained how he and Rachel Bonner had become involved.

"Hey Dad, it's your life," Gordon had said as he paced the length of his wood-paneled den several times. "It's none of my business whom you choose to spend time with."

But Gordon's face had betrayed his claim of disinterest. Terrance wasn't surprised. Although Gordon knew his father dated on occasion, he'd never seen Terrance touch any other woman but Eleanor. Tonight, Gordon had seen him embracing Rachel, a woman closer to Gordon's age than to his own. It must have been particularly jolting. And Terrance could see that his son did not approve at all.

Who in his social or business world would approve of such a relationship? Terrance wondered as he sped past a cluster of Boston University buildings. Hell, that kind of approval didn't seem to matter much now.

But Gordon and Kerry mattered. They meant the world to him, and Terrance never wanted anything to come between them. Perhaps anticipating the boys' misgivings, he had purposely put off telling them about Rachel. Terrance knew now that was wrong and unfair to the boys.

And terribly unfair to Rachel.

If it was all so unfair, why had he kept silent? Why indeed? Terrance thought as his grip on the steering wheel tightened. Only now as he agonized over the pain he caused Rachel could he acknowledge his motivations. The problem was that in coming to terms with his questionable actions, his own pain was aroused—the pain caused by his loss of the past and his fear of the future.

Tonight, however, it was all so clear to him. Telling his sons about Rachel constituted a risk, for it would've established her in his life and inevitably led him to have expectations, *hope* for the future. But Eleanor's death had taught him the fallacy of such expectations, and he'd been left behind alone and empty. How could he allow Rachel to become entrenched in his existence when she could, for many reasons having nothing to do with death, so easily be out of his life tomorrow? Snap! Just like that it could be over. She'd be gone and he would be alone. Again.

When Terrance finally arrived at the museum's entrance gate, the security guard recognized him right away. "Mr. Nelson, good evening. What can I do for you?"

"I'm here to see Mrs. Bonner, Larry."

"She didn't leave word you were coming by. She usually does."

"I know. Would you call and tell her I'm here, please?"

Larry glanced at his wristwatch. "Gee, Mr. Nelson, it's almost midnight. What if Mrs. Bonner's already turned in?"

"It's important I see her, Larry. I'm sure she won't be angry with you."

Terrance wished he could be equally as sure that Rachel wasn't too angry to see him. Even if she wasn't, he didn't know how to explain his conflicting feelings to her. Why couldn't he believe her when she said their age difference didn't faze her? Where she was so accepting, he was full of questions. What if a man closer to her own age came into the picture? Wouldn't a vibrant young woman like Rachel prefer to be with a younger man? Even if another man didn't come along, how long would it be before their own attraction came crashing into the hard cold reality of twenty years?

How long would he have her in his life? Ah, that was the crux of the whole matter, Terrance mused wearily.

Larry hung up the phone in his booth and set the electronic gate in motion. "All right, Mr. Nelson, you can go ahead."

When he drove up to her house she was standing inside the screen door, waiting. A stream of light behind her and the single lamp above the front door bathed her in a softening warmth. Terrance was relieved that her face was no longer taut with anger. But she wasn't smiling, either. She just watched silently as he walked toward her.

Wrapped in a simple dark blue silk robe, she looked even lovelier than she had in that sexy green evening dress. Terrance slowly mounted the three porch steps and then stopped. Gazing across the short distance that now separated him from Rachel, he tried desperately to find the right words.

"Thanks for seeing me." When she made no reply, he continued on. "Rachel, in a few months I'll be forty-nine years old. You're just thirty-one. When we're alone together those years between us seem to magically vanish. But we're not alone in this world, are we?"

Slowly, Rachel swung open the screen door. Its creaking spring pierced the quiet night. "Come inside," she said lowly, reaching for his arm to draw him into the house.

Her touch was light, yet Terrance was strongly aware of it. As she led him to the living room, her hair moved soft and full against her neck. He could still recall how lush it felt beneath his fingers when he'd stroked it just hours ago. His muscles tensed as a renewed desire washed over him.

Rachel switched on the table lamp next to the sofa and then sat down. She patted the empty cushion to her right. Wordlessly, he sat beside her. Finally she turned to him, and even in the dimly lit room her simple beauty shone. Now scrubbed clean of the evening's makeup, her face was fresh, glowing.

Rachel watched Terrance lean back into the sofa. Still dressed in his elegant evening clothes, his tall, angular frame dominated the room, made it seem smaller. What a waste to worry about their age difference, she thought. In her eyes, Terrance was as vital and as appealing as any man of thirty-five—maybe even more so. And Lord, what an affect he had on her. For she knew she should be angry at him; she knew she should give him hell. But instead, she was just glad that he was with her. She gazed into his smoky gray-blue eyes and saw that they were waiting.

"Perhaps you can tell me, Terrance," she said calmly, "why I'm never able to stay mad at you. No matter how richly you deserve it."

Surprise, and then relief flashed across his face. But he still said nothing—as if he weren't sure what to say. This reaction struck a chord of tenderness in Rachel; she identified with it. There were so many things she'd been wanting to say to Terrance, only the right words had never seemed to come to her.

His reaction touched her heart for another reason as well. From the very first, Terrance had been unfailingly poised, clever, sophisticated and always the master of any situation he might be in. Now, in his uncertainty, he seemed more real, more human somehow and more accessible. Almost involuntarily, her fingers reached out to graze his hand.

He enclosed his hand around hers in an impassioned grip. His touch warmed the depths of her heart. She held on tightly to his hand and her eyes never wavered from his.

"Rachel, we have something special."

She nodded silently.

"But the gap in our ages is very real and wide."

His message was disheartening. Yet there was something in the passionate resonance of his voice and the torn emotions glistening in his usually smiling eyes that quickened a desire in her soul. At that moment, Rachel knew she wasn't going to simply give up. She'd wanted

Terrance before that unfortunate encounter with Gordon; she wanted him now. All consequence dissolved from her mind as the feelings she'd been wanting to express for weeks now crystallized and took form.

"It's too late—for me anyway—to worry and wonder," she murmured gently. "I'm already falling in love with you."

A long silence ensued until Terrance pulled her closer to him. Holding her head between his hands, he kissed her hair, her forehead, her eyes. Finally his cheek came to rest against her hair. Rachel could feel his breath against her ear as he spoke. "Too late for me as well."

He kissed her fully and with a strength of emotion that spurred her own passion. She returned his kiss and deepened it. This was what she wanted, to show him how she felt, to reveal her emotions, her desires, without holding back. Curling her fingers in Terrance's dark hair, she lost herself in their kiss. Drawing her even closer now, his hand caressed her shoulder blade as he trailed urgent kisses along her throat and across her cheek until his lips found hers again.

It was wonderful and dizzying, and soon Rachel's head was spinning with memories of the happy times they'd shared in recent weeks. Her days had been so full since she met Terrance, her happiness more than just fleeting. Those good times far outweighed any uncomfortable moments. What had happened between them earlier this evening couldn't possibly matter when they could hold each other like this. Opening up to each other's true feelings was what was important. It was what made them right.

Terrance's fingers were now stroking the curve of her neck, taunting her bare skin with delightful tingles. Rachel sighed against his lips, tightening her arms around his muscular back as she sought yet another kiss. Now, despite the haze of sensual pleasure that befogged her mind, Rachel could almost see those twenty years "magically vanish" from all reason. Surely Terrance must see that, too.

Finally, gasping for air, she eased herself away from Terrance's embrace. Searching his eyes, she heard herself ask, "You are falling in love with me?"

He kissed her lips. "I must be."

"But?" She couldn't help saying it; this was all too good to be true.

"No 'buts' Rachel—not after tonight. Tonight I discovered you're more precious to me than I'd realized— more than I wanted you to be."

Rachel felt a twinge of uneasiness. "More than you wanted? Because of the age difference."

"Twenty minutes ago, before I walked into this house, I would've said yes, that's exactly why. But now… here…Rachel, we feel so right together. It's not so clear-cut anymore." Terrance paused briefly, then he shook his head. "So to hell with what anyone else thinks."

"You may not care about what others think, but it still concerns you doesn't it?"

"I'd be lying if I said it didn't, Rachel. It's a fact of our lives. We can never completely dismiss it. I don't want our age difference to keep us apart. I do think we should be prepared for our share of obstacles because of it. I mean it hasn't been exactly easy so far, has it?"

Rachel nestled her head on his shoulder. "No, it hasn't. But I feel like everything's changed now that we've admitted how we feel."

His lips brushed her forehead. "I made it harder for both of us by holding back. I guess I was operating under the theory that you can't lose what you never had in the first place. Maybe I was being a little too sensible for my own good."

"It sounds more like an emotional reaction to me," Rachel offered. And that very fact made her want to reassure him. She reached for his hand, kissed it and then pressed it gently against her heart. "Terrance, we're just beginning. Let's just see where our feelings lead us."

He smiled warmly. "Darling, I love your hope, your resolve."

"And my indignation?"

"Definitely. That fiery gleam in your eyes is very sexy."

His smoky gaze thrilled her. She touched his cheek and then her fingers combed through his dark hair. Gently she pulled his head closer to hers until Terrance's lips hovered just over hers. His eyes were so close that she could see her own eyes reflected in their bluish depths. She kissed him with all the longing in her heart.

"Rachel," he finally said in a husky whisper, "we're not alone, are we? Danny's home tonight."

Reluctantly, she nodded yes. "His room is right next to mine."

"Then I better go. Now."

That he was struggling with his desires was written all over his face. And oh, how she wanted him to stay. Yet Rachel knew they weren't in a position to allow themselves to be carried away by the intensity of the moment.

As if he had read Rachel's mind, Terrance assured her, "There'll be time for us . . . soon."

Rachel was feeling a bit desolate. "Sometimes I wonder, Terrance."

"I promise you, we will be together." He squeezed her arm gently. "Then we'll be sure, and then it'll be right."

"LOOK DAD, I don't have time for a family powwow the first thing on a Monday morning," Gordon claimed acidly. "Besides, I know what you want to say to Kerry and me, and I've already heard it. Frankly Dad, I should be downstairs at my desk, not here in your office discussing your..."

From behind his massive old mahogany desk, Terrance regarded his son with a stern eye. "My what, Gordon?"

"Mrs. Bonner."

"I want to tell you and your brother what is happening between Rachel and me."

"Dad, I know what's happening. I saw it with my own eyes last night. Remember? I also told you it's none of my business. Why should I have to sit through this again?"

"Because you were in no frame of mind to listen to me last night. And because there's much more that I have to say about it."

"Dad, save the speeches for Kerry. He's the sensitive one. But why make a big deal about it all? Go ahead, have your fun and get it out of your system."

Terrance slapped his hand on his desk in despair. "Gordon, why do you refuse to take this seriously?"

Gordon stood in front of the desk, calmly peering down at Terrance. "How can I? She's young enough to be your daughter." Then his voice sounded more compassionate. "I know you've been lonely without Mom all these years. I'm sure it's your loneliness that's made you susceptible to someone like her. I'm sure she knows that, too. Look, the woman is no dummy. The first time I met her she was looking for money for her museum. Maybe now she's looking out for her own interests."

Terrance glared angrily at Gordon as protective feelings for Rachel grew fiercely within him. If there was one thing Rachel was not, it was a gold digger. And he didn't want anyone thinking that about her.

"I'm sorry to say that, Dad," Gordon went on, "but you've taught me to be honest about my feelings. And that is exactly how I feel about Rachel Bonner."

"So, even though you scarcely know the woman, you think she's after me for my money?" Terrance said, derision piercing his tone. "Your old man is too over-the-hill to interest the young woman on his own, nonmonetary merits?"

"You're putting words in my mouth, Dad. You know exactly what I mean. In time, I'm sure you'll realize I'm right about the whole thing." Gordon started edging his way toward the door. "So as I said, enjoy yourself. I'm not worried. You're much too shrewd to get caught in any traps."

At that moment, Kerry appeared in the doorway. "What traps?"

Grinning slyly, Gordon turned to his brother. "You'll know soon enough." Then he eyed Kerry from head to toe. "Ten minutes late and inappropriately dressed for the office to boot. Have you got a lot to learn, little brother. Good luck."

"Hey, where are you going?" Kerry asked as Gordon whisked by him. Stepping inside the office, he looked to Terrance. "I thought you said this was a family meeting."

"Apparently Gordon's decided to abdicate from the family—for this morning at least." Terrance wearily leaned back in his leather desk chair and waved to Kerry to take a seat.

Watching his younger son stride into the room, he found himself seconding Gordon's opinion about Kerry's attire. Denim jacket, T-shirt, jeans. Not exactly what Terrance would wish his son to wear to his place of business—where Kerry himself would soon be holding a responsible position. But Terrance understood that Kerry's dress reflected his casual student life-style, not that of a nine-to-five businessman. Well, they would straighten out his wardrobe soon enough. A pre-wedding shopping trip to Brooks Brothers would take care of that.

Kerry lowered his lanky frame into the nearest chair, stretching his long legs lazily before him. "So Dad, what's this all about? You must really mean business if you haul us in here at nine on a Monday morning."

Terrance sensed a defensiveness in Kerry's tone, which puzzled him. Had Gordon already tipped him off about Rachel? But why would that put him on the defensive? No, Terrance thought, he must be imagining it.

"How's Martha?" Terrance asked. "Have you two set a date for the wedding yet?"

Terrance observed his son leaning so far back into his chair that its two front legs were precariously tilted off the floor—a careless childhood habit that Kerry still hadn't outgrown.

"We've narrowed it down to either the end of September or the beginning of October. We'll be deciding for sure any day now. But don't worry Dad, we'll let you know in plenty of time." Kerry suddenly straightened the chair. "That's what this is all about, right? You and Gordon wanted to know how soon to add my name to the office door."

The defensiveness was real after all. Still, Terrance wasn't sure why Kerry would feel that way. "Actually, the reason I asked you here has nothing to do with your future plans, Son. I asked about you and Martha because I haven't seen you in a couple of weeks."

"So we're not here to talk about me?" Kerry asked, appearing rather surprised and a shade relieved.

"No, we're here to talk about me."

"You?"

"And about a woman I've been seeing."

"Dad, just a few weeks ago, you told me you weren't seeing anyone in particular. Now this?"

"A lot has happened since then."

"I guess so. But why did you have to call me in here like this? Are you planning to get married or something?"

Terrance smiled broadly and shook his head. "Not that much has happened—not yet anyway."

"Dad, come out with it," Kerry insisted as he slouched back into the chair. "What's this all about?"

Carefully and deliberately, Terrance told Kerry about Rachel Bonner. He tried to be as matter-of-fact about it as possible, especially when he revealed what had happened with Gordon the previous night.

"Old Gordo didn't take this too well, did he?" Kerry mused when Terrance had finished explaining.

"That's why he refused to stay this morning. He thinks it's just a passing fancy."

"Well, isn't it, Dad?" Kerry asked pointedly. "I mean, she is only thirty-one."

"It most definitely is not," Terrance adamantly replied, although he was disappointed in Kerry's reaction. For some reason, he thought his younger son would be more understanding about it.

But Kerry was shaking his head with no small degree of incredulity. "I just can't see it, Dad. I mean you've always been so down-to-earth. This isn't like you at all."

"Perhaps you don't know me as well as you think."

"Guess not."

"I'm not drawn to Rachel Bonner just because she's young and attractive. I care about her because she's a warm, sincere person. You understand that, don't you?"

Kerry shrugged. "If you say so. But I bet she's a looker. Right?"

Terrance decided it was best to keep quiet about how beautiful he thought Rachel was. "You can see for yourself next Sunday afternoon. Two o'clock at the company's box seats at Fenway. I want you and Gordon to meet Rachel and her little boy, Danny. We'll go out to dinner after the game."

"Hmm, sounds like a command appearance."

"It is. And bring Martha if she's free. She'll be part of this family soon enough. And Kerry?"

"Yeah, Dad?"

"I've always thought you less rigid, not as quick to judge as your brother. Rachel's a good person."

"Ah, Dad, I don't really believe she's a gold digger or anything like that," Kerry declared, staring down at his hands self-consciously. "It just seems strange. You know, you and someone so different from Mom."

"I know," Terrance said gently, glad that Kerry had opened up to him. "It's even taken me some getting used to."

"Well, Dad, you know I'm on your side. I promise to give your Rachel the benefit of the doubt."

Terrance gazed at his son fondly. They talked—really talked—so rarely these days. He realized how much he missed it. But now, the special closeness he and Kerry had shared throughout the years felt as if it had been revived. For the moment anyway. He wanted to hug him, but didn't. It might be too embarrassing for Kerry to have his father go sentimental on him. Instead Terrance invited him to lunch. "We haven't had a chance to talk alone in a long time."

"Ah, Dad, I'd really like that, but I can't. Not today," Kerry said regretfully as he rose from the chair. "How about a rain check?"

"Anytime. I mean that." Trying to keep his disappointment from showing, he quickly got to his feet and moved from behind the desk. He walked Kerry to the door. "We'll see you on Sunday, then?"

"Absolutely. Sunday at Fenway at two." Then, with his hand on the doorknob, Kerry paused and turned around slowly. "Dad, there is something I've been wanting to talk to you about."

Terrance thought Kerry sounded awkward, and his blue eyes seemed anxious. "Something troubling you, Son?"

Kerry's body stiffened as he released his grip on the doorknob. "Yes—no—I mean nothing's troubling me," he stammered nervously. "I'm concerned about something—about my coming to work here."

"Why should you be concerned about it? You decided to join us months ago. Everything's been arranged. You just have to say when. You know that."

"Well, I was thinking, maybe I'm not suited for NBM."

"What do you mean 'not suited'?" Terrance asked, unable to hide his concern. "This company belongs to you—to you and Gordon."

"But that's it. Gordon has a brilliant mind for business—he's like you. I mean, let's face it, Dad, I'll never be that good. I'd probably be more of a hindrance than a help."

"Nonsense. You have many fine qualities that will benefit the business," Terrance insisted, realizing for the first time that Kerry's delay in joining the company was due to a lack of confidence. Terrance had never doubted his son's capabilities for a minute. But he'd been remiss about telling him so.

He hastened to reassure Kerry. "You are different from Gordon, and your skills will counterbalance his beautifully. Frankly, I can't wait to see my two sons working together. The sooner you start the better as far as I'm concerned. I was very happy when you decided to join the company after you became engaged to Martha."

"You were?"

"Of course. Your mother and I always hoped that's what you boys would want to do. We built this company for you." Terrance looked closely at Kerry. He had hoped his reassurances would put Kerry's mind at ease. Still, his eyes seemed clouded, his expression was strained.

"Don't worry, Kerry. I'll be here to help you, to guide you. It's going to work out just fine."

Kerry nodded with a slight smile. "Great, Dad. That's just great."

"ISN'T IT LOVELY to have a nice grown-up brunch without the kids running all about?" Ilsa remarked, leaning back in the white mesh patio chair. Shading her eyes against the bright late morning sun, she quickly added, "Not that I'm not crazy about them."

"Well, it is nice to have a break from them now and then," Rachel added before addressing the two men sitting across the table from her. "Jim, Terrance, more coffee, pie?"

Terrance pushed his dessert plate aside. "Just coffee this time around. But save me a second helping of that pie for later on."

"Well, I won't be here later on," Jim Baird piped in, handing his plate to Rachel, "so I'll just take you up on that offer, thank you."

Ilsa sat up instantly. "Jimmy, that is your third helping of pie!"

"I know, I know, and I shouldn't indulge," Jim responded, not sounding the least bit contrite. "But how often do I get fresh homemade blueberry pie? You certainly don't make it for me."

"That is quite so," retorted Ilsa, pretending to be miffed. "I may not be much of a baker, but I do have other talents."

Reaching across the table for his wife's hand, Jim growled lowly, "That you have, my sweet. And I love you madly for them." He drew Ilsa's hand to his lips and made a great show of kissing it passionately.

"Okay, you two. Let's have a little propriety at the meal table, please," teased Rachel.

She was thoroughly enjoying her role as hostess on this blissfully sunny Saturday morning. She had pulled out all the stops with a menu of mimosas, fruit compote, cheese soufflé, hot rolls and freshly baked blueberry pie. Even her tiny backyard looked elegant with the patio table set with crisp linen and her best china and crystal. With Terrance at her side and the congenial company of Ilsa and Jim Baird, the small get-together was proving to be quite a success.

Rachel hadn't entertained much in recent years—she rarely had the reason or the desire to. But the urge had finally hit her, and she had thrown herself into the preparations for this Saturday morning brunch, loving every minute of it. Gazing across the table at Terrance, she flashed him a warm smile. She knew very well that he was the reason and the desire behind this new urge to entertain. He made her feel festive.

Terrance answered her smile with a playful wink just as Jim Baird plopped back in his chair with a groan. "I'm stuffed," he declared, having just finished his last morsel of pie. "Rachel, this has been wonderful. Everything. You are one good cook."

"Thank you, Jim. I'm glad you enjoyed it."

Jim shook his blond head in protest. "Don't thank me yet. I may not be able to move from this chair for a week. You'll be stuck with me, Rachel."

"Oh no, no, darling," Ilsa said, leaving her chair to stand behind her husband. Leaning over, she curled her arms affectionately around his shoulders. "You may have made a pig of yourself here, but I will not let you make a nuisance of yourself." She planted a kiss on top of his head. "Now start digesting while I help Rachel clean up. Then we must leave."

"You certainly will not help clean up, Ilsa. You're my guest."

"But there are so many dishes."

Terrance stood up, tossing his napkin back onto the table. "Ilsa, don't give it another thought. I'll help Rachel with the dishes."

Jim Baird let out a laugh and peered up at Terrance through his horn-rimmed eyeglasses. "I never thought I'd see Terrance Nelson, the founder and owner of one of the largest computer companies in America, offering to do drudge work like washing dishes. As they say in the press, you are a maverick of the industry."

"Don't let my public image fool you, Jim. I've been doing my own dishes for years." Then Terrance glanced fondly at Rachel. Extending her his hand, he helped her to her feet. "Besides, helping this lovely lady is no drudge work, believe me."

To her surprise, Terrance pulled her back against his chest, wrapped his arms around her waist and then playfully nuzzled her neck. Still holding her firmly, he looked again at Jim. "As you can see, I'm crazy about her."

Rachel gave him a curious sidelong glance. "Is that the mimosas talking, sir?"

"No, the blueberry pie." Terrance kissed her cheek.

"Ah ha! It always comes back to food," Rachel quipped, although she was basking in Terrance's affectionate behavior. Since the night of that awkward scene with Gordon, Terrance had genuinely been trying to be more open and honest about his feelings, to let their relationship follow its own natural course. For him to be so openly demonstrative toward her in front of the Bairds was of no small significance. Yes, Terrance really was trying—he knew it meant a lot to her. She could really love him for that.

Rachel noticed that Ilsa was taking this all in with faintly scoffing eyes. "Is his offer to do the dishes just a ruse to get rid of us so you two can be alone?" she finally said. "My experience has taught me that a man never offers to do dishes unless he has ulterior motives in mind."

Rachel shook her head. "Oh no, it's nothing like that, Ilsa. Terrance is a true Boy Scout. You know, good deeds and all that."

"Ilsa, my love," Jim interjected, managing to drag himself out of his chair. "Don't look a gift horse in the mouth. If they want to be alone now, that means we can be alone. We don't have to pick up the kids for another two hours."

"But Jimmy, I thought you were too stuffed to move?"

Sliding his arm around her waist, he pulled Ilsa close to his side. "Suddenly I feel the need for a little...recreation to help me work off that last piece of pie."

Although her cheeks reddened noticeably, Ilsa managed to answer gamely, "Well, in that case we'd better be off. Exercise is good for the metabolism, no?"

Rachel got a kick out of seeing Ilsa blush. She knew that Jim was the only person on earth who could make her turn pink..

After the Bairds departed, Terrance proposed they put off doing the dishes for a while. "Let's have one more cup of coffee," he suggested as he led Rachel back outside to the patio.

"Wait a minute, was all the business about helping with the dishes actually just a ruse to get me alone?" she baited.

Terrance poured more coffee into her empty cup. "Oh I'll help all right. But not right away. I do want to spend some time with you."

This kind of attention pleased Rachel to no end. Her mood light, she watched him with loving eyes as he sat back down at the table. "This has been a wonderful morning," she mused.

"Yes it has. I've had a fine time. In fact it's been so good that I'm getting excited about the outing with our kids."

"How do you think it will go tomorrow, Terrance?" she couldn't help but ask. "Do you think we'll all get along?"

"I know you're nervous about tomorrow. Hell, I'm nervous about it," Terrance admitted. "And I wish I could say everything's going to work out just fine. But I just don't know. We can only try."

Squinting against the sun, Rachel looked across the patio table at Terrance. Even though he, too, was wary about tomorrow's outing at the Red Sox game, his eyes shone with a certain contentment—something she hoped came because they were together. She shared that contentment, and she knew she had to lock it into her consciousness in order to survive tomorrow.

"Maybe Gordon and Kerry will be less skeptical when they see us together," she suggested.

"It might do the trick. Although I'm still concerned about whether or not Gordon actually shows up. He never really committed himself to coming." Terrance shook his head wearily. "At least Danny is taking all this in stride."

Rachel nodded. "So far. I told him that after he gets back from his father's tomorrow morning, we'd be going to meet your family at the ball game. But I've got to tell you, I think he's more excited about the front row seats near the Red Sox dugout than he is about seeing you or your sons."

Terrance chuckled. "A tried-and-true all-American boy. He'll probably make the afternoon a little easier for everybody."

"I'm not sure how he'll be tomorrow," she said listlessly, before taking another sip of coffee.

"What do you mean?"

"Today, Danny's father and stepmother are going to tell him about the new baby they're expecting. I'm worried about how he'll react."

"I see. Well, that is pretty momentous news for a boy who's been an only child all his life. But surely he's asked about brothers and sisters before this. All kids do. Haven't you ever discussed the possibility with him?''

Rachel suddenly felt uncomfortable. "Greg may have. I haven't," she said flatly, wanting very much to drop this subject.

Fortunately Terrance didn't notice her abrupt reply. He reached across the table for her hand and gave it an affectionate squeeze. "You've just got to stop worrying about your son and mine. Let's see, how can we get your mind off tomorrow's outing?''

"I don't think it's possible."

"Nonsense. Just let me think a minute or two."

While he was thinking he smiled across the table at her, his twinkling eyes irresistibly lifting her spirits. "How about a game of tennis?" he said at last.

"Are you kidding? Me play against you?"

"Why not? You've been taking lessons for weeks now. I'd love to see how well you're doing."

"Sure, if I was doing well," Rachel briskly quipped. "Terrance, I'm just a beginner—"

"For the third time. You must have learned something by now," he added slyly. "I'm not asking for the game of my life."

"You might as well be. It'll be years before I'd get on the same court as you. Terrance, I'm terrible, uncoordinated and slow. It'd be too embarrassing."

Terrance laughed heartily. "Rachel, you can't be that bad."

"Trust me."

"Well, I have more faith in you than that. Come on, it'll be fun." With a teasing glint in his eyes and a sly grin on his lips, Terrance took her hand again. "We could play a couple of quick sets. Come back here, shower, send out for dinner." His gaze became more intense as his voice deepened with romantic suggestiveness. "Then we'd have the rest of the night . . . alone under the stars."

Then Terrance lifted her hand to his lips for a brief whisper of a kiss.

"Hmm," Rachel murmured dreamily, her hand and arm tingling pleasantly. "Don't stop now. I could be convinced." She thought about what it would be like to finally be alone with Terrance—really alone. It was something that she'd been longing for, a longing that his open affection of today had only heightened.

"Wonderful," he said lowly before kissing her hand again.

She felt flush as a pleasurable yielding sensation rushed through her body. She leaned toward him as she answered in a taunting, yet breathy, whisper, "Yet your price seems high. I would have to expose my incompetence on the tennis courts." Rachel gazed at him provocatively. "Couldn't we negotiate?"

"Perhaps." His reply sounded like a weakening growl. "If the terms are right, I could be bought."

Drawing closer to her, he met her lips in a long, languid kiss. Rachel didn't want it to end. For not only did this sweet kiss hold the promise of more kisses to come, it also blotted out her anxiety about the following day. She liked the feeling of living for the moment—no yesterday, no tomorrow. When she and Terrance were in tune like this, the rest of the world seemed to vanish.

Then the kitchen telephone rang, its clanging somewhat muffled but just as insistent sounding from the patio. At the second ring she shifted her mouth slightly away from Terrance's. "Forget about it," he murmured.

She wanted to. Oh, how she wanted to. But whenever Danny was away from her, she found it impossible to ignore a ringing telephone. Maternal instinct overruled passion. Terrance groaned as she pulled away. "I have to answer that. It might be about Danny." Terrance reluctantly released her hand. "But don't move an inch," she urged. "I'll be right back."

"Two minutes or I'm coming after you," Terrance playfully warned as she went inside the house.

Rachel was surprised to hear Greg's anxious voice when she answered the phone. "Rachel, Danny wants to go home. As soon as possible."

"Oh no. He's upset about the baby?"

"That would be my guess, although he won't admit it. I've never seen him behave like this before."

"What happened?"

"Last night we took him to the restaurant at the turkey farm he likes so much, and we told him during dinner. He seemed to take the news calmly enough. He asked a few questions, and then didn't say anything else about it for the rest of the evening. This morning, while Nancy was helping him make his bed, he asked her if the baby was going to have his room. Of course she said no. But he's been acting up all morning long, answering us back, getting into things he knows are off limits. When we reprimand him he cries and says he wants to go home."

"Oh, God," Rachel sighed.

Greg continued. "So I said I'd take him home. But he doesn't want that. He wants you to come get him. He insists upon it. Normally I wouldn't give in, Rachel, but he's so upset. Anything I say only seems to make matters worse. Can you drive up here and get him?"

"I'll leave right away."

Chapter Seven

Traffic on I-93 was rather light for a summer Saturday, so Rachel reached Greg's home on the outskirts of Peterborough in about an hour. She had only been to her ex-husband's house once before, so she followed his landmarks as she drove along the narrow country roads. When she reached the mailbox marked Bonner, she turned onto the long winding driveway. Apprehensive, she took a deep breath. Now she wished she had accepted Terrance's offer to accompany her. Rachel wasn't sure what awaited her at the end of the driveway.

She had turned Terrance down exactly because she didn't know what to expect. Danny was upset—that's all she knew. Her gut instinct told her this was a situation she'd better handle by herself. Terrance's presence would've been reassuring for her, true. But Danny's reaction might be another story altogether. He might regard Terrance as an intruder.

Danny was sitting, alone, on the front steps when Rachel reached the house. He looked downcast, lonely. Her heart ached for what he must be feeling. With his baseball cap pulled low over his eyes and his weekend duffle bag bunched beneath his arms, her little boy looked so small and vulnerable. He didn't even lift his head when she stopped the car in front of the house.

Greg apparently had heard her drive up because he opened the screen door just as she got out of the car. His head of unruly sandy hair, jeans, blue chamois shirt and workboots made Greg look very much the rugged outdoorsman. He seemed perfectly suited to his home's rural environment. Rachel glanced up at the large old house before her. She knew it had a lot of rooms to fill up with lots of children, and the surrounding wooded acres provided plenty of space for children to run and play. This is exactly what Greg had wanted since he was a kid. How often he'd spoken about it before and during their marriage.

The gravel driveway crunched beneath her feet as she approached Danny. "Hi, sweetheart."

"Hi, Mom," he said glumly without looking up at her. His eyes remained fixed on the step below him, still shielded by the bill of his cap.

Rachel sensed that Danny might also be feeling embarrassed by the uproar he'd created this morning. She thought it better not to press him about what had happened in front of Greg. "If you're ready to leave, why don't you go ahead and get into the car?"

He was on his feet in an instant and he hurried past her. "Hey wait a minute," Rachel called. "Aren't you going to say goodbye to your father?"

Danny glanced back at the house. "Bye Dad, thank you," he said solemnly.

Greg stepped to the edge of the front porch. "Sure thing, Dan. We want you to come back real soon." He paused, his eyes searching the sky awkwardly for something else to say. "Maybe I'll give you a call tomorrow morning."

Danny nodded and then got into the car. Rachel turned to Greg.

He was shaking his head. "I didn't think he would take the news this hard, Rachel. We've talked about his having brothers and sisters since Nancy and I got married."

"I guess the reality of it is something else again. From what you said on the phone, he's afraid the baby will take his place in your life."

"I know. And I tried to tell him that just wasn't so."

"It'll take a while for him to get used to the idea. I'll keep talking to him about it. And you should keep in touch with him more than ever."

"Definitely," Greg agreed. "And Rachel?"

"Yes?"

"Thanks for coming so quickly. I know you'll help us get this matter straightened out. You've always been a wonderful mother to Danny."

"Thanks, that's nice to hear," Rachel said, awkwardly looking away from Greg's gaze. "Speaking of mothers, where is the mother to be?"

"In the bathroom, I'm afraid. She's not as lucky as you were when you were expecting Danny. She gets morning sickness pretty bad. And in her case, it strikes in the afternoon."

The subject made her feel a little uncomfortable. "I'm sorry to hear that," she said, wanting nothing more than to get away from Greg and his pregnant wife and this house that was perfect for a big family. "We'd better be heading out now. Tell Nancy I said hello."

On the way home, Danny didn't say much until they were on the interstate. "Mom, I'm hungry. Can we stop at Wendy's or something?"

"I think so." Rachel gave a quick sidelong glance at Danny, securely belted in the seat beside her. "Feeling a little better now?"

"A little."

"Feel like talking about what happened?"

"Not yet. Maybe later."

"Okay."

Danny stared out the window awhile before looking thoughtfully at Rachel. "Mom, do we still have to go to the ball game with Terrance tomorrow?"

"Well honey, everything's been arranged. I thought you were looking forward to sitting near the Red Sox dugout."

Danny just shrugged.

"Terrance wants you to meet his family. And I want them to meet you. Besides, it'll be fun." Rachel winced as she said that for she had no idea what to expect tomorrow. And now this sudden spurt of reluctance on Danny's part was just something else for her to contend with. "You'll see, you'll enjoy yourself."

Danny just sighed. "I guess so."

DANNY'S MELANCHOLY MOOD continued through to the next day. He remained closemouthed about what had happened at his dad's, and when Terrance arrived to take them to Fenway, he was uncharacteristically subdued. Rachel had hoped Danny's spirits would lift once they got to the ballpark, but instead he insistently stayed by her side and said little.

The charming green-walled ballpark was humming with pregame activity as the usher led them to the NBM box. It was a pleasantly warm summer day. The bright sun felt good on Rachel's bare arms, and a gentle afternoon breeze blew her full, cotton floral skirt against her legs.

"I see we're the first to arrive," Terrance said as the usher dusted off the front row seats with a white cloth.

Once they were settled in their seats, Terrance gave her hand a squeeze of encouragement. She smiled and shook her head. "My nerves must be showing."

He leaned his head close to her ear. "Just a bit. But remember, we're in this together." Then he winked playfully.

She could feel herself starting to relax as she gazed back into his twinkling eyes. Their color seemed to match the cloudless summer sky, and his smile warmed her more than the afternoon sun.

Terrance leaned over her lap to speak to Danny. "I'll take you over near the dugout if you like, Danny. Sometimes the players sign autographs before the game starts. How about it?"

Danny shook his head. "No thanks. I'd rather stay here."

"If you change your mind, let me know," Terrance said as he shot Rachel a puzzled look.

Rachel was disheartened by Danny's behavior. She wished he wouldn't take his distress about his father's new baby out on Terrance. Before today, she'd been pleased by how well Danny had been getting along with Terrance. Rachel prayed that his indifference toward Terrance would pass quickly. Already it was making a difficult day even more so.

A cheery feminine voice caught her attention. "There's your father, Kerry."

Apprehension tightened the knots already present in her stomach. Rachel slowly looked over her shoulder as Terrance stood up to wave at the approaching young couple. The girl was pale, blond, flatteringly thin, and her pretty smile revealed perfect teeth. Rachel noted that Martha's yellow and cream-colored outfit was the latest in expensive casual chic.

Then Rachel's eyes fell on Kerry. He wasn't anything like what she had expected. With his slight, boyish build, five-nine or five-ten height and unruly mass of curly brown hair, Kerry resembled Terrance less than Gordon did. Yet when they shook hands after being introduced, Rachel saw immediately that Kerry's gentle blue-gray eyes were just like his father's.

Kerry mumbled a shy greeting, and then was silent while his friendly fiancée talked effusively. Rachel relaxed a bit. For all Martha's youthful enthusiasm, Rachel liked the young woman right off. And although Kerry didn't seem as outgoing and warm as Terrance, at least he wasn't pompous like his older brother. She thought she could get along with Kerry quite nicely—if he'd give her the chance.

She did think Martha and Kerry made an odd couple, at least on the surface. Wearing well-worn blue jeans, a faded red Lacoste shirt and black high-top sneakers, Kerry contrasted starkly with the well-groomed, fashionably dressed Martha. Young love does work in wondrous ways, Rachel mused.

Kerry and Martha sat in the row directly behind Terrance, Rachel and Danny. "Gordon is joining us, isn't he?" Martha asked.

Terrance glanced at his watch. "It's still twenty minutes until game time. He'll be here."

"He better be," Martha asserted, fidgeting in her seat. "You three Nelsons are rarely ever at the same place at the same time. Kerry and I have something to tell the family."

Grinning slyly, Terrance turned around to Martha and Kerry. "And what might that be?" he asked, sounding as though he knew the answer already.

"Oh, I should wait until Gordon gets here," she claimed halfheartedly. She cast a questioning look at Kerry.

An indulgent smile crossed his lips. "Go ahead if you want to. Believe me, Gordon won't mind hearing the news ten minutes later than everyone else."

Martha planted a quick peck on Kerry's cheek. "Ooh I love you," she said happily.

"So tell us this news," urged Terrance.

Martha was beaming. "We've finally set the date—Saturday, October twelfth. It's Columbus Day weekend, so we've already reserved the church and booked a reception room at the Ritz. The ball is rolling."

Throughout the ensuing round of congratulations Rachel felt that Kerry was being curiously subdued about the announcement—especially when Martha seemed to be literally bursting with excitement. Maybe it was just her imagination, or perhaps Kerry was just naturally shy.

Yet, within seconds Kerry cut the subject of the wedding short by standing up rather abruptly. "Hey kid," he said to Danny, "let's go over by the dugout and see if we can talk to a player or two."

"Do you think there's time before the game starts?" Danny asked somewhat shyly.

"Plenty. Come on."

Rachel watched Kerry and Danny weave their way toward the Red Sox dugout. Maybe she hadn't been imagining Kerry's reticence after all, but that was just a fleeting thought. She was much more disconcerted by Danny's ready acceptance of Kerry's offer—an offer he'd previously turned down from Terrance.

No sooner had Danny and Kerry disappeared from her line of vision when Gordon arrived on the scene. He stiffly shook Rachel's hand. "When you first came to my office, I had no idea we'd be meeting again so often," Gordon said.

Rachel smiled politely, but gave no reply. She reminded herself to stay on her guard around Gordon. Terrance had told her about his older son's disapproval of their relationship. And seeing Gordon again today, slick talking and impeccably dressed even for a Sunday afternoon ball game, reconfirmed her hunch that he'd never make things easy for her and his father.

Fortunately, Martha was there to fill the breach caused by everyone else's discomfort. She filled in Gordon about all her wedding plans until Kerry and Danny came back.

"Look, Mom," Danny cried with delight, waving a white slip of paper in his hands. "We got a player's autograph. He even shook my hand."

"That's wonderful honey." Rachel was relieved to see Danny feeling more chipper.

"And Kerry's gonna teach me how to keep a score-card during the game." Danny looked directly at Martha and Gordon. "But I'll have to sit next to him."

"Danny, that's not very nice," admonished Rachel. "Please ask politely if Martha or Gordon would mind trading seats."

Danny lowered his eyes to the ground. "Would you mind trading seats with me, please?"

"Sure, sweetheart. I don't mind," Martha responded quickly.

The game started shortly after Martha and Danny had exchanged seats. The first few innings passed uneventfully. Except for Danny and Kerry conferring about their scorecard, noticeably little conversation passed between the rest of the group. Although Terrance tried to keep some sort of banter about the game going in between innings, Gordon was keeping almost adamantly tight-lipped, Martha understood little about baseball, and Rachel found it difficult to keep up a cheery facade. So far things were not going well.

Before the start of the fifth inning, a Red Sox trivia question was flashed across the huge electronic scoreboard. "What does it say, Kerry? What does it say?" Danny asked impatiently. "I can't read it."

Kerry read the question on the scoreboard out loud. "Which Red Sox player had the most runs batted in in the 1946 World Series against St. Louis? Say, Danny," Kerry continued, "you couldn't read any of that?"

Rachel heard her son reply in a low voice, "Just a couple of the words. I don't read so good. I have to take a special class this summer."

"I bet that'll help," Kerry said kindly, and then smoothly changed the subject. "Does anyone know the answer? It sounds like a toughy to me."

Terrance nodded in agreement. "It is tough. Ted Williams, Dom DiMaggio, Johnny Pesky, Bobby Doerr were all on the '46 team. They were all superstars."

"Well, I'm gonna put my money on DiMaggio," Kerry decided. "What about you Danny? Wanna guess?"

"Ted Williams! He's my dad's all-time favorite player. Him and Yaz."

Martha refused to guess, claiming total ignorance about baseball. Although Rachel knew next to nothing about Red Sox history, she made a point to second Danny's choice.

Gordon was more than resolute about his pick. "You guys have selected the obvious, which is how they trick you. I prefer a more subtle answer—Bobby Doerr. He's well-known, yet a bit more obscure than Williams and DiMaggio. Doerr has to be the one," he flatly concluded.

"I don't know, Gordon," Terrance said as he rubbed his chin thoughtfully. "I seem to recall a fella named Rudy York making something of a splash during that series. I was just a boy back then, mind you, but he could be the one."

"Come on, Dad, Rudy York? He's too obscure," Gordon said.

"No, I think that's just who hit the most RBI's," Terrance continued. "The answer is Rudy York."

Gordon shook his head. "Not a chance, Dad."

Terrance smiled. "We'll just have to wait until the seventh inning for the answer, won't we?"

Suddenly Martha got to her feet. "This is beyond me. I'm dying of thirst. Does anyone want anything from the refreshment stand?"

Since everyone expressed a desire for cold drinks and snacks, Rachel went with Martha to help her carry back the refreshments.

"Gee, will you look at those lines," Martha said when they reached one of the snack bars beneath the stands. "Looks like everyone else had the same idea."

"I don't mind waiting in line if you don't," Rachel told her.

"Anything's better than hearing those guys debate between Rudy York and whomever." Martha's eyes twinkled merrily. "Besides, I'd much rather talk to you. You know, when Kerry first told me that Mr. Nelson was seeing you, I was amazed."

"I see," Rachel said, unsure of how she should take Martha's remark.

"Oh no, I didn't mean that the way it sounded, Rachel. I'm sorry," Martha apologized in a rush of embarrassment. "It's just that he hasn't dated much since Mrs. Nelson died. So it came as a surprise."

"It's all right. I understand," Rachel reassured.

"But you know I think it's wonderful. You're so nice, and your little boy is darling." Martha gave Rachel a meaningful look. "Mr. Nelson's been lonely. A man like that is not meant to be alone. He's very attractive. All my mother's widowed and divorced friends have been after him."

"Oh really?" Rachel smiled in spite of herself.

Martha wrinkled up her nose in doubt. "Maybe I shouldn't have said that."

"It's okay, Martha. I understand perfectly why he'd be so sought after." Rachel decided to change the subject as they gradually moved up in the line. "I've been admiring your ring all afternoon, Martha. May I take a closer look?"

Martha extended her left hand for Rachel's inspection. Although the diamond itself was fairly large, it didn't overwhelm the simple platinum setting, and Martha's long slender finger carried the ring well. "It's really lovely," commented Rachel. "The setting is so elegantly old-fashioned. Is this a family ring?"

"No it's not. But I chose it because of its antique look. I collect antique jewelry, you know." The line shuffled ahead a few spaces as Martha spoke. "Actually, Kerry had thought about giving me his mother's engagement ring. But it turned out that Gordon had already asked his father if he could have it—not that he has any immediate plans to use it."

Rachel's curiosity was aroused. "Was Gordon very close to his mother?"

"Not that I could see. But then Gordon's never been a particularly demonstrative person. That's why that ring business came as such a surprise. You know, it's not like it's an extremely valuable diamond or anything. Mr. Nelson bought it for Mrs. Nelson after his family lost all their money."

"Then Gordon probably wanted the ring for sentimental reasons."

"Which is really the amazing thing about it," Martha said, shaking her head. "I've known Gordon all my life, and I didn't think the guy had a sentimental bone in his body."

Finally they reached the head of the line and put in their order. While they waited for the food, Martha started rattling on about some engagement party.

"I know this is terrible of me to say, Rachel, but I can't wait until you walk into the party with Terrance. Everyone will go bananas."

"You think so?" Rachel said lightly, pretending she knew what Martha was speaking about. What engagement party? she wondered. This was the first she'd heard about it. Terrance hadn't mentioned it to her—at least not yet. Either he hadn't gotten around to inviting her or he wasn't going to, period. With everything else going on, Rachel decided it wasn't worth worrying about. Not today.

It was already the bottom of the seventh inning by the time the two women returned to their seats. "We were about to send a search party after you," Terrance greeted, looking warmly into Rachel's eyes.

"What have we missed?" she asked.

"Just three innings of superbly pitched shutout ball," Terrance told them. "Both pitchers are hot."

Martha took her seat next to Rachel. "Sounds boring. At least we didn't miss any home runs or anything."

Gordon turned to his brother with a scowl. "For Pete's sake, Kerry, will you teach this woman something about baseball before you bring her again. The damn Yankee pitcher has a seven-inning no-hitter going!"

"Give me a break, Gordon," Martha sneered.

Although Martha didn't appear to be that miffed by Gordon's comment, Kerry still patted her head affectionately. "Don't mind him, sweetheart. Besides, you're just in time for the answer to Red Sox Trivia."

Martha grimaced. "Oh joy."

Everyone's attention was diverted to the scoreboard where the trivia question was being repeated. When the answer appeared on the board, the Fenway crowd cheered and applauded.

"Ah ha, Rudy York," Martha exclaimed. "Good old obscure Rudy York." She turned to Gordon with a smug grin on her face. "Gee, Gordon, I thought you had that one all figured out. Looks like you still don't know absolutely everything."

Apparently Martha had no qualms about putting Gordon in his place, and Rachel secretly enjoyed witnessing it. She soon realized, however, that Gordon was bent on having the last word.

"Seeing that Dad has a few decades on everybody else here, of course he had an edge," Gordon said, staring down at Martha, his voice brittle. "Hell, he's the only one here who was alive in 1946."

Everyone was astonished into embarrassed silence. Stunned, Rachel thought she could almost hear her heart thumping frantically. She couldn't move. Gordon's implication was painfully clear. Everyone else seemed as uncomfortable as she. And for what seemed like an eternity, no one else said a word.

Finally, Martha broke the silence. "I can't believe you said that," she gasped, aghast. "What a pompous a—"

"Okay, that's enough you two," Terrance broke in, visibly struggling to keep his temper. His voice was tight, restrained. His eyes were stone-gray cold.

No one, save Danny, said much during the rest of the game. The no-hitter was lost in the bottom of the eighth, but by then no one in their party seemed to care. Terrance gave Rachel's hand a reassuring squeeze now and then, but it scarcely helped her frame of mind. The afternoon that had gotten off to a so-so start, was now virtually ruined. Gordon's dislike of her and Kerry's obvious indifference felt much worse than anything she'd imagined. Each in his own way had made her feel like a suspect intruder into their family circle.

Rachel was relieved when Gordon backed out of dinner after the game. Terrance didn't even argue about it with him. Yet Gordon's absence didn't help the situation as much as she thought it would. During dinner at Anthony's, Kerry had very little to say to anyone except Danny. Although he was shutting out Martha and Terrance as well, Rachel couldn't help but feel Kerry's aloofness was due to her presence.

Paranoid? Rachel asked herself. After today, she felt she had every right to be.

Her head was pounding by the time dinner was over, and she was depressed. As Terrance drove Danny and her home, she took a sidelong glance at him behind the wheel. Despite all her intentions to fight for her man, she had been overwhelmed by the cold shoulder she'd received from his sons. It brought back the initial fear of being out of Terrance's league—something she hadn't thought about in a long time. It made her feel wretched.

"Danny's fallen asleep already," Terrance said, his voice low.

Looking over her shoulder at the backseat, Rachel saw Danny slumped behind the confines of his seat belt. Mouth open, but breathing evenly, Danny was dead to the world. "At least he had a reasonably good time today," Rachel mumbled more to herself than to Terrance.

"Rachel, I'm sorry it went so badly."

"Why?" she asked, staring out the passenger window. "It's not your fault."

"I don't understand those two boys. You'd think they'd want me to be happy," Terrance despaired. "Hell, if they weren't grown men, I'd take them both over my knees and—"

Rachel looked around at Terrance. "Well, they are grown men. Nothing you can do will make them accept me if they don't want to. And they obviously don't want to."

Terrance shot her a worried look. Then, before she realized what was happening, he was pulling the car over to the side of the road. "Terrance, what?"

Cutting off the car's engine, he glanced back quickly at Danny. Her son was still sound asleep. Terrance unbuckled his seat belt and shifted his lean torso and long legs in order to look directly at Rachel. His face was grave, his eyes intense.

"Now that you've had your first bitter taste of what it can be like for us, Rachel, I'll understand if you're having a change of heart," he said, keeping his voice deliberately low so as not to wake Danny. Yet, in light of what he was broaching to her, he sounded so calm, so controlled.

His composure bewildered Rachel; her heart was in utter panic. After only one meeting with Terrance's family, her mind was being besieged by unhappy questions and doubts. And she was the one who was going to go down fighting for her man! She felt like such a wimp.

Still, Terrance calmly continued on. "Obviously, my sons' behavior was much worse than what you'd been expecting. Maybe worse than anything you'd imagined. In light of that, second thoughts about us would be understandable. I might not like it, but I'd understand." He lowered his gaze to the car's leather upholstery for a moment.

"It's totally up to you," he said lifting his eyes to hers. His gaze was now as direct and as steady as the tone of his voice. "What do you want to do, Rachel? Call it quits?"

Chapter Eight

"Absolutely not!" Rachel said with a vehemence that came from her soul. "I love you."

Terrance folded her in his arms. "Thank God for that."

She held onto him tightly, resting her head against his chest. She could feel his heart beating wildly, and she was at once exhilarated and contented. Terrance was all that mattered. What a fool she'd be to let him go.

Straightening in his arms, Rachel clasped his head between her hands. "Terrance, what happened today really did throw me for a loop. I won't lie to you about that."

"I know it did. It tore me up to see you hurt like that. I felt like I'd let you down."

"But you didn't let me down, Terrance. I hated today, but I survived it. We survived it." She gently pulled his lips to hers and kissed him passionately. When she emerged from the kiss she was breathless and happy. She whispered in his ear, "I'm all right now."

Terrance peered down at her, his own breathing still ragged form their deep kiss. "Are you sure?"

"I'm ready and raring for the next round with your kids."

"Well I'm not. Let them stew about it for a while." He gave her a wry wink.

She kissed his cheek.

Smiling, he squeezed her waist. "I'm a bit too old for necking in the car in the middle of Commonwealth Avenue. Even you'd have to admit that."

"I admit nothing of the kind," she replied breezily. "Because that was the best kiss I've ever gotten in a car."

Terrance laughed, hugging her close. "I'm crazy about you, you know."

"Just keep it that way." She kissed the tip of his nose.

"We'd better be going anyway. We still have your kid in the backseat."

She checked on Danny. He was fast asleep. Rachel sighed and reluctantly moved away from Terrance. "Will we ever be alone?"

Terrance started the car again. "We're going to talk about exactly that right after we put Danny to bed."

When they arrived back at her house, Terrance carried Danny inside. Rachel pulled down the covers on Danny's bed and Terrance carefully put him down without waking him. Rachel went to the bureau for a clean pair of Danny's pajamas, and when she returned Terrance had begun undressing him.

She watched Terrance slowly easing off her sleeping son's clothes. Tenderness filled her heart. What a good, gentle man Terrance was.

He looked up at her and smiled. "Guess I haven't lost my touch," he whispered, "even though I haven't done this in years." He reached out for Danny's pajamas.

Handing them to him, Rachel found herself recalling the remark Terrance had made after they'd gone sailing on the Charles with Danny. Fathers were more involved with their children these days—he had said—it was enough to make a man wish for a second chance. She wondered if Terrance really might want more children. She supposed that would be a benefit of his becoming involved with a younger woman—a younger woman other than herself of course, she thought uncomfortably. Perhaps he and his wife had wanted or even had tried to have more children. Had they privately hoped to have a daughter in addition to their two sons? On occasion, Rachel had wistfully daydreamed about having a little girl in addition to Danny. Although that could never happen, the thought still crossed her mind from time to time.

"I think he's all set," Terrance said when he finished dressing Danny. "This kid could sleep through a five-alarm fire."

"He's had a hectic few days," Rachel said, pulling the sheet and summer-weight blanket up to Danny's chin. She kissed his forehead. "Poor kid's exhausted."

Nodding sympathetically, Terrance reached over the bed for Rachel's hand. "Come along, Mom. It's time for us to talk."

He led her out to the front porch to the old wicker settee she had bought secondhand and for which she had spent several winter nights sewing new bright blue cushions. As they sat down, Terrance pulled her back against his chest, neatly tucking her head beneath his chin. Feeling protected and very comfortable, Rachel wanted to remain in that position forever.

"Rachel, you and I have to have some time for ourselves. Time alone away from work, and away from our kids."

"I say amen to that. But when? Where?"

Terrance chuckled, and Rachel could feel it vibrate through his chest. "I have a plan," he said. "I worked it all out during dinner."

Shifting in his arms, Rachel slanted her head to look at him. "So that's why you were so quiet."

"Uh-huh. I was trying to save my sanity."

"Will you save mine, too, please?"

"My pleasure," Terrance murmured in her ear. "How about next weekend at my cabin outside Stockbridge? It's the Fourth of July weekend. Four days and three long nights of just you and me." He tightened his arms around her. "I want to make love to you. It's time."

"I know."

"Then we'll go?"

Although she wanted very much to go away with him, she hesitated.

"You don't want to?" Terrance asked, troubled.

"I do want to. There are things to consider...."

"Such as?"

"Well, Danny for one. He's supposed to spend the holiday with Greg. But after what happened this weekend, I'm not sure he'll go. I won't force him."

Terrance tenderly stroked her cheek with his thumb. "You're a good mother, Rachel. But you're allowed to be selfish once in a while. Maybe you could make other arrangements for Danny."

"I suppose he could visit my folks."

"And they'd probably be thrilled to have him. Right?"

"Of course," she said flatly. "Then I guess we can go."

"You guess? Now wait a minute here." Turning her around by the shoulders, Terrance looked at her with questioning eyes. "Rachel, are you nervous about being alone with me next weekend?"

Rachel lowered her gaze. "A little bit, maybe. It's silly."

"Oh darling," he said, hugging her close, "nothing about you is silly. And you'll see, we'll have a wonderful time."

AS RACHEL FEARED, Danny was reluctant to spend the Fourth of July weekend with his father. Following two days' worth of telephone calls between Brookline and Peterborough, Greg finally drove down to talk to Danny in person.

Rachel was thankful for that. Although her parents had already tentatively agreed to take Danny for the weekend, she really wanted him to be with Greg. That's where Danny belonged this weekend. Danny was so lucky to have such a caring, involved father. She would hate to see this painful rift between Danny and Greg become permanent.

Greg took Danny to the backyard to talk. While she nervously waited, Rachel kept herself occupied by washing the kitchen floor. Now and then, as she pushed the sponge mop across the no-wax tile, she'd sneak a peak out the kitchen window. Each time she looked, Danny appeared sullen, his head bowed as Greg tried to make some headway with him. Rachel wished she could go out there and help them. But it just wasn't her place to do so. This was between father and son.

Instead, Rachel opened all the kitchen windows, tugged on thick rubber gloves and attacked the oven with a vile smelling cleaner. Wiping out the oven's greasy grime did the trick though. Time passed quickly. Before she knew it, Greg was standing over her as she scrubbed the oven door.

"Rachel, how can you do that at a time like this?" Greg asked as he waved off the strong oven cleaner fumes.

"It beats sitting around wringing my hands," she said, pulling off the rubber gloves. "How did it go?"

"Once that kid gets an idea into his head, it's really hard to talk him out of it." Then Greg added in a curt aside, "He sort of takes after you in that way."

Rachel chose to ignore his remark. "So what happened?"

"We compromised. We're all going to spend the Fourth with my folks up at Lake Sunapee."

"He's still embarrassed about the fuss he made at your house."

Greg nodded. "This works out fine, though. My folks were coming down to Peterborough anyway. And by the way, who is Kerry?"

"A son of the man I'm seeing. He mentioned Kerry?"

"Oh yes. Once I got Danny thinking about what it would be like to be a big brother and how he could teach the baby to do things, he started raving about Kerry, scorecards, Red Sox trivia and you name it." Smiling, Greg shook his head. "The upshot was that he wants to be like Kerry and teach the baby all those neat things."

"Kerry made a bigger impression on him than I thought," Rachel remarked.

"I admit I was a tad jealous of how much Danny likes this Kerry. But now that I know he's your boyfriend's child . . ."

"Kerry's no child," Rachel said without thinking, "he's twenty-three."

"Oh?" Greg's eyes widened in surprise.

Damn! Why couldn't she just keep her big mouth shut? she thought. Although Greg's expression was just oozing curiosity, Rachel knew he wouldn't come right out and ask her about the boyfriend with a twenty-three-year-old son. And she wasn't about to explain a thing. Without so much as batting an eye, she proceeded to change the subject. "So what time are you picking up Danny on Friday?" she asked.

THE NEXT MORNING at the office, Rachel and Ilsa lingered over their first cups of coffee as they discussed the upcoming holiday.

Sighing lazily, Ilsa leaned back in her chair. "You know I am getting such vicarious pleasure thinking about your weekend of passion."

Rachel gulped down a mouthful of coffee, nearly choking. "That says a lot about your sex life, Ilsa."

"At least for this weekend it does. Jimmy's mother is coming down from Bar Harbor."

"Uh-oh." Rachel knew Ilsa and her mother-in-law did not get along.

"Uh-oh is right. Now you know why I much rather fantasize about your weekend with Terrance than even think of mine with the *Grande Dame*."

"I just hope the reality of my weekend matches your fantasy," Rachel commented skeptically.

Ilsa's head jerked to attention, her pale blond hair flinging across her eyes. Rolling her chair right up against her desk, she peered across at Rachel. "Don't tell me there is trouble in paradise before you even get there?"

"It's nothing quite so dramatic, Ilsa. Sorry."

"But something is worrying you, I can tell. Danny is all set now, so what could it be?" When Rachel shook her head, Ilsa railed on in accented, but precise English. "Don't lie. I know something is the matter."

"Okay, okay." Rachel tossed up her hands. "I've decided I should tell Terrance I can't have more children before we go away this weekend. And I'm kind of worried about it."

"Why haven't you told him already?"

"There's never been a right time."

"Now you absolutely have to tell him before you go away?" Ilsa queried with disbelief. "And you're worried about it. Rachel, what on earth happened?"

She repeated what Terrance had said about wishing for a second chance with children. Then she told Ilsa how Terrance had helped her put Danny to bed—how it made her feel. "Ilsa, it dawned on me that Terrance might want more children if we...I mean he could expect that I'd want a baby some day." With her emotions getting the better of her, Rachel paused to compose herself. Then she added calmly, "He has a right to know."

"Of course he has. But Terrance is not Tom French. He won't dump you because you cannot have children. Besides, you are getting ahead of yourself talking about babies. You two have not even slept together yet."

Wearily rubbing her forehead with her fingers, Rachel nodded. "Intellectually, I know you're right. But emotionally I'm terrified. I've really fallen for him, Ilsa. God help me, I haven't felt this vulnerable in years."

Ilsa's manner softened. "Rachel, I consider you a strong person. You are also very sensitive about your sterility, which is understandable. But for your own sake, you must calm down. Talk to Terrance today and get this all straightened out."

Rachel glanced at the phone on her desk. "I'm so afraid of disappointing him."

"Believe me, you will be a bigger disappointment to him if you are in this frame of mind all weekend," Ilsa observed as she pushed the telephone closer to Rachel. "Now call."

TERRANCE COULDN'T HELP but be alarmed. The person stammering and hedging her way through the phone call didn't sound like the forthright Rachel he knew. All she would say was she needed to talk—she wouldn't even say about what. He promised to meet her on the Common at noon. Terrance checked his wristwatch. Hell, two more hours to go, he thought, irritated. What on earth was the matter with her?

He arrived at the Park Street station doors a full ten minutes early. Already the Common was filling up with the lunch hour crowd. He locked his attention on the subway exit doors, watching for Rachel to emerge. He was hot and he was worried. She was not ill and neither was Danny. He had at least gotten her to tell him that much over the phone. His gut feeling told him this had something to do with this weekend. Was she having cold feet? Or worse, had she changed her mind completely about going away with him? He hadn't felt like celebrating the Fourth of July in years. It had become just another three-day weekend for him to endure until the return of normal business routine. But this year was different because of Rachel. After the planning and anticipation, he just wasn't prepared to spend the holiday alone.

Finally giving into the midday heat, Terrance took off his blue suit jacket and rolled up his shirt sleeves. Just then, Rachel quietly stepped up to him.

"I'm not late, am I?" she asked.

"No. Actually, I was early," he said, regarding her carefully. She was smiling warmly. Her eyes looked as bright as the summery green color of her dress. But those gorgeous eyes also revealed a certain nervousness. What was bothering her? "I've been puzzled over your phone call all morning," he added, trying to appear calm.

She looked up at him. "I'm sorry. I shouldn't have been so mysterious."

"True." Tossing his jacket over his shoulder, he folded her slender arm beneath his and held her hand tightly. "I want you to tell me what this is all about right now."

As they began strolling along one of the Common's shaded walks, Rachel was slow to respond. Terrance sensed that she was really struggling with herself, and this bewildered him all the more. Stopping in his tracks, he turned her around to face him. "Rachel, what's the matter? You're not acting like yourself at all."

Her lips trembled slightly, as though she was about to cry. But then she shook her head as if to shake off the onslaught of tears. "I'm sorry. This is just so hard for me to talk about."

"It's about this weekend isn't it?"

"In a way." Rachel turned to survey their surroundings. She pointed to an empty park bench a few yards away. "Let's sit down."

Mystified, Terrance followed her. The bench was beneath a massive old oak tree, and its shade provided welcome relief from the hot sun. After neatly folding his jacket over the back of the bench, he turned to Rachel. "Now out with it," he commanded, reaching for her hand.

"Terrance, this is a very difficult thing for me to talk about. And maybe I should have told you sooner." She nodded as she rambled. "Yes, I should've said something before now."

"Rachel, please."

Lifting her head to meet his gaze, Rachel's face was expressionless. Her eyes were unwavering, her voice flat and direct. "I can't have children, Terrance. I'm sterile."

"Sterile?" he repeated, scarcely believing what he'd heard. He hadn't been expecting anything like it. "But Danny? What about Danny?"

"It happened when I had Danny. Complications developed during his delivery." Rachel looked away for a moment.

Terrance wracked his brain for the right thing to say, but could only sputter his sympathy. "It must have been hard for you," he added solemnly. Once the initial shock of Rachel's revelation dissipated, it occurred to Terrance why she'd been so nervous. "You were afraid this would make a difference to me, weren't you?"

"Well, it might. I mean I'd understand."

"First of all you shouldn't have put yourself through the wringer like that, or me, either. I can't tell you what's been going through my head since you phoned me this morning."

"I'm sorry, Terrance. I was afraid."

"Surely you guessed having more children isn't a concern of mine. How could this possibly change the way I feel about you?"

"Oh it could. It wouldn't have been the first time."

Her words stung. Uneasiness churned his insides. Then something buried in his memory resurfaced with crystallizing force. "Your close call in Washington?" he offered automatically.

Rachel was surprised. "You remembered?"

"The man from your past? Of course I've wondered about him and about what happened."

"What happened was I told him I couldn't have any more children and he broke it off. But that was years ago."

"You make it sound so cut-and-dried."

"Well, it was to him."

"What an unfeeling man," Terrance muttered.

"Why? Because he wanted children?" she retorted, her voice breaking.

"Oh, darling, never mind about him," he consoled, clasping her shoulders tightly. "I love you. And I certainly don't care about having more children." He wryly added, "Especially after the way my two have been behaving lately."

Her eyes filling with tears, Rachel looked away.

Moved, Terrance held her closer. "I'm just sorry for the pain this has caused you all these years. I wish I could make that hurt go away." He paused to kiss her forehead. "And I wish you had told me about this sooner."

"It's hard for me to talk about this. It always has been. I can't tell you what it does to a woman's sense of herself to be told, at twenty-three, that she can no longer bear children," she explained. "That was the final nail in the coffin for my marriage. We'd been having trouble all along."

Her face was strained with the agony of her memories, and his heart ached for her. "You don't have to go on about this."

"I want to," she insisted. "Last time I kept silent until it was too late. It's part of me, and you should know about it."

Terrance wasn't sure he wanted to know more about it. For the flash of an instant he thought it might be the reason she was drawn to him, an older man. But he discarded the notion immediately. If wasn't fair to Rachel at all, and now she was much too important to him. Her inability to bear children made no difference in how he felt about her. But bringing up the man she'd been involved with before disturbed him. He wasn't jealous, just wary. And he couldn't say exactly why.

"Rachel, isn't it enough for you to know that it doesn't change how I feel about you?"

"It's more than enough if it's true."

"You know it is."

Relief softened the corners of Rachel's mouth as her whole body seemed to relax. "You're the most wonderful man. How did I get so lucky?"

Her bright, sexy smile delighted him. "Oh darling, I'm the one who's lucky. And I'm going to show you how lucky I feel all weekend long."

Feeling as if the weight of the world had been lifted off her shoulders, Rachel spent the next two days looking forward to the holiday weekend with excitement. Even the last-minute errands and tedious packing she had to do for herself and Danny didn't faze her. Danny, too, was feeling better about his weekend plans. He was gradually getting used to the idea of sharing his father with a new sibling, although he still worried that the new baby might replace him in Greg's heart.

Fortunately the museum was closed for the Fourth of July weekend, so Rachel spent part of Friday morning reassuring Danny about Greg and the new baby as she readied him and his gear for the trip to New Hampshire. By the time his father arrived, Danny was raring to go. She gave Greg the phone number where she could be reached in case of an emergency before hugging Danny goodbye.

"Aw, Mom." Danny sighed when Rachel's hug extended into a big emotional kiss.

"Don't worry, Rachel," Greg said, slamming the car trunk shut. "Danny's going to have the time of his life this weekend."

Well it was all very well and good to tell her not to worry, she thought as Greg's car slowly eased out of sight. But she would anyway. Oh, she planned to have a wonderful time with Terrance. In fact she could hardly wait for him to come and get her. Still, Rachel knew that she'd wonder how Danny was doing more than once or twice.

She went back inside to shower and change before Terrance came for her. She happened to be tossing some last-minute items into her weekend bag when the entrance gate guard rang her up.

"There's a young man to see you here, Mrs. Bonner," the guard advised. "And he's not on the list of expected visitors you gave me yesterday. Name's Kerry Nelson."

Kerry? What on earth? She instructed the guard to let him in. "It's okay, Nate. I know him."

Completely bewildered, Rachel decided to wait for Kerry out on the porch. He drove up in a shiny red sports car. Rachel had no idea what make it was, although it looked very expensive. She half expected to see Martha but Kerry was alone.

Rachel sat on the top front step as Kerry got out of his car. "Hi Kerry. It's nice to see you again."

"Thanks." He was wearing blue jeans and a T-shirt again, clean but well-worn. He stopped at the foot of the steps and looked back at the Wrentham mansion. "I remember visiting the museum with my sixth-grade class. It must be kind of neat living here on the grounds."

"We enjoy it."

Combing his fingers through his thick curls, Kerry turned to her. "I'm looking for my father. He'd already left his office when I called there, and his secretary said he was coming here. I need to talk to him."

A chord of urgency underlined his tone, which struck Rachel as curious. "Is there something wrong, Kerry?"

Averting his eyes, he fidgeted with the keys in his hands. "Not at all. I just wanted to tell him something before he leaves. His secretary told me he's going out to Stockbridge for the weekend."

"Yes I know."

"You know? You mean you're going with him?"

"Why, yes." Kerry's reaction surprised Rachel. Lord, she hoped she hadn't let slip a deep dark secret. If Kerry seemed preoccupied before, he now looked troubled. "Does that bother you?" she had to ask.

"That you and Dad are going off for the weekend? Of course not. You're two consenting adults. Why should it bother me?"

Well if that wasn't troubling him, something else surely was. Something in Kerry's nervous manner hinted that it had nothing to do with her—thank goodness. Still, she felt a little sorry for him; he seemed awfully anxious.

"Your father should be here in a half hour or so. You're welcome to come inside and wait."

Kerry shook his head. "No, maybe I should wait until next week. You guys certainly don't need your fun disrupted by me." He started edging toward his car.

Rachel got to her feet. "Disrupted? Kerry wait."

"Don't worry, it's no big deal. Really. Just wanted to talk to him about the office. That's all." After opening the car door he paused for a moment. "Tell him I said to have a great time. And that I'm glad."

His car roared out of sight, leaving Rachel wondering what exactly had happened here. When Terrance arrived later, she told him about Kerry's strange visit right away.

"What do you think was on his mind, Terrance?" she asked as he carried her weekend bag out to the car.

"I'm not sure. But if he said it can wait until next week, then it can wait," Terrance claimed. "It probably has something to do about when he plans to start working at NBM."

"Why would he rush over here to talk about that?"

Terrance finished loading the trunk of his car. "Rachel, he knows I'm anxious for him to get started on his career. I'm sure he wanted to tell me the good news before I went away."

"But he was so edgy."

"Kerry gets easily worked up over things. He's always been a bit emotional. When he realized we were going away together, he probably got embarrassed about coming over here. That's why he was nervous."

"Do you really think that's all it was?" she asked skeptically.

Terrance grasped her elbow and guided her toward the passenger door. "Darling, if I thought anything was really wrong, I'd go after him in a minute. Whatever it is can wait. Kerry said so himself. Remember when I told you mothers were allowed to be selfish now and then?" he asked while opening the door for her. "Well, the same thing applies to fathers. And from this moment on, this dad is not going to think about anyone but you."

Chapter Nine

They escaped the city before the early rush of heavy holiday traffic. As Terrance drove west on the Mass. Pike, Rachel felt both festive and relaxed. The car stereo serenaded them with the delightful sounds of Terrance's favorite classical music. The ride was smooth; the day was glorious and warm. Soon they reached the less populated stretch of highway through central Massachusetts where the road was lined with rows of lush green trees.

Rachel could see nothing but clear sailing ahead for their first weekend alone together. Alone at last! Rachel marveled. And not a moment too soon, either. No jobs to distract, no kids to interrupt and no goodbyes to say at the end of an evening. How many times had she lain awake in bed—restless—after a night out with Terrance? How often she had wished their passionate kisses and embraces could continue unhampered by their responsibilities. She longed to go home with him at night, and she longed to wake up beside him in the morning. Tonight it would all be theirs.

"I'd give a million dollars to know the reason for that sly and very satisfied looking grin on your face," Terrance said, glancing over at her.

Startled, Rachel's face reddened. Still, she answered gamely, "All will be revealed tonight."

"That's all you're going to say?"

She turned to him, grinning. "I will say this—I'm very happy right now."

His eyes remained fixed on the highway as he reached across the seat for her hand. He lifted it to his lips and kissed it once. Returning her hand to her lap, he softly added, "I am, too."

It was early evening when they reached the low mountains and verdant countryside of the Berkshires. Daylight was still with them when Terrance drove into the town of Stockbridge, Massachusetts. Rachel had heard the town was quaint, but in reality it was lovelier than she'd imagined. As Terrance slowly cruised down Main Street, Rachel was fascinated by the grand old homes with their manicured lawns and well kept gardens. It looked like something out of a storybook.

"I made reservations for an early dinner at the Red Lion," Terrance was saying as he pulled the car up near the huge white hotel. "I thought we'd eat here before going on to the cabin."

Once they were seated in the dining room and handed menus, Rachel realized she was starving. On Terrance's recommendation, she ordered prime rib, and to her own amazement, she ate it all—and dessert, too. "Must be the fresh mountain air," she explained, slightly embarrassed by her huge appetite. "It was just so delicious, but I shouldn't have eaten so much."

Terrance's eyes twinkled in amusement. "Don't worry. We'll work it off you with a tennis match in the morning."

"Gosh darn, Terrance," Rachel said, snapping her fingers and shaking her head coyly. "I forgot to bring my racket."

"Somehow I'm not surprised," Terrance replied, in turn. "That's all right though, I've a spare at the cabin."

"Not a chance, buster," Rachel asserted firmly—just in case he was serious. "I need a few more lessons before I'm ready to take you on."

He gave her a sly wink. "I'll be waiting."

Dusk had fallen when they emerged from the restaurant. Rachel suggested a short walk to work off their heavy meal. Arm in arm, they strolled beneath the stately old trees gracing the wide Main Street. In dusty shadows of the young evening, the center of town was quiet, tranquil.

Rachel rested her head on Terrance's shoulder. "This must be a wonderful place to have a summer home," she said, feeling quite content at the moment.

"Mmm, one really can feel away from it all out here. That's always been its charm for me."

Smiling inwardly, she murmured, "You like to escape?"

"In my line of work it's been essential—especially when the company was new. Eleanor liked it here. She always used to be after me to buy a place. But we had the beach house on the Cape, which the boys loved and it was closer to Boston. So I never got around to finding something until after she died."

Rachel found Terrance's mention of his late wife disconcerting. He'd spoken of her now and again, but it had never really bothered Rachel. Still, she thought it odd that Terrance would bring up Eleanor on what was to be *their* night. Her concern passed quickly, however, for Terrance was soon entertaining her with colorful stories about the town and its inhabitants. He smiled and he joked. Eleanor apparently had vanished from his thoughts.

Although he was trying to keep the conversation upbeat as he drove along, Terrance regretted having mentioned Eleanor. Why tonight of all nights? he asked himself. He could tell it had disturbed Rachel. Still, for reasons not even his heart could understand, the memory of his dead wife was very much with him. A sense of sadness crept over him, a sadness for what was lost forever. How odd to feel that way when he was embarking on a relationship that held such promise. He glanced over at Rachel. His life was moving again because of her; she was the future. Terrance knew he had to fight his inexplicable sadness or risk ruining their weekend together. He tried to steel himself against the past. He had to—for both their sakes.

Pulling himself together, Terrance turned to Rachel with a smile. He squeezed her hand. "We'll be at the cabin soon. I know you're going to love it."

Terrance's touch was reassuring, and Rachel felt optimistic. Not until they were driving along the rolling hills outside Stockbridge did Rachel again feel uneasy. Outwardly, Terrance seemed animated and carefree as they headed for his house on the outskirts of town. Yet the rhythm of their warm, usually easy banter was off. He seemed distracted, as if his mind were miles—or maybe years—away.

Hoping she was imagining things, Rachel kept her fears to herself. Maybe her own nervousness about beginning a physically intimate stage of the relationship was making her overly sensitive. She told herself that once they were settled in at the cabin, they both would feel better.

It was pitch dark by the time they arrived at the cabin, yet lights were on and windows were open. "I called ahead to have the place aired, cleaned and ready for you," Terrance explained, leading her inside.

The recently renovated cabin was roomy yet cozy. Early American pine and oak furnishings, hand-braided rugs on wide-planked wood floors and exposed ceiling beams retained the structure's rustic character, while a spanking new kitchen and remodeled bathrooms provided up-to-date creature comforts. Terrance continued the house tour upstairs where there was a master bedroom, a smaller second bedroom and a fair-sized bath.

"Perhaps you'd like to freshen up while I get our bags from the car," Terrance cordially suggested.

Rachel agreed, although she was perturbed by his tone. It was *too* cordial. Distant. What was happening to him? Washing her face with cool water, Rachel despaired of the invisible wall that had seemed to pop up between them. She felt it so strongly, how could she be imagining it?

After reapplying blusher and lipstick, Rachel left the second-floor bathroom only to be stopped short by the sight of the luggage in the hallway. Terrance left both unpacked bags between his room and the spare bedroom—as if he'd been undecided about just which room she should sleep in tonight. At least that's how it seemed to Rachel.

Now she knew she wasn't imagining things. Terrance's vague signals of withdrawal had been real after all. Their night at last, she thought with bitter irony, not knowing whether to laugh or cry. And she didn't know what, if anything, she could do to save it.

She found Terrance in the kitchen uncorking a bottle of red wine. "I thought we might have some wine out on the back porch,'' he said without looking at her. "It's such a nice night."

Dazed, she just nodded. What would happen now? she wondered.

Still manipulating the bottle's cork, Terrance glanced briefly at her. "It's gotten much cooler outside. You can toss a sweater of mine over your shoulders. It's over there on the sofa."

"Thanks," she said softly, noticing that he had donned a navy crewneck sweater over his shirt. She went into the combination living room and dining room that comprised most of the first floor. She found his tan cardigan and draped it over her shoulders. The wool held his familiar musky scent, and she thought her heart would break. It reminded her of how she'd come to love him.

Rachel followed Terrance out to the back porch. An old wood porch swing swayed crookedly with the light evening breeze. It squeaked when they first sat down, but then settled into an easy rhythmic pace as they sipped wine. They sat just far enough apart not to touch. Conversation came slowly.

"You look very pretty tonight," Terrance finally said. "Blue looks lovely on you."

Rachel glanced down at her dress of soft summer cotton. "I'm glad you like it," she replied offhandedly, remembering the pale blue negligée packed in her bag upstairs. She couldn't think of what else to say. His flattery, though probably sincere, rang hollow. She sensed he knew it, too.

Nothing more was said for endless minutes. Only the creaking porch swing and a choir of crickets echoed in the silence. Finally, frustrated beyond endurance, Rachel jerked her head up to search Terrance's eyes. He met her gaze and held it. His gray-blue irises flickered with kaleidoscopic confusion—the emotions too profuse to read. For Rachel, not knowing what was in his heart felt like separation, and that pained her greatly. She had to look away.

The pained expression in her eyes made it all too clear to Terrance that his effort to appear lighthearted and carefree had failed dismally. She truly didn't deserve this from him, she who was so warm and giving...so loving. Lord, he had wanted her so much. But now that the moment was at hand, he felt torn, as if the past were tugging him backward just when he so desperately wanted to reach out to the future.

And yet, her turning away in sad confusion had resparked his longing for her. His determination to take the happiness Rachel offered was renewed. He would not let her slip away.

"I do love you, Rachel," Terrance finally said, his voice solemn.

Her heart was beating rapidly. She was afraid to respond.

Terrance continued calmly. "Almost since the day I met you, I've dreamed of bringing you here to my special place. I've dreamed of making love to you here, sleeping beside you, waking you in the morning." He cupped her chin with his hand, turning her face back to him. "I've wanted that so very much."

"Then why are my bags still sitting upstairs in the hallway?"

"It's a big step, Rachel. There might not be any turning back." He caressed her cheek with his hand.

The first impassioned touch from him in hours stirred her deeply. Yes, her heart ached for his fears, but her body was aching for him. This longing trembled deep within her being.

"I don't want to turn back," she declared, her voice a breathless murmur.

His fingers combed through her hair. "Even now?"

"Especially now." She inched closer to him on the swing, her hands moving across the navy wool covering his chest. "From the very first, I was attracted to you, Terrance. So handsome, witty, sophisticated and kind— I was bedazzled."

His hands tightened around her shoulders considerably as she continued. "Yet it wasn't until the night in your car when you first kissed me, really kissed me, that I knew I could love you, knew that I wanted to love you."

Leaning her head back slightly, she quickly scanned the dark sky as she groped for the right words to say. Then she looked into Terrance's eyes again. "It goes beyond sophistication and attractiveness now. It's just you...the man you are." Rachel shrugged in frustration. "I'm not expressing this very well."

Terrance bent his head over hers, his eyes gleaming. He kissed her fully, with an emotional forcefulness that took her breath away. When he finally released her lips, he took her in his arms, holding her firmly against him. His voice was husky from the impact of their kiss as he murmured against her hair. "There's been enough talk tonight."

She pulled her head back to look at him. Pure desire—desire for her—shone in his eyes, making her pulse race with excitement. "Entirely too much talk," she barely whispered, wrapping her arms around his shoulders to claim a kiss for herself.

Propelled by a passion restrained too long, Rachel kissed Terrance with uncharacteristic boldness. Her tongue caressed and taunted his lips until they surrendered to a deeper kiss. Her fingers tingling with excitement, danced lightly over his neck, his jaw, his hair, his ears. A groan vibrated deep within his throat, and the sound and sensation of it flooded her lower body with tantalizing warmth. She pressed closer against him and she felt his body stiff and tense with desire.

Terrance finally broke from her kiss and gently held her head between his hands. "We've waited so long—too long." His eyes glowed with fiery intensity. "I want you so much."

He rose from the porch swing and took her by the hand. Rachel heard the screen door's muffled slam when he led her inside. Then the rest was all fluid, unconscious movement—as if in a dream. Before she knew it they were upstairs, walking past the luggage sitting unceremoniously in the hallway. Terrance's grip on her hand was reassuring in its firmness as they crossed the threshold into his room.

Without turning on a single light, Terrance led her across the room to his double bed. Yet the summer moon's pale glow illuminated the room just enough to allow her to see his face and body. Pausing at the side of the bed, Terrance pulled her into his arms again. He trailed liquid-smooth kisses along her neck and shoulders—kisses that sent thrilling shocks up and down her spine.

These kisses only made her hunger for more of him. A short, husky moan escaped from Terrance's lips when she pressed herself urgently against his body. He kissed her passionately then, his hand gliding around to her back. She felt him pulling at the zipper of her dress, heard its popping sound as it became unfastened. With his mouth still claiming hers, Terrance eased the blue dress off her shoulders and her arms until it slipped down the length of her body and onto the floor.

The cool evening air washed over her body, making her skin tingle with both excitement and anticipation. Keeping her eyes riveted to Terrance's admiring gaze, Rachel removed her lacy white bra and panties. Then she melted back into his arms.

"You are so beautiful, so exciting," he whispered in her ear, his hands feverishly roaming along her bare skin.

"Then love me."

Terrance gently lowered her onto the bed. He kissed her warmly before standing up again to take off his own clothes. Rachel watched with fascination as he undressed. While tugging and pulling off his clothes, he moved with an agile grace. And even in the shadowy dimness, she was able to admire Terrance's tall, trim figure. Naked now, his shoulders seemed broader, his arms and chest more muscular. Her body tingled as her desire mounted. He was a beautiful man and she wanted him.

She welcomed him into her arms with a sigh of sheer delight. After years of being alone, the touch of his skin, the feel of his weight against her were richly satisfying. She and Terrance were one now. Their bodies entwined, he showered her with more kisses. His hand caressed one breast, stroking its firm roundness with maddening results. Writhing under his touch, Rachel delighted in the sensation. Finally, Terrance lowered his mouth to her other breast, and his tongue played equally maddening games with its taut nipple.

Just when she thought she could endure no more, Terrance's hand slithered down along her stomach to the softness between her thighs. She sighed at this new touch, and then gave herself up to the immense pleasure he was giving her. She felt like a sky diver floating effortlessly, riding the air with a smoothness that would shatter as soon as she hit the ground. As Terrance's fingers became more insistent, she felt herself falling faster and faster, her body enjoying his caressing touch.

"Terrance," she murmured, her voice breathless and dry. But the words to express how she felt escaped her. She could only hold him closer, wanting him to feel her excitement.

Holding her in his arms, he pulled her onto his chest. She stared into his eyes, their color sparkling with love. His expression was so intimate, so intense, Rachel felt sure he could see into her soul. That Terrance could gaze at her with such a depth of emotion filled her heart immeasurably. She wove her fingers through his thick hair, her thumbs caressing his temples. "I love you so."

"Show me."

That's all she wanted to do. She brushed his throat, lips, cheeks and eyelids with soft as butterfly kisses. Then shifting in his arms, she let her hand glide across his muscular chest. She playfully fingered its silvering curls of hair for a moment before taunting his hard, tense body with languorous strokes and kisses. She could feel his body vibrate with pleasure—the pleasure she was giving him. Her excitement grew with his.

"I need you so much," Terrance whispered. He gently rolled her over onto her back and gazed lovingly into her eyes.

He tenderly traced the outline of her face. She clasped her arms tightly across his back, her fingers kneading his smooth damp skin. For a few moments they lingered in each other's embrace, enjoying the feel of their naked bodies. Oh, how she wanted him and this closeness. The passion that had been growing within her needed to be released, freeing her to express the love she felt for the man beside her.

Their bodies were one now. Terrance moved deeply in her, his breath warm against her neck. Rachel felt the intensity of his desire, and then gradual release.

They remained in this intimate embrace for some time, saying nothing, just basking in the glow of their lovemaking. She couldn't hold him close enough. She wanted him to feel the same pleasure and peace she herself was experiencing—to know that he was no longer alone, that she was there for him.

Terrance nuzzled her neck affectionately and murmured in her ear, "I love you, Rachel."

"You better be careful when you say that from now on, especially when we happen to be in bed," she declared, her voice unmistakably happy. How could she be otherwise?

"Why's that?"

"Well, the last time I said those three little words—right here on this bed—I was instructed to prove it."

Chuckling, Terrance lifted his face above hers. "Is that right?"

"That's right." Basking in the happiness shining on his own face, Rachel knew that whatever had been troubling him earlier was gone. He was hers alone now. They were united in both body and spirit, and that was her true ecstasy.

TERRANCE WOKE UP first. Outside the blue jays, sparrows and robins seemed to be involved in a rousing squawking match. He glanced out the screened window. The morning was sunny and brisk, just the way he liked them. A perfect Berkshire summer morning was quite in line with his happy frame of mind. The years of lonely mornings were gone, replaced by the warmth of love filling his heart. He realized it was the first time he had woken up beside a woman since Eleanor's death.

Terrance looked down at Rachel sleeping soundly in his arms. He smiled. Even the racket of rowdy birds couldn't stir her. She looked so lovely in the morning light, her auburn hair and creamy skin a warm contrast with the crisp white bedsheets. He hoped he was the reason for the peaceful smile gently curving her lips. It matched the peace he felt inside, a peace that came with lovemaking.

Although their lovemaking lasted long into the night, Terrance felt refreshed and energized this morning. It had been so good between them. And the contentment shimmering in her eyes last night had been gratifying. Terrance leaned back into the pillows, his hold on Rachel still secure. His thoughts continued wandering back to their lovemaking: the feathery light sensation of Rachel's hair across his chest, the compelling impact of her lithe body, the sound of her soft, breathless whispers and his own exquisite pleasure.

With a lazy sigh Rachel shifted in his arms, yet she was still sound asleep. Terrance's heart filled with tenderness for her. And love. How he did love her. She was continually in his thoughts and in his heart.

Rachel was the best thing to happen to him in a long time. He knew that. She said she loved him, and he was secure with the knowledge.

He had to admit that he'd thought about asking her to marry him. Still, that stubborn Yankee common sense of his prevailed. A marriage proposal would be asking too much too soon. They needed to adjust to this new aspect of their relationship. He wanted to make sure that Rachel had enough time to think about a permanent future with him. Losing a woman you loved was devastating and he didn't want to go through that again. Yes, loving Rachel was indeed a risk, and as their love intensified, the stakes grew higher.

Terrance looked at Rachel's still face. His fingers carefully combed back a wayward strand of hair from her closed eyes. He must be crazy, worrying about losing her just when they were closer than ever. Here he was holding this wonderful woman in his arms, his heart full of love for her. How could their future be anything but bright? They had the rest of this glorious weekend ahead of them. He promised himself then and there that he would do everything to make sure they both enjoyed this time together to the fullest.

TERRANCE KEPT THAT PROMISE, and the next three days were happy ones. They bicycled along the rolling back roads, ate the huge meals they cooked together and then spent the long lazy afternoons making love. At night they would sit out on the porch swing, enveloped in each other's arms, talking and drinking wine until it was time for bed. And although they managed to take in a performance at Tanglewood in nearby Lenox, and to watch the local Fourth of July fireworks amidst a large holiday crowd, Terrance felt as if they were the sole two inhabitants in a blissful world of their own.

"Terrance, I don't know how many rolls of film you've wasted on me so far this weekend," Rachel chided playfully as they took an afternoon stroll through a wooded section of Terrance's property. "But enough is enough. The beautiful woods and hills are much more worthwhile subjects than me."

Terrance snapped one more shot of her before letting the camera dangle against his chest. "Ah, but I can't resist that gorgeous smile of yours," he replied, drawing her close to his side as they carefully walked down a narrow trail. "Besides, I spent years taking pictures of all this beautiful scenery. I can't tell you what a treat it is to photograph a beautiful woman for a change. Especially when the beautiful woman is you." He paused on the path to punctuate his claim with a warm kiss.

The taste of his kiss remained with her as they resumed their hike. For Rachel, its sweet warmth only reinforced the happiness they'd been sharing this weekend. She had never felt as in tune with another human being as she now was feeling with Terrance. It wasn't just the new, physically intimate side of their relationship that made her feel that way, although their lovemaking had been gloriously satisfying. No, there was more involved than that—like the low, languorous talks they had in bed at night after making love, or the secret smiles they shared even when standing in the midst of the crowds watching the holiday fireworks display, or the evenings they sat outside gazing at the starry sky, saying nothing, just enjoying the summer quiet and each other. They shared a harmony, a unity, as if their hearts and minds actually had combined into one spirit. The very notion made her sigh.

Hearing Rachel, Terrance looked down at her with a bemused smile. "Now what was that about?"

"Happiness, I think. I feel as if I've died and gone to heaven. Everything is just about perfect."

Terrance just smiled back at her, without saying anything in reply. But from the warm gleam in his eyes, Rachel knew he felt the same way. Her gaze then turned back to the shady patch of forest stretched out before them. The warm sunlight that streamed down through the occasional clearing of trees seemed to form into mystical golden arches, welcoming her and Terrance to their own private paradise.

With Terrance carefully guiding her along, they continued along the haphazardly marked trail. Only the sound of their footsteps as they tread upon broken twigs and dried leaves pierced the peaceful silence. Eventually reaching a rocky incline, Terrance gripped her hand tightly. "Watch your step now," he cautioned as he led the way down the hill.

The sound of gushing water reached Rachel's ears, and she realized they must be approaching the mountain stream Terrance had wanted to show her. Soon she could see the stream for herself, its crystalline waters flowing gently over slick stones and around larger moss-covered rocks. "Oh, Terrance," she exclaimed, "this is as lovely as—"

"Shh!" Terrance warned suddenly as he stopped short on the hill.

Following his gaze, Rachel discovered the reason he had hushed her up. Off to their right a doe and her fawn were also traipsing down the rocky slope. At first she had difficulty distinguishing the two deer from the surroundings as their grayish-brown coloring and white markings camouflaged them well. But as the two came closer to the stream, she could see them clearly.

Terrance drew Rachel against his chest, encircling her shoulders with his arms. "Isn't that a sight?" he whispered in her ear.

She and Terrance stood perfectly still, watching with fascination as the doe and fawn waded into the stream and leisurely drank of its cool waters. Finally, the deer crossed the stream and slowly made their way back into the woods. When they were out of sight, Terrance released Rachel from his embrace and they resumed their descent down the rocky hill.

"Those two would've been beautiful subjects for a photograph," she commented as they reached level ground. "Why didn't you take a picture of them?"

"I didn't want to frighten them away. The slightest sound or movement would've made them bolt."

"You're probably right," she said, nodding.

"Besides, I was so caught up with just watching them," Terrance explained. "I always marvel at how deer seem so serene and yet so vulnerable at the same time. Sometimes I worry about what might happen to them once hunting season starts."

His tone was so wistful, his gaze so thoughtful, that Rachel felt overwhelmed by a combination of emotions. Tenderness, respect and longing were all bubbling up inside her with potent force. She had known all along that Terrance was a good man, and his sensitivity about the deer didn't really come as any surprise to her. She had seen how kind he'd been to Danny, how patient he tried to be with his own sons and how thoughtful and gentle he had been with her. But spending this weekend completely alone with the man brought all her emotions about him to full boil.

Turning to him, Rachel curled her arms around his neck and kissed Terrance with all the love and longing brimming in her heart. The kiss seemed blissfully endless as Terrance was returning it with an emotional force of his own. Although her head was spinning and her heart was beating wildly, Rachel felt as if she'd been suspended in time. And as their kiss finally came to a breathless conclusion, she believed she would be very happy indeed to remain in that one static moment forever.

With her arms still wrapped around him, Rachel peered up into his clear gray eyes. "Terrance, I do love you," she declared in a low, unsteady voice.

Terrance cupped her face between his two hands. "I know that."

"Yes, and I've said it to you before. But today—now— I mean it more than ever. I feel so close to you. And I don't mean just because we've been intimate—although being with you has been wonderful. There's more—" Rachel dropped her arms to her side in frustration. "I'm not being very articulate about this, am I?"

She felt him brush his lips across her forehead. "Oh Rachel, you're so giving, so loving," he murmured lowly, an unmistakable tinge of regret coloring his voice, "and I've been so unfair to you."

Although his remark confused her, she answered it at once. "Don't say that. You've been wonderful."

"Not when we first arrived here on Friday night," he claimed flatly. "My behavior was not the least bit wonderful."

"Terrance, you don't have to bring that up. It's water under the bridge now." The thought of their first few hours in Stockbridge made her feel uneasy.

"We should talk about it, Rachel. I need to talk about it," he admitted. "I want things to be straight between us, to make this closeness you're feeling genuine. I want to feel it, too." Taking her by the hand, Terrance urged gently, "Come on, let's sit down."

He led her to a mossy bank above the stream. The dark green moss felt softly luxuriant against her skin when she leaned back on her bare arms. As Terrance lowered himself beside her, Rachel's apprehension mounted. She wasn't sure she was ready to hear what he had to say.

Sliding its strap off his shoulder, Terrance put his camera on the ground. Then he stretched out on his side, resting his weight on his elbow and his head on his hand. His eyes were fixed firmly on her face. "Things have happened quickly between us, haven't they, Rachel? Just a matter of weeks, really."

"Yes, I suppose."

"And from the beginning I know I've given you a hard time because of our age difference." Terrance paused to collect his thoughts. "Except something else was holding me back, something I buried way down deep because I didn't want to face it. But my behavior on Friday night and what's happened between us since then has made me realize I can't avoid it any longer."

Rachel was perplexed. All along Terrance had been maintaining that he was too old for her. Now there was something else?

Terrance's fingers raked at some tufts of heavy moss. "I told you once that I'd never been really drawn to a much younger woman before I met you."

"I remember that. We were at Maison Robert."

"There's more to it than that. You see, Rachel, you're the first woman—the only woman—that I've felt so strongly about, that I've loved, since my wife's death."

"Oh, Terrance." A wave of compassion rushed over her.

"Sometimes it seems strange to want you so much even when being with you feels absolutely right. Maybe I didn't think love would come to me again. Maybe I didn't think I'd feel a desire this intense. You took me by surprise, Rachel. And then this feeling of—of—disloyalty to Eleanor gradually crept over me as you and I became closer. That feeling very nearly paralyzed me the other night."

"I had no idea."

"How could you when up until then I had convinced myself that age was the only reason for my hesitance?" Terrance shook his head in disbelief. "Seems the past has a hold on me, Rachel."

"It has a hold on all of us in one way or another. I have my ghosts, too. You know that. And sure, we both have doubts and fears. But what new loving relationship is without them?"

"Perhaps I'm afraid I'll lose you," Terrance admitted with painful honesty.

"You mean the way you lost Eleanor?"

"Loss is loss, no matter what way it comes about. Eleanor suddenly became ill and died within months. But there are afflictions of many kinds, Rachel. Like change of heart, loss of nerve."

"We both should know there are no guarantees." Rachel sought his gaze. "Will I have a change of heart about you? I hope not. As for loss of nerve, you should ask yourself about that, Terrance. Because the bottom line is that the difference in our ages bothers you much more than it does me."

"I guess I'm as susceptible as anyone."

"Still, I'm willing to take my chances with you," she declared. "I wouldn't be here if I wasn't."

"You are a fearless risk taker, aren't you?" he said lightly, his hand now stroking her bare arm.

Rachel was relieved to see him cheering up. "Maybe I just know a good thing when I see it."

"I'm going to do everything possible to prove you right," Terrance reassured, his eyes bright with hope. "You've made life worth living again, Rachel, and it's a wonderful feeling. Almost as wonderful as how close I feel to you right now."

Rachel was delighted. "You feel it too then?"

"Very much so."

His stroking hand thrilled her almost as much as the exciting glint in his eye. Her whole body glowed with contentment. His revelation about Eleanor had actually strengthened the new bond between her and Terrance.

Shifting his body so that his head was now resting in her lap, Terrance gave her a beaming smile. "Maybe you were right, Rachel, maybe we are in heaven. Or at least as close to a heaven on earth that two people can get."

She breathed a wistful sigh. "I wish we could stay here forever."

Although they both knew they'd have to return to the real world eventually, the remainder of the holiday weekend was spent happily, without a care of what tomorrow might bring. Yet hours before they were scheduled to leave for Boston, the real world came crashing down on them. They were in the kitchen, preparing themselves an early light supper when Terrance noticed that Rachel seemed preoccupied. As he beat the egg whites for a cheese soufflé, he watched her slicing onions and cucumbers for the accompanying salad. She said little. Since talk had flowed so freely between them all weekend long, Terrance knew something was bothering her.

"What's on your mind, Rachel?" he asked matter-of-factly as he poured the soufflé mixture into a white baking dish.

Apparently surprised by his question, Rachel looked at him with a sheepish grin. "Actually, I was wondering how someone like you learned to make soufflés."

He didn't believe that for a second, but decided to play along with her anyway. "Hey, just because I came of age during the Eisenhower era doesn't mean I believe cooking is strictly women's work."

"But soufflés, Terrance? I couldn't make one to save my life."

"Actually, Gordon showed me how. He's quite a good cook you know—learned from the housekeeper when Eleanor and I were working long hours at the office. Good thing too," he added, sliding the soufflé dish into the oven, "because I was one widower who was sick and tired of eating at restaurants every night. He taught me everything I know about cooking. He even bought pots and pans for my kitchen."

"I can't believe it. Gordon?"

Terrance nodded. "You know, there's more to Gordon than meets the eye, just as there's more on your mind than my culinary skills."

Rachel averted her eyes and busied herself with the salad again.

After she tore lettuce leaves into the wooden salad bowl for a minute or two, Terrance finally interrupted her. "We've been so open with each other this weekend, Rachel. Don't close up on me now. Talk to me."

Rachel dropped the remainder of the lettuce into the bowl and stood very still, her head bowed. She looked sad.

Terrance sensed the reason for her sadness. "I wish we didn't have to leave tonight. But we will come back. Soon."

She smiled wanly. "I know," she said. "Everything's been perfect here. But at home—"

"Not so perfect?" Terrance went to her side, putting his arms around her.

Rachel nodded and cradled her head against his shoulder.

"Well, it's the real world and we have to face it," he said, his voice soothing and low. "And we will—together."

"I know. Still, I wonder if we can be as happy back home as we've been here this weekend?"

"Why shouldn't we?"

She took a long time to answer. Too long, Terrance thought. He couldn't understand why she would be holding back now. Then it finally dawned on him. Even after the closeness they had shared this weekend, the one subject she'd still be reluctant to speak up about would be his sons.

He turned her by the shoulders to face him. "This is about Gordon and Kerry, isn't it?"

She grimaced, nodding her head. "Any fool can see how much you love them. And let's face it, Terrance, neither one approves of me at all. I'm afraid of what might happen."

He pulled her close. "There's enough room in my life for all of you."

"Do you think they know that?"

"They'll come around. You'll see," he reassured. "We'll just have to spend more time with them so they can get to know you."

"And I want to get to know them better. If they'd give me a chance, I just know we'd all get along."

"Maybe we should take them one at a time," he suggested. "We'll start with Kerry. He'll be easy to win over."

"And you call me an optimist," she observed dryly.

Terrance ignored her remark. "Now that we know how well we collaborate in the kitchen, let's invite Kerry and Martha over to my place for dinner. Just the four of us.

Martha already likes you, and I think Kerry will feel comfortable in that setting.''

Rachel seemed to like the idea, for her mood lightened considerably. ''The old win his heart through his stomach trick?'' she reflected, squinting thoughtfully up at him. ''But it might work. We'll make it work,'' she added resolutely.

Relieved to hear the playful lilt in her voice, he pressed his lips on her forehead in a light kiss. ''With your charm and my cooking, we'll just bowl him over,'' he teased. ''I guarantee it.''

Chapter Ten

Kerry and Martha agreed to come to Terrance's for dinner on Wednesday night. In the interim, Rachel was determined not to work herself into a state of high anxiety. Besides, Terrance was confident that the evening would go beautifully, and Rachel decided to believe him. A positive attitude seemed to help. She found herself enjoying planning the dinner menu and other preparations with Terrance. And as the big day approached, she discovered she was actually looking forward to spending time with Kerry and his fiancée.

Even the situation with Danny had improved vastly over the Fourth of July weekend, much to Rachel's relief. Apparently, Greg spent a lot of time talking about the new baby with Danny. Danny returned from New Hampshire bubbling with news about early morning fishing expeditions, holiday parades, barbecues and boating trips on Lake Sunapee. Best of all, however, was Danny's growing acceptance of his dad and stepmother's expected baby. He revealed, with great enthusiasm, that Nancy wanted him to help shop for pictures for the baby's room and toys for its playpen.

Rachel realized that this baby was still an abstract concept in Danny's mind, and that his new enthusiasm would occasionally lapse before and after the baby's birth. For now, at least, the long face was gone, and her little boy was himself again.

This was especially true where Danny's behavior toward Terrance was concerned. They were able to resume their earlier easygoing relationship following Danny's weekend with his father in New Hampshire. The night before they were to entertain Kerry and Martha, Terrance took her and Danny out to eat and then to shop for groceries for the next evening's meal. Danny seemed glad to be with Terrance, and he was thrilled to have a fresh, receptive ear to hear all about his holiday adventures up north. Terrance, bless him, gave Danny his undivided attention, listening and responding to her son with avid interest.

Later, after Terrance had dropped them off at home, Danny again asked Rachel if she was going to marry Terrance.

"I still don't know the answer to that," she told him, tucking him into bed.

"Well, I hope you do," he announced in between yawns. "Because that will make Kerry my brother. Then I'll have a big brother who lives in Boston and a little brother who lives in New Hampshire."

"I see, you'd like to have some brothers."

"Sure. And it'd work the same way with dads. I'd have my real dad in New Hampshire and a dad—a sort of dad—who lives here."

"You wouldn't mind having Terrance for a 'sort of dad'?"

"Na. He's nice. But he wouldn't replace my real dad just like Dad's new baby wouldn't replace me. Right?"

"Right," she agreed, planting a good-night kiss on his cheek. "No one can take your daddy's place. And he'll always love you very very much, even if you don't live with him. Right?''

"Right."

The next morning at work, Rachel repeated her conversation with Danny to Ilsa. "Maybe things are finally falling into place," she added, trying not to sound too hopeful. "I'm not even that nervous about dinner tonight."

"That's because Kerry is the nice son," Ilsa reminded her. "But I am sure everything will be just fine. Remember, I want to hear all about it when you pick up Danny afterward. And I mean details."

The remainder of the day passed quickly. She and Ilsa finished off a great deal of routine paper work in the morning. In the afternoon, she escorted a small group of VIP visitors, sent over by the Swiss Consulate, through the Hudson River school exhibit and then served them tea in John Hollings' spacious office suite. By four o'clock she was back at her desk, taking advantage of the late-afternoon quiet by reading a few of the professional journals she had been ignoring of late. Then Terrance called from his office.

"I'm sorely tempted to skip out of here early," he declared in an enticing, sexy voice. "Any chance you could meet me at my place in about twenty minutes?"

Rachel glanced at her wristwatch. It was only four-thirty, a full hour and a half before they had originally planned to meet. "Well, I am all alone here. Ilsa's already left with Danny. He's having dinner over there tonight."

"Sounds like the perfect opportunity to leave early. Wouldn't you like to spend an hour or so alone with your sweetheart? I don't believe you've had a personal tour of my bedroom."

Rachel smiled inwardly as arousing tingles danced up and down her spine. An hour alone with her "sweetheart" was just what she'd been longing for. Although it had only been two days since they'd left Stockbridge, it felt like forever since she'd been in his arms. "I'll be there in twenty minutes," she told him.

She arrived at Terrance's condominium just as he was unlocking the door. Grinning widely, he nodded at his watch. "That's nineteen minutes flat, my dear. You must have every traffic cop in Boston trailing you."

"Not me," she replied, breathless with excitement. "I took a cab and offered him double fare."

Terrance laughed as he curved an arm around her shoulder. "That's my kind of lady." Once inside the apartment though, he dropped his briefcase to the floor and took her in his arms for a long, satisfying kiss.

It was so good to be in his arms again, to lose herself in the hypnotic sensations his touch evoked without having to worry about any outside intrusions. The weekend in Stockbridge seemed like an eternity ago. There they had been spoiled by having all the time in the world together, by the freedom to express their love whenever and wherever they had wanted. In contrast, the practical restraints of their everyday lives felt like sheer torture. At least it felt that way to Rachel. She knew she had to live this moment alone with Terrance to its fullest. Who knew when they could be alone together like this again?

Finally breaking away from his kiss, Rachel gasped for air. Pressing her cheek against his, she whispered lowly in his ear, "How about that tour you promised me?"

At first, Terrance seemed reluctant to release her from his arms. He lowered his eyes, his gaze locking on hers with a darkened intensity. Without his saying a word,

Rachel knew his need to make up for lost time matched her own.

His breathing was labored, his voice raspy when he finally eased his embrace. "Come with me," he beckoned.

Terrance's bedroom was actually a suite with its own separate den and a huge bathroom. In an odd turn-about, Terrance seemed to be taking his dear sweet time showing her the antique rolltop desk in the den and fidgeting with the elaborate controls in the bathroom Jacuzzi. At first Rachel didn't understand. Surely he must know she wasn't the least interested in the room's decor. Not now anyway.

When he stopped at the foot of his king-sized bed, he turned to her with a knowing smile, unmasked desire gleaming in his eyes. Then it dawned on her that he'd been playing a game with her, taunting her deliberately.

"You're a devil, Terrance Nelson," she accused.

"Why? Because I saved the best for last?" he said slyly as he loosened the knot of his dark necktie. "Ah, Rachel, don't ever underestimate the excitement of anticipation. It makes this moment all the more sweet."

Indeed it had, she thought, unable to take her eyes off him as he moved to take off his suit jacket. Her skin was flush with excitement and her limbs seemed to literally ache with the need to touch him again. Rachel covered his hands with hers to stop him. "Let me," she requested in a husky murmur, her hands then gliding across the fine blue pin-striped fabric. Slowly, she lowered the jacket's sleeves down his arms and dropped it carefully over the back of a nearby chair. The next thing she knew, she was hastily unbuttoning his shirt until she felt the silky strength of his bare skin against her fingers.

"I love you," she said, brushing her lips against Terrance's chest.

He lifted her onto his huge bed and helped her undress. Two days' worth of unrequited passion spurred them on to exquisite planes—each caress, each stroke, each kiss heightening both their pleasure and their love. Rachel wanted to lock the harmony of sensations of their lovemaking into her heart. She longed to capture forever the feeling of being one with Terrance. For better and for worse, Rachel realized that part of her soul would be missing whenever they were not together.

Afterward, they held each other close. With her head cradled against his chest, Rachel could feel Terrance's breathing gradually become peacefully even. And her own pounding heart finally returned to a calmer rhythm.

"The more I make love to you, the more I want," Terrance said nuzzling her neck. "After this past weekend, being apart from you is much harder to take."

"We'll just have to make a serious effort to find time to be alone like this," she acknowledged. "Actually, stolen moments can be quite exciting, don't you think?"

His chest vibrated with a sexy rumble. "I love the way you think. And I'd love to steal a few more moments with you, but Kerry and Martha will be arriving in less than an hour."

Rachel sighed. "And we have an entire meal to cook."

To her delighted surprise, Terrance carried her off to his shower where they were able to make the most of a few extra moments. Rachel emerged from the shower, refreshed and happy. She quickly changed into the yellow cotton pullover sweater, crisp white slacks and sandals she had brought along with her. She and Terrance had previously decided to make this evening as casual and as comfortable as possible—right down to their clothes.

When she joined Terrance in his kitchen, he was already piercing the chunks of marinated lamb, green peppers, tomatoes and zucchini with long metal skewers. He smiled when she stepped into the room. He looked relaxed, and roguishly handsome, she thought, in forest-green T-shirt and tan trousers.

He provided her with a clean white chef's apron so she could start making the corn bread batter and the rice pilaf. They worked side by side talking and laughing, just as they had at the cabin in Stockbridge, until the doorbell announced their guests' arrival.

Kerry and Martha appeared to be in great spirits after a day of sailing near Gloucester with friends. Kerry's greeting to Rachel was friendly, and he was definitely more relaxed than the previous times they'd met. Her hopes for the evening soared. She decided she too should relax and just have a good time.

Lots of lighthearted banter and laughter carried them through drinks and much of the meal, interspersed with getting acquainted topics like Rachel's job at the museum and Kerry's backpacking trip through Europe last summer. Rachel enjoyed picking up on the similarities between Terrance and his son. The way Kerry shook his head and smiled, the timbre of his voice when he was trying to make a point and his resonant laugh were some of the physical and vocal mannerisms he shared with his father.

Eventually the dinner conversation turned to Martha and Kerry's wedding. Martha's eyes shone as she talked of bridesmaids' gowns, church music and floral arrangements. Kerry interjected a comment here and there, but he gradually became subdued as the talk drifted from possible honeymoon spots to their post-honeymoon plans.

Rachel noticed how Kerry's eyes slowly glazed over when Martha began describing to Terrance the Back Bay town house they hoped to lease from her uncle. "It's a bit too far from the office for Kerry to walk to work," Martha explained. "But he can pick up the T at Copley Square and get there in no time."

At this point, Kerry was nervously twisting his unused dessert fork between his fingers and not saying a word. Rachel knew then and there something was bothering the young man. She wondered if she was the only one who sensed this? Terrance and Martha didn't seem as if they noticed anything was amiss.

Finally she tapped Kerry on the shoulder. "How about helping me in the kitchen with the desserts?" she whispered while Martha was describing the layout of the town house to Terrance.

Kerry nodded with a smile, apparently glad to have the chance to excuse himself from the table. He followed Rachel into the kitchen. "Dinner's been great, Rachel. I hope Martha hasn't been boring you talking about the wedding so much. She's just so excited about it."

"Her enthusiasm is understandable. A wedding is an important event in a person's life." Rachel handed him a package of shortcake shells and asked him to put them on the four dessert plates she had set on the counter. Keeping a thoughtful eye on him as he did this, she decided to draw him out a little bit.

"You must be getting excited about the wedding too," she suggested offhandedly.

"Actually, I try not to think about it that much," Kerry said, keeping his gaze lowered on the task at hand.

"Oh?"

Realizing what he'd said, Kerry hastened to correct himself. "I mean it seems so far off to me. Thinking about the wedding now will just make me nervous that much sooner.''

"I see," she said, placing a bowl of whipped cream and a bowl of sliced strawberries on the counter next to the plates. Kerry's explanation wasn't very convincing. She didn't believe it. As he helped her spread the shortcake with strawberries and cream, Rachel watched him out of the corner of her eye. He seemed so tense, as if he were keeping something bottled up inside of him. Feeling sorry for him, she contemplated saying something about it. Yet she reminded herself that there was a fine line between helping and interfering. And Kerry didn't exactly think of her as a friend—of that she was certain.

But when they finished making the strawberry short-cakes, Kerry's expression got to her. He looked like a lost little boy, and a trace of weariness in his eyes indicated that perhaps her earlier remark had touched a nerve. Compassion got the better of her and she had to speak up.

"Kerry, forgive me for prying, but you look a bit down right now," she said awkwardly. "Is there something on your mind?"

His body stiffened uncomfortably, although he did force a clumsy smile. "Maybe I'm nervous already after all. Happens to everyone I imagine. I didn't realize I looked so gloomy, though. Sorry if I upset you, Rachel."

"No need to be sorry. I guess I was mistaken."

"I guess so," he replied lightly.

Still unconvinced by his cavalier reaction, Rachel felt she could say no more.

Kerry, however, took it upon himself to change the subject. He inquired about Danny.

"This hasn't been the best summer for him, so far," she revealed, first explaining about Danny's reaction to his father's new baby and then about the remedial reading program he was taking at summer school. "He's not making much progress even after two weeks of classes. I'm probably going to have to hire a tutor to help him catch up."

Kerry made an immediate offer. "I'd be happy to tutor him."

"You?"

"Sure. I used to tutor disadvantaged kids in reading when I was in college. Did it every semester. I think I helped my kids a lot, and I enjoyed it tremendously. Maybe I can help Danny."

"It's really generous of you, but I couldn't ask you to give up so much time."

"You're not asking, I'm offering. And I'm not caught up in the corporate grind yet—my time is still my own. I can't think of a better way to utilize it." Kerry then shrugged. "Besides I like Danny. He's a good kid."

"He does think the world of you. But are you sure you want to do this?"

Kerry nodded. "Positive. It'll probably do us both some good."

At that moment, Martha and Terrance came into the kitchen. "Did you two forget about us?" Martha asked.

Placing an arm around Martha's shoulder, Kerry gave her a playful squeeze. "You are one person who is hard to forget."

Martha beamed with happiness. "Now that's what I like to hear."

While Kerry and Martha were becoming absorbed in their affectionate banter, Terrance slipped by them to be near Rachel. "I tried to keep Martha occupied as long as I could," he said low enough for just Rachel to hear. "Did you and Kerry get along all right?"

"Fine, I think. I'll tell you about it later." She pointed to the freshly brewed pot of coffee still sitting under the drip coffee maker. "Why don't you pour the coffee while I bring in the desserts?"

Hearing Rachel, Kerry offered to help carry the strawberry shortcakes. While he followed Terrance back into the dining room, Martha stayed behind. Being a well mannered young woman, she made a point to say how much she was enjoying herself and to compliment Rachel on the good meal. Although Martha's compliments were the result of good breeding, Rachel could tell she was also being sincere. Martha was a genuinely sweet person with something of an innocent air about her. Yet, after spending time with her on two separate occasions, Rachel began to wonder if the younger woman's guilelessness bordered on naïveté. Martha seemed so sure of Kerry and their impending marriage—much surer than she ought to be.

As Rachel emerged from this quiet speculation, she realized Martha had begun talking about Terrance. "He seems so much happier since he met you, Rachel. And much more relaxed. Even Kerry thinks so."

Rachel was hopeful. "Did he actually say that?"

"Oh yes. As a matter of fact we were at my Aunt Allison's house at the time—discussing the engagement party she's giving us," Martha explained. Then she leaned closer to Rachel, a conspiratorial glint in her blue eyes. "I should warn you, though, both my aunt and my mother are very curious about you. All Mr. Nelson's old friends are."

"Really? Then they know about me?"

"Well, it's kind of hard to keep things quiet among that circle. They've all been friends for years and years," Martha revealed. "And they haven't seen hide nor hair of Mr. Nelson in weeks. My mother calls you Mr. Nelson's mystery woman."

"Oh, dear."

Martha was quick to reassure her. "Oh, she doesn't mean any harm by it. Besides, I've told her and my aunt how wonderful you are. I can't wait for them to meet you at the engagement party. I know they're going to love you."

Martha's engagement party! Rachel had only thought about it in passing since Martha had first mentioned it to her at Fenway Park. And Terrance hadn't yet mentioned it to her at all. Now that oversight struck her as odd. Or was it an oversight?

Terrance poked his head around the kitchen door. "Ladies, your coffee's getting cold."

Grateful for the interruption before Martha said any more about the engagement party, Rachel picked up the last plate of strawberry shortcake and hurried into the dining room.

As the four of them lingered over dessert and coffee, Rachel contributed little to the conversation. She couldn't stop thinking about this engagement party business. Was Terrance planning to invite her to it or not? Martha had made it clear that much of his family and many of his friends would be there. The party presented an opportune time for her to meet some of the other people in his life—if he wanted them to meet her, that is. Maybe after all was said and done, he was still embarrassed by their relationship, she thought resentfully. But no, that couldn't be, not after the past few weeks. Perhaps Kerry had asked his father not to bring her. She realized her presence could be disruptive. And maybe, just maybe, Terrance felt he would be protecting her by keeping her away from disapproving friends. They might not be as receptive to her as Martha believed.

Damn it! Stop analyzing this thing to death, she scolded herself.

She looked across the table at Terrance. He caught her gaze, winked and smiled. She smiled back, her heart filling with love. Suddenly the engagement party didn't seem so important. If they loved each other, what did it matter? Certainly not enough for her to make a big deal out of it. She was sure Terrance would tell her about the party soon enough. He wouldn't keep it a secret from her.

By the time Kerry and Martha left, everyone was in good spirits. Declaring the evening a success, Terrance plunked himself down on his living room sofa and pulled Rachel onto his lap. "I knew Kerry would warm up to you if given half a chance."

"Don't go overboard, Terrance. He may think I'm an okay person, but I'm not sure he approves of us yet."

"Say, what were you two talking about all that time you were alone in the kitchen?"

Rachel repeated her entire conversation with Kerry. Then, with some trepidation, she told Terrance she thought Kerry might be having doubts about marrying.

"It's possible," agreed Terrance. "He is young. When he first got engaged, we had a long talk about this. He assured me he was ready and that marrying Martha was what he wanted." Terrance chuckled lightly, shaking his head. "You know, I always thought it would be Gordon who would end up with Martha."

Rachel's green eyes widened. "Gordon and Martha? You must be kidding."

"Not at all. Martha has always been a sweet, gentle, kind girl—gets along with everyone. Except Gordon, that is. The two of them have been at odds since they were babes. By the time they reached adolescence, I began to wonder if there wasn't some deeper emotion behind all that antagonism.''

"I don't see it, Terrance."

"Well, it was just a theory, and obviously a wrong one," he admitted. "In any case, I will talk to Kerry soon. He's probably suffering from a premature case of cold feet."

"I hope that's all it is. He does seem very fond of Martha."

Terrance nodded in agreement. "One thing I wish Kerry would do is start working at the company," he said, his face clouded with concern. "He'd be better off starting a new job before the wedding than after it. He'll have plenty of other adjustments to make then. And he has nothing else to do this summer."

"I told you he wants to tutor Danny," she reminded.

He glanced quickly at her. "And I think that's great, don't misunderstand. I want them to become friends. But Kerry can tutor Danny and still work at least part-time at NBM until after the wedding."

"Maybe he's also having doubts about joining the business," Rachel said without thinking.

Terrance's gray eyes narrowed. "The only doubt he has about that is whether or not he's good enough. And I've already reassured him that he's more than capable and that we want him. Though sometimes I think he takes his opportunities for granted."

"As you said yourself, Kerry is young."

"So I did." A grin gradually emerged from his concerned face, and he tightened his arms around her waist. "Let's talk about you now. Any chance you can spend the night?"

"I wish I could, but Danny is waiting for me at Ilsa's. And as a matter of fact I should call and let her know that I'll be coming for him soon."

Remaining on the sofa, Terrance watched Rachel head over to the telephone on the hallway table. The evening had been a success, an enjoyable one at that. He knew Kerry would come around to liking Rachel. Well, one son down, one to go, he mused. But thinking about how to get Rachel and Gordon together couldn't overshadow the guilt Terrance had been experiencing for the past couple of hours. All Martha's talk about the wedding had reminded him about that damn engagement party, a party he had managed to push out of his mind these past weeks.

His relationship with Rachel had been going so well that he had been loath to even mention the party to her. And now he felt guilty because he was still reluctant to do so. He had such mixed feelings about the engagement party, feelings he hadn't yet sorted out for himself. Although it was a celebration for his son and his fiancée, the party also seemed like a return to a life that he was fast losing touch with. Old friends of his and Eleanor's, vague acquaintances from country clubs and summers on the Cape, all people he had scant contact with over the past five years—that was what this party meant to him. It was bad enough for him to take a step back into the past, but why drag Rachel with him?

"Terrance, have I got news for you," Rachel called out brightly, interrupting his train of thought.

She looked pleased when she plunked herself back down on the sofa. Her smile delighted him so. He didn't have the heart to bring up any touchy subject now. He curved his arm around her shoulder. "Tell me this news. By the grin on your face it must be good."

"Ilsa has already put Danny to bed at her house," Rachel revealed. "Apparently he was exhausted from playing with Johanna all evening." Then she added with considerable glee, "So, tonight is ours. And Ilsa expects us to take full advantage of it."

Terrance drew Rachel closer. "She does, does she?"

"Yes, and I quote." Rachel giggled slightly before attempting to imitate Ilsa's German accent. "'Lovey, think of it as a surprise package from your good pal Ilsa.'"

DURING THE WEEKS FOLLOWING the dinner with Kerry and Martha, Rachel's life settled into a pleasant routine. Each day was full, rich, happy. She and Terrance spent part of every day together, enjoying each other and treasuring each precious, intimate moment.

Kerry had begun tutoring Danny. The one-on-one attention was creating a gradual, yet noticeable improvement in her son's reading skills. The two of them were also becoming friends. Sometimes Terrance would join Kerry and Danny for a simple game of catch or for an all-day sailing outing. Rachel found those get-togethers especially gratifying. Seeing Terrance interact with her little boy and his own grown-up son revealed what a good father he'd been and still continued to be.

Only two things kept Rachel's happiness from being complete. One was Gordon's displeasure over his father's relationship with her. When Terrance tried to arrange get-togethers, Gordon usually bowed out at the last minute. The one time he did bother to show up, he scarcely spoke to her. He seemed determined to keep a cold distance from Rachel in spite of—or because of—how much his father cared for her.

The other problem for Rachel was Terrance's surprising silence about Kerry and Martha's engagement party.

With each passing day, his failure to even mention it bothered her more and more. Now, with the party only three days away, Rachel knew Terrance wasn't going to invite her. But that was really beside the point. What really irked her was that he hadn't even talked the situation over with her. It was this secretiveness and the unknown reasons behind it that were getting to her. She probably should have said something to him about it earlier, but she had hoped he'd bring it up himself. Now, when it was apparent he wasn't going to say anything about the party, she was still hesitant to mention it.

What good would it do now that the party was a mere three days away? If she told Terrance she knew about it, he would then feel compelled to invite her. She'd hate that. No, better to wait until after the party to discuss it, she decided. Part of her, however, didn't want to ever talk about that damn party. She was wary of those unknown reasons behind Terrance's silence. Things between them were so wonderful otherwise.

Yet for something that had seemed rather incidental weeks ago, this engagement party situation had grown to annoyingly troublesome proportions in her own mind. Rachel knew she had to keep it from dominating her thoughts—as was now happening during a meeting with her boss. Twice John had had to call her attention back to the subject at hand when her mind had drifted off to her own problems.

Returning to her office after the meeting, she chastised herself for behaving so unprofessionally. John had been understanding about it. But Rachel considered dwelling on personal problems during business hours unacceptable. She'd always been able to keep her private life from interfering with her work before—before Terrance that is.

Ilsa was clacking away at her typewriter when Rachel asked if there were any phone messages for her. Her fingers now motionless, Ilsa stared down at the keys. She took a second or two before replying, "You don't want to know."

"What?"

Ilsa tossed up her long arms with resignation. Shifting position in her wheeled secretarial chair, she rolled it over to the center of her desk. "Your old boyfriend is in Boston for the historical archivists conference," she explained, handing Rachel a pink message slip. "Here's his number at the Sheraton. I think he wants to get together with you."

Rachel glanced at the name and number on the pink paper. Tom French. She couldn't believe it. She hadn't spoken to him since the day they broke up all those years ago. This was like hearing from a ghost out of the past.

"Don't call him back Rachel," Ilsa urged, her accent thickening. "You do not need any hassles from him."

"For heaven's sake, Ilsa. It's been five years—he's not going to hassle me."

"But why bother with him? You have Terrance now."

"This has nothing to do with Terrance," Rachel scoffed. "Besides, what's wrong with getting in touch with someone for old times' sake?"

"I do not believe in old times' sake," Ilsa declared with a firm slap of her hand against the desk. "If Jimmy wanted to see an old girlfriend for old times' sake, I'd lock him in our bedroom."

Chuckling, Rachel shook her head. "Ah, such a trusting wife you are, Ilsa." Then, peering at her friend with a mischievous glint in her eyes, she asked, "Aren't you the least bit curious about what he has to say?"

"Of course I am. But I do not like this whole thing."

Still, Ilsa watched Rachel intently as she dialed the Sheraton's number. Bracing herself for hearing Tom's voice for the first time in five years, Rachel breathed deeply while his room phone rang. His effusive greeting immediately put her at ease. Since he had to attend a seminar within a few minutes, he quickly explained that he wanted to see her. She invited him to dinner on Saturday night.

After Rachel hung up, Ilsa drilled her impatiently. "Now that you've done the dirty deed, please tell me why you invited him over for dinner on Saturday?"

"Because I'm not busy then. Danny will be at his dad's," she replied, thinking with some irony that Saturday night was the night of Kerry and Martha's engagement party.

"Well, what does he want?"

"I'm not exactly sure," Rachel admitted rather uncomfortably. "He said he's been making big changes in his life and he's been thinking about me a lot."

Ilsa shook her head. "I do not like the sound of that."

"Honestly, Ilsa. I really don't think it's anything to worry about." Yet Tom did make it sound urgent, she thought to herself. He really needed to talk to her is what he said. What could it be about?

"What will Terrance think of this?" Ilsa asked belligerently. "You are planning to tell him of this?"

"Yes, I plan to tell him," she said. "*I* do not keep secrets."

Chapter Eleven

Terrance was at war with himself. He had been for weeks. Why hadn't he even told Rachel about the kids' engagement party? he asked himself as he drove to Rachel's to have dinner with her and Danny. He wanted to bring her to it; he knew he should bring her. Yet he always held back, deliberately keeping her in the dark.

He already knew the answer all too well. To escape the past and to protect her, he had thought. With family and old friends watching, speculating, passing judgment, it would be no picnic. And Eleanor's family would be there, too. That would be rough. He honestly didn't want to subject Rachel to that. Not yet—not when they'd been so happy.

Who was he trying to kid? He and Rachel would have to confront those people sooner or later. Despite his earlier apprehensions, theirs was a serious relationship. For better or for worse, their children already knew it. And Rachel had been open with her family and friends about her relationship with him.

So why couldn't he be as open about the relationship as Rachel? Because the crowd attending that engagement party was an altogether different story from their children and close friends. All Terrance had to do was recall the criticism that had been blasted at Max and Laurie Windom for him to realize even old friends could be derisive and judgmental.

Subjecting Rachel to any unfortunate scene was a consideration for not inviting her to the party. But it wasn't his ultimate concern. With the party only a few days off, Terrance was finally able to admit to himself the real reason for keeping silent. He didn't want to risk losing Rachel. He was afraid the party was one test their relationship might not survive.

When he'd finally acknowledged that fact, Terrance knew the only thing they could do was try. As he approached her house on the museum grounds, he hoped to God she'd forgive him for not saying anything sooner.

He found her in the kitchen preparing dinner. Through the window over the kitchen sink he could see Danny playing with some toys outside on the patio. Terrance was glad he'd have some time alone with Rachel. He wanted to explain to her about the party right away.

She greeted him with a long, fervent kiss before helping him ease off his suit jacket. "It's awfully muggy tonight. You should have gone home first to change into cooler clothes."

As he loosened his necktie, he watched Rachel hang his jacket in the hall closet. Her auburn hair was pulled back off her neck and twisted into a thick braid. She looked comfortable and sexy in deep blue shorts and matching tank T-shirt. "I'll keep cool by looking at you," he remarked slyly, eyeing her great pair of legs.

Returning to the kitchen, she offered him a glass of wine.

"I think we both better have a glass. We have to talk," he informed her.

Her eyes widened. Their color was as luminous and as green as the sea. "That sounds ominous," she said, handing him a chilled bottle of Chablis to open.

"I'm afraid I have a confession to make."

The surprise evaporated from her expression. Now her steady gaze made him suspect that Rachel already knew what he had to tell her. After he said his peace, explaining about the engagement party and apologizing for not saying anything to her about it sooner, she was still clear-eyed and calm.

"I've known about the party for weeks," she admitted. "Martha's mentioned it a couple of times."

"Of course. I should've known you'd hear about it some way or another. Why didn't you say something to me about it?"

She glowered at him. "I was waiting for *you* to say something to me, Terrance."

"Rachel, I'm sorry. I wouldn't blame you if you were furious with me." He meant every word. For frankly, he was surprised that she was being so coolheaded about it. He half expected biting anger or tears of hurt.

"I'm not furious, just disappointed," she claimed, composed and matter-of-fact. "And I do understand why you might be hesitant to bring me to the party, Terrance. I really do. I wish you hadn't deliberately kept it secret from me, that's all."

"It was an asinine thing to do—something I truly regret. I want you to come to the party very much. I'd be proud to have you at my side and to introduce you to everyone. It's short notice I know, but will you come with me?"

Her face turned pale as she stared at him with obvious distress. "I wish you had said something sooner. It's too late now. I've already made plans for Saturday night."

"But it's a special night. I know Kerry and Martha would be happy to have you there. Can't you rearrange whatever it is?"

"No I can't," she snapped.

Stunned by her sharp reply, Terrance stared at her in bewilderment.

Looking contrite, Rachel moved close against him and curled her arms around his shoulders. "As much as I want to be with you Saturday night, something else has come up," she revealed, her voice softly tender. "A former colleague is in town on business and he wants to visit me. He's going back to Washington Sunday morning, and Saturday is the only day he has a few spare hours. Besides Terrance, I'd honestly given up on the party."

"You had every reason to," he reassured, despite his great disappointment. "My loss though, and entirely all my own fault."

At least Rachel had forgiven his lapse of good sense. They said little else about the engagement party or her visiting colleague. The rest of the evening passed pleasantly—as if all had been resolved. But had it really? This question lingered on in Terrance's mind for the next three days. For although Rachel's behavior was as loving as ever, Terrance sensed an air of apprehension about her. She seemed uncharacteristically tense at times. And often, in the midst of a conversation, she would get a look in her eyes that indicated her mind had just drifted away to who knew where.

Terrance wondered if she was angrier about the engagement party than she'd let on. Or perhaps her apprehension had something to do with her Saturday night dinner guest. The thought made him uneasy. She hadn't made much of this fellow—Tom French, he thought Rachel said his name was. Just an old friend from

Washington, she said. But she also had said it was important for her to see him. Why important?

By Saturday, Terrance was distracted enough by these questions that he made an unplanned stop at Rachel's on his way to the party out in Wellesley. Although she hadn't been expecting him, she welcomed him with a broad smile.

"Come into the kitchen," she said, leading the way. "I have a white sauce just starting to bubble on the stove. Got to keep an eye on it."

Right away he knew he shouldn't have come. After cooking and enjoying so many meals with her, to watch her cook for another man felt strangely disturbing. He noticed that the table in the dining alcove was elegantly set for two. He knew Danny was in New Hampshire with his father. And the fact that she looked so radiant in a casual, loose-flowing turquoise dress didn't help matters much. He acknowledged that there wasn't any actual justification for the feeling these things aroused in him. Yet, justified or not, he was jealous.

"Your guest hasn't arrived yet, I see," he noted nonchalantly.

"He should be here any minute. Why don't you wait?"

Considering his frame of mind, Terrance didn't think that was good idea. "I can't sweetheart. I promised Kerry I'd get there early. I just dropped by to tell you I'll miss you tonight." He meant it with all his heart.

Gazing at him with much tenderness, Rachel turned off the heat beneath the pan of white sauce. She came up to him and kissed him on the lips. He wrapped his arms around her and held her warm body hard against him. Her lovely, subtle fragrance was arousing.

He murmured lowly into her ear. "I've been a fool about this damn party. I wish you were coming with me."

"It's probably for the best," she said, resting her head on his chest. "It's Kerry and Martha's night. Together, you and I might attract too much attention at the party. That wouldn't be right."

When the doorbell rang, Terrance instinctively tightened his arms around her. She gradually eased away from him, however, to go open the door.

"Rachel, it's been so long," the man declared, swooping her into his arms.

Rachel returned the sentiment, hugging him briefly. "It's so good to see you, Tom. I'm glad you got in touch with me."

For just a moment, Tom seemed hesitant. "Are you sure?"

"Of course, I'm sure," she replied, her face beaming.

That's when it struck Terrance who this visitor was. Although Rachel had never put a name to the man she was involved with in Washington, he had no doubt that Tom French had to be that person. All the pieces started to fit, and with it his uneasiness grew.

While she was introducing Tom to him, Terrance surmised that he was around the same age as Rachel. Fair-haired, deeply tanned, well dressed and neatly groomed right down to his trim mustache, Tom was a good-looking young man in his prime. Experiencing an involuntary pang of jealousy, Terrance wondered about their past relationship. Rachel never had gone into much detail about her feelings for the man.

Terrance knew he'd better leave. He was reacting like a lovesick young teenager rather than a forty-eight-year-old man. By tomorrow morning the engagement party would be history, and Tom French would be heading back to Washington. Then he and Rachel could get their lives back on track.

Rachel folded her arm around his and walked him to the front door. He had to admit her fervent goodbye kiss was gratifying. Unfortunately, Terrance caught French's startled reaction to Rachel's demonstrative farewell. Was Tom wondering why Rachel was mixed up with an old guy like him? Terrance mused as the door clicked shut behind him.

He found it hard not to think about Rachel and Tom as he drove out to Wellesley. Terrance soon realized that French's look of surprise when Rachel kissed him was bothering him much more than it should have. He wondered if Rachel had seen Tom's response.

When he arrived at the party, Kerry was the first person he saw. Oddly enough, his younger son was standing alone in the entrance hallway, drinking a glass of champagne. Still, Terrance was glad to see that Kerry had cleaned up his act for the occasion. With a haircut, new dark suit and black shoes, his son looked quite presentable. Reaching out to straighten the knot in Kerry's conservative tie, Terrance winked at him fondly. "You look great tonight, son. Nice suit."

Kerry strained his neck against his shirt's crisp collar. "You like it?" he asked. "Gordon helped pick it out. It was a compromise actually. Martha and her Aunt Allison were really pushing to make this a formal party. But that's where I drew the line. Wearing this is one thing, but black tie? No way."

"Well, I hope Martha wasn't too disappointed."

"She got over it," Kerry said. "This time anyway," he added with a shrug.

Kerry's offhanded remark reminded Terrance that he hadn't yet had that talk with Kerry. The two of them never seemed to have the opportunity to sit down alone and talk. This engagement party, however, was not the place to discuss the second thoughts Kerry might have about marrying.

"Is Gordon here yet?" Terrance asked, scanning the room for a sign of his older son.

"Oh yeah. He was with Martha just a while ago. I left them debating the merits of domestic versus imported champagne. A real heavy-duty conversation," Kerry cracked with a trace of disdain. "Of course Gordon favors French, so Martha calls him a snob, and then the two of them are off and running. That's when I left."

"You think you should've left those two arguing?"

"I haven't heard any fireworks yet. Martha's too well-mannered to start a yelling match with Gordon at her own engagement party. Once a debutante, always a debutante. Besides, she knows her mother would have a fit."

Hearing Kerry speak with such uncharacteristic scorn shocked Terrance. He made every effort to keep his voice low. "What the hell's gotten into you, son?" he demanded.

Kerry gave him a blank stare. His eyes were glassy and unfocused.

"How much have you had to drink already?"

"It's only champagne, Dad—imported of course. Besides, who's counting?" Kerry asked, his voice getting louder. "It's a party. A party for me."

Checking around them, Terrance was thankful to see they were still alone in the hallway. He knew, however, that he'd better get his son out of there before Kerry said or did something he'd regret.

Although Kerry balked at first, he finally allowed Terrance to escort him outside. Terrance kept a firm arm around Kerry's shoulder as his son walked on unsteady feet. "How much of that stuff did you drink?" he asked as Kerry stumbled across the driveway.

"Just a couple of glasses, Dad. Honest."

Smiling to himself, Terrance shook his head. "I believe you, son. We Nelsons never could hold our liquor."

"Aw Dad, I'm not drunk."

"Yet," Terrance warned as they reached a secluded part of the grounds. It was very dark outside as murky clouds hid the moon and stars. His eyes gradually adjusted to the gray darkness. The night air was crisp, however, which was just what Kerry needed to clear his head. He instructed Kerry to take a few deep breaths. Then Terrance looked him straight in the eye. "Now tell me, what is the matter with you?"

"Too much to drink."

"Besides that."

"Nothing, Dad. You're making a big deal out of nothing."

Exasperated, Terrance realized he couldn't wait on that talk with Kerry any longer. "Do you still want to get married to Martha this fall?"

Staring wide-eyed at Terrance, Kerry was clearly taken aback by his directness.

"If you're having second thoughts you should say something," Terrance urged. "If not to me then at least to Martha."

Kerry moved away from Terrance, stuffing his hands in his pockets and staring down at the grass. "I love Martha."

"Enough to marry her?"

"Of course," Kerry replied without hesitation. "I've always loved Martha, Dad. You know that."

"But enough to get married, Kerry?" Terrance implored. "It's a tremendous step to take."

Kerry lifted his head, his blue eyes defiant. "Don't you think I know that? Martha and I love each other and we're going to get married. It's what she wants and what I want."

Terrance studied Kerry's intense expression. "Are you sure?"

"What do I have to do, Dad? Make an oath in blood or something?" he belligerently suggested. "Why don't you trust me to know what I'm doing?"

"That's difficult to do when I arrive here to find you already tipsy and making arrogant, almost snide comments about your fiancée."

Suddenly Kerry's intensity shattered into peals of laughter. Terrance was bewildered, and getting angry. "Damn it, Kerry. I don't understand you at all."

"Dad, I'm sorry. Really," Kerry said, his manner softening toward Terrance. "Now I understand why you're getting bent out of shape. But you've got it all wrong, Dad. Believe me."

His gaze narrowed. "I've got it all wrong?"

"About the way I was acting. It's this party, this extravaganza. It's not my kind of scene," Kerry explained. "I guess just being here put me on edge. So I drank more than I should have and said some things I really didn't mean. You know I think the world of Martha."

"Yes I do," Terrance concurred. "And I also know that this type of party is very much Martha's kind of scene. How are you going to manage a lifetime full of them if they disturb you so much? Get drunk every time?"

"No! It won't be like that—"

"Hey, Dad! Kerry!"

Gordon's voice echoed through the darkness. Terrance looked back toward the house, spotting his older son's silhouette emerging from the shadows. "I've been looking all over for you two," he announced. "Martha's frantic, Kerry. Everyone's asking her where you are."

"I'd better go in," Kerry muttered, straightening his shoulders. He hurried off, no longer staggering. Terrance was relieved that the fresh air had done Kerry some good. But he was still terribly concerned for Kerry.

"I assume it's not going to do me any good to ask what was going on out here," Gordon remarked as he and Terrance headed back toward the house.

"You assume correctly."

"Trouble in the youngster's paradise no doubt."

Terrance didn't bother to reply.

Keeping in step with Terrance's brisk pace, Gordon dropped the subject of his brother in favor of another. "Well, I'm glad I found you. Now you can answer all the questions about your lady friend."

Terrance stopped abruptly. "What do you mean?"

"Everyone kept asking me if she was coming to the party with you. But, since Mrs. Bonner is nowhere to be seen, I gather you came stag. That was probably a wise choice, Dad."

"It wasn't a choice, Gordon. Just circumstance. I wish Rachel *was* here."

"Okay, okay. I get the picture," Gordon said as they resumed walking. "At least I warned you. There are a lot of curious people inside."

Indeed there were. The people he cared for the most, like his sister, Liz, and Martha's parents, were open and friendly in inquiring about Rachel. The others didn't matter. Terrance was oblivious to much of what was happening around him. He found it difficult to get into a festive mood when he was thinking about Rachel and how much he missed having her by his side.

He did manage to keep a watchful eye on his son. Kerry seemed subdued, yet he was trying hard to live up to his position as guest of honor of this elaborate affair. He remained at Martha's side for the rest of the party, politely greeting their many well-wishers. And he didn't touch another drop of liquor.

Terrance realized he wasn't doing nearly as well in his own role as father of the groom to be. He was too distracted by thoughts of what might be happening back at Rachel's house to concentrate on the niceties of party conversation. The fourth time he caught himself blankly staring into space when another guest was speaking to him, Terrance decided to get out of there.

By that time he could no longer ignore what had been gnawing at his subconscious for hours. At least now he could admit it to himself, Terrance thought as he said his goodbyes to the hosts and to the kids. Hell, Kerry wasn't the only one he was worried about having second thoughts. Terrance knew now that he was worried—no, afraid—that the reappearance of Tom French might have given Rachel some second thoughts of her own.

The need to see Rachel, to talk to her about his fears, helped him drive the stretch of Route 9 from Wellesley to Brookline in record time. Larry, the night guard, waved Terrance's car through the museum gates without calling ahead to Rachel. She had instructed all the guards to let Terrance in at any time.

As he slowly drove up the long, winding driveway, Terrance hoped Rachel was still awake. The illuminated dial on his car's dashboard revealed that it was almost midnight. "Be awake Rachel, please," he muttered under his breath.

He knew his fears were probably groundless. After all, Rachel loved him now, not a man of the past. Still, Terrance needed to see that special smile meant only for him and to feel her arms around him in a welcoming embrace. He wanted to kiss her, hold her and make love to her all night long—to know, to be reassured that she was indeed his, no matter what.

But just as his car rounded the last curve before Rachel's house, Terrance spotted the beige sedan still parked in her yard. He recognized it at once. It was Tom French's rental car.

Feeling as though he'd just had the wind knocked out of him, Terrance grasped the steering wheel tightly, so tightly his knuckles turned white. His foot gently tapped the brake and he dimmed his car's headlights. He relaxed his grip on the wheel, but otherwise he didn't move a muscle. He couldn't.

Dazed, he stared at Rachel's cozy little house for quite some time. The lights in the house were on—just as they'd been when he left for the party hours earlier. Terrance glanced at the dashboard clock again. Obviously she and Tom had a lot to talk about, a lot of years to catch up on.

Suddenly he felt weary and about a hundred years old. With a stiff, deliberate yank of the gear stick, he shifted the car into reverse and slowly backed away from her house.

Chapter Twelve

It was an unusually brisk morning for late July. The sun was bright in the cloudless sky, yet the air was dry. This Sunday morning had the snap of early autumn rather than the enervating humidity more commonplace in midsummer Boston. Rachel was pleased. Gazing out her bedroom window, she considered the weather a gift—a gorgeous, comfortable Sunday to spend with the man she loved.

Last night had helped her realize just how deeply she loved Terrance. Her visit with Tom had been a healing one. They had talked late into the night, resolving the loose ends that had frayed the memory of their former relationship for years. Rachel could see how much Tom had changed over the years. He had definitely matured. But then, she supposed, so had she.

Now Tom was planning to get married. He had claimed he was ready and that he had finally found the right woman. Rachel was happy for him. She could also identify with his feeling about having found the right person. For that was exactly how she felt about Terrance.

Yes, Greg had been her first love, the love of an inexperienced young girl who hadn't yet realized what she really wanted out of life. And yes, she had once been in love with Tom. But she had never *loved* either one of them the way she loved Terrance. The intervening years had changed her. The mistakes, the pain and the triumphs had molded her, strengthened her, helped her grow until she was ready, really ready to love someone again. She was so glad that Terrance was that someone. Now she couldn't wait for him to arrive; there was so much she wanted to tell him.

She showered quickly and carefully chose an outfit to wear. Although they were just driving out to Concord for brunch at The Colonial Inn, a date they'd made days ago, Rachel wanted to look as good as she felt today. Knowing Terrance liked her best in green, she selected the mint-colored sundress she had bought last summer. She hadn't worn it yet this year because of the weight she had gained. When she slipped the dress over her head today, however, the soft cotton knit clung gently to the same curves it had hugged too tightly in early June. Apparently the tennis lessons with Ilsa and all those lowcal lunches had finally started working, Rachel thought happily as she checked the mirror. Stepping into a pair of tan open-toed pumps, she heard a car door slam outside.

Terrance was a good twenty minutes early. Not that she minded at all. She hurried to the door to let him in, fully prepared to throw her arms around him. When she swung open the front door, however, she was taken aback by his appearance. Wearing white slacks and a royal-blue knit shirt, he looked as neatly dressed and groomed as ever. But it was his face, tired and drawn, as well as the weary cast in his usually twinkling eyes that caught her attention.

"Boy, that must have been some party last night," she joked, hoping to elicit a smile from Terrance.

His expression remained flat as he breezed past her. "It was interesting."

Terrance was obviously not himself this morning. Had something awful happened at the party last night? Before she had a chance to question him, Terrance walked into the living room. He didn't kiss her hello, didn't touch her. In fact, he gave her nothing more than a perfunctory glance, which wasn't like him at all.

Suddenly, apprehension threatened her good spirits. She followed him into the living room. She sat on the sofa; he sat in the blue velvet wing chair on the other side of the coffee table. Exasperated, she finally spoke up. "Terrance, what's the matter? Did something happen last night?"

"A lot happened last night."

She gasped, leaning forward anxiously. "Kerry and Martha?"

"Kerry got drunk and then promptly declared his love for Martha. Seems like the wedding is on," he said dryly. Eyeing her coolly, he added, "Could I have a cup of coffee?"

Bewildered by his tone of voice, Rachel glanced at the clock on the mantel. "I'll have to brew some. Do you think we have time? Our reservation at the inn is for eleven."

"We have time."

"All right," she said calmly, masking her growing irritation.

Rachel marched straight into the kitchen and began making a small pot of coffee. What the heck had gotten into him? she asked herself. Here she'd been feeling so gloriously happy all morning long, and then Terrance shows up acting like he'd gotten up on the wrong side of bed. Her resentment grew as she measured and poured.

Too bad she didn't have any instant coffee in the house, she mused ruefully, knowing full well that Terrance hated the stuff. It's just what he deserved.

She decided to wait until the coffee finished brewing before returning to the living room. Maybe a good strong cup of black coffee would cure whatever ailed him. She honestly loved the man, but he did have his moments. Although Terrance was pretty wonderful, he wasn't perfect. But then, she probably wouldn't love him so much if he was perfect.

Standing at the counter as the automatic drip coffee maker gurgled and swished, Rachel wondered what had sparked Terrance's strange behavior. She suspected it had something to do with Kerry. Whatever it was, she hoped he'd get over it by the time she brought him his coffee.

To her surprise, Rachel heard his approaching footsteps on the tile floor. Stubbornly refusing to look at Terrance, she kept her gaze glued to the rapidly filling glass coffeepot.

She turned to him briefly. His face was pale and lined with fatigue. She detected a sadness in his gray eyes. Returning her gaze to the coffee maker, she said softly. "Care to tell me what's bothering you?"

He didn't answer for an alarmingly long time. Her heart began pounding frantically; her entire body became rigid with fear. She felt his hand on her shoulder. He gave it an affectionate squeeze, but his touch did little to relieve her mounting tension. She bowed her head, waiting for him to say something—anything.

And then he finally did. "Was Tom French your close call in Washington?"

Rachel spun around to face him. "Is that what this is all about? Tom?"

Terrance gaze was expectant. And unhappy. "Is he the one?" he asked again.

"Yes, but there's no reason for you to be upset. We just had dinner and talked. We had an awful lot to catch up on."

"I know. I came back here last night around midnight. Tom was still here, so I left," he explained. The hand that had been resting on her shoulder fell to his side.

Desperately wanting to keep some physical contact with Terrance, Rachel grasped each of his hands in her own. "Why didn't you come in? You should have."

"I assumed you two had a lot to talk about. I didn't want to intrude."

"You wouldn't have," she implored, her eyes searching his. "In fact we talked about you. And Tom told me about the woman he's marrying in just a few weeks. We also discussed what had happened between us all those years ago. And I'm glad we did, because it helped me to finally resolve the hurt I still felt about why he and I broke up." She squeezed Terrance's hands firmly.

"And why did you and Tom break up?"

"You know why," she replied, puzzled that he'd even asked.

"Because you wouldn't be able to bear him children, and he couldn't accept that."

The tone of his voice, detached, unemotional, was unnerving. It was as if he were deliberately trying to distance himself from her. That made her angry—and scared. "Terrance, why are you being so cold?" she pleaded, holding onto his hands for dear life.

"I don't mean to be, but I'm very tired. I was up most of the night thinking."

"About us?"

"About you." He looked directly into her eyes. Then he led her to the kitchen table. "Come sit down."

The physical distance between them widened as Terrance sat across the round oak table from her. Emotions ranging from panic to irritation were whirling inside her like a tornado. "Tell me what you thought," she finally said, her voice sounding raspy to her ear.

"I know you care for me. But maybe, just maybe, your feelings for me have more to do with your sterility than either of us has wanted to admit."

His words pierced her heart like a knife. "Terrance, why?"

His eyes were filled with compassion, but his reply held nothing back. "Perhaps, deep down, you were afraid that another young man would reject you for the same reason Tom did. Then I came along—an older man with grown children of his own, a man who couldn't care less about having more children. Maybe, subconsciously, I seemed like a safe choice to you."

Rachel was stunned. She didn't know what to say.

Realizing this, Terrance continued. "I strongly feel this is something you should think about long and hard, Rachel. In the long run, you might be happier with a man closer to your own age, someone who has enough sense to want you for the wonderful woman you are and nothing more."

"I thought you were that man, Terrance," she said with a composure that belied the hurt and resentment welling up in her heart.

"For the wrong reasons, I'm afraid," he said, rising from the table. He walked over to her, stopping behind her chair, caressing her shoulders with his hands. "If we don't face it now, we'll both end up with regrets."

She shrank from his touch and got to her feet at once. She felt betrayed by Terrance's assertion. After all they had been through together, all those bridges they had to cross and did, all the pain and joy. Even after all that, Terrance's everlasting ambivalence was rearing its ugly head again. Rachel's anger came to a furious boil.

"You know what you're doing, don't you?" she lashed out at him, bitterness rising in her voice. "You're pushing me away—again—by claiming it's for my own good. In the end I'll be happier with someone my own age, you say. Why can't you accept that these past weeks with you have been the happiest of my life?" She backed away from him. "You're the one who always, *always* had trouble handling our age difference, not me. That's why you waited until the last minute to invite me to Kerry's engagement party. I knew about it for weeks before you said one word about it. How do you think that made me feel?"

"Obviously a lot angrier than you had let on a few days ago. Why didn't you tell me how upset you were then, instead of keeping it all bottled up inside?"

"Because I was trying to be understanding. Patient. I wanted to give you a chance to work things out for yourself. But you know, Terrance, I've just about had it," she declared, throwing her hands up in frustration. "Your concern about how your friends and family will react to me is really just a smoke screen. After all, why should you worry about other people accepting us as a couple, when deep down you can't even accept it yourself?"

Terrance didn't flinch at her charge. He nodded his head, his voice steady but solemn when he responded. "You may very well be right about that, Rachel," he said simply. "I weigh the pros and cons, I analyze the costs. When we're alone, I'm so happy that I can't imagine my life without you in it. But there are also times when reality slaps me in the face. Then it all seems like a gamble, the risks too great for both of us." Terrance looked at her with regret. "I wish it wasn't so."

But his words couldn't temper her ire. She started pacing around the kitchen table. "I hope you realize the real reason you can't accept us, because it's all too clear to me. It's not those blasted eighteen years. Not really," she asserted, pausing to look Terrance straight in the eye. "You're afraid you might lose me somehow. You lost your wife, so you're not about to take a risk like that again."

She half expected him to deny it, but he didn't. He reached for her hand. When he took it, she realized her hand was clenched into a fist. Terrance looked at it, shaking his head sadly. He gently uncurled her tense fingers and held them flat between his hands. "I'm sorry I hurt you, Rachel."

His tender gesture almost made her fall apart, but she fought hard against it. "What really hurts me, Terrance," she began haltingly, blinking back unwanted tears, "is that I would've risked anything for your love. Until now that is. My head may have needed a few go-arounds with a brick wall before reality sunk in. But now I finally know that you won't or you can't love me enough to overcome those problems."

Terrance breathed a forlorn sigh. "Oh, Rachel, I've learned that sometimes just loving someone isn't enough. I've already lost someone I loved dearly, and the aftermath was like a living death. I've been trying to fight the memory of that pain since the day I met you. But it's still too vivid. Even now."

"You could be right," she commented, withdrawing her hand from his grasp. Suddenly she felt calm and in control. "Maybe we never really had a chance."

Terrance nodded wordlessly. Shadows of fatigue darkened his eyes. He looked older than she'd ever seen him before. "Not now perhaps. Things between us happened so fast, I was caught off guard. I just wasn't ready for this. But if we spent some time apart—a few months to catch up with ourselves—then we could try again."

"No. We couldn't," she replied. "This will have to be a clean break. It's the only way."

"But Rachel—"

"No calls, no contact. It has to be over. Otherwise I don't think I can take it. So please, please promise you'll stay away."

"Stay away? Rachel, that's not what I want."

"This can't go on, Terrance," she insisted. "I can't take it."

A pained expression crossed his face. "If that's what you really want."

Her heart was breaking, but somehow she was able to maintain her composure. "It's what I want."

TERRANCE KEPT HIS WORD and stayed away from her, just as she knew he would. The old school gentleman in him would ensure that he'd honor her wishes. And although she missed him terribly, Rachel was grateful. With each passing week, the pain of their breakup became a little more bearable. She was intent on rebuilding the course of her life, and one visit, one phone call could make a shambles of her progress.

Yet a day never passed by without her thinking about him, worrying if he was all right, or wondering if he was perhaps as lonely as she. Some days were worse than others, and the weekends were always difficult, especially when Danny was visiting Greg and Nancy. Nevertheless, she always remained stubbornly firm against the occasional urge to call Terrance.

The museum was closed to the public during the month of August. While Rachel still went to the office every day, the pace was maddeningly slow, making the quiet summer afternoons seem endless. So when Ilsa suggested they take their kids to Montreal and Quebec City for a week while her husband was in California on business, Rachel jumped at the chance.

Vacationing in Quebec with four kids, the au pair and Ilsa, was more than enough to get her mind off her troubles. The days were full of fun activities with the children. She enjoyed them tremendously. But evenings in those two romantic cities seemed to drag slowly once the kids were in bed. She and Ilsa tried to go out for a few hours each night. As companionable and amusing as Ilsa was, Rachel couldn't completely shake the loneliness that had haunted her since the day she and Terrance had said goodbye.

Ilsa had kept remarkably quiet on the subject of Terrance during the trip—until their last night in Quebec City. The two of them were dining at a highly recommended restaurant that specialized in French Canadian cuisine, when Rachel pushed away her bowl of split pea soup. She had eaten only a couple of spoonfuls.

"No appetite again, Rachel?" Ilsa said, frowning. "We have several more courses to go, and you are quitting already? You have eaten so little this week, even with all this marvelously fattening food surrounding us. You are wasting away to nothing. I can't stand it!"

"You're getting carried away," Rachel scoffed. "The only part of me that has wasted away is the last of that weight I gained last year. And personally, I'm pleased."

Ilsa scrunched her face into a disparaging grimace. "Personally, I'd rather have you plump and happy, than svelte and depressed. Please call Terrance when we get home."

Rachel stared down at her bowl of soup. "I don't want to."

"Ooh, Terrance may have been a fool, but you are a stubborn fool," Ilsa accused. "All you have to do is snap your fingers and he would come running. I know it. Why not forgive him?"

"It's not a question of forgiving, Ilsa. I'll admit I was extremely angry with him that last morning we were together, but only because he was pushing me away for what felt like the umpteenth time," Rachel explained. "Except this last time I could tell he was backing off for good, and frankly I was just fed up. How much can a person put up with?"

Ilsa's reply surprised Rachel. "As much as it takes to be with the man you love," she said, obviously sincere. "For me, it was leaving my family and my country to make a home in a city I had never seen, a place where I knew no one. It was the only way to convince Jimmy that we were meant to be together. Otherwise he would have left me behind in Germany forever, believing he was doing what was best for both of us."

"Like Terrance believes he's doing for us."

"Exactly," Ilsa said, nodding. "Sometimes men are too noble for their own good."

"I'm afraid it's not as simple as that, at least not for Terrance and me. The problems run too deep."

"Maybe. All I am saying is that sometimes a woman has to put up with a lot or possibly end up with nothing."

Rachel contemplated Ilsa's words for several days. But once she and Danny were back home and settled into their daily routines, she decided that her friend's supposition had little to do with the reality of her own situation.

The Labor Day holiday arrived, marking the end of the summer and the end of Danny's reading sessions with Kerry. Despite her breakup with his father, Kerry kept diligently working with Danny. She never said a word to Kerry about what had happened, and thankfully, neither did he. Now Danny was going back to school and Kerry had to concentrate on his wedding, which was little more than a month away.

Kerry had been her last real link with Terrance. Now he too was gone. Her relationship with Terrance seemed to be drifting away into yesterday's hazy memories, becoming yet another ghost for her past. The thought made her sad.

Unfortunately, the end of Kerry's tutorial had an unanticipated affect on Danny. It made him feel Terrance's absence in their lives much more keenly. At the time of the breakup, Rachel had explained to him that Terrance wouldn't be coming around anymore. He had understood and accepted it, or so she had thought. She realized now, however, that Danny had been so wrapped up with Kerry that he hadn't yet fully experienced the void caused by Terrance's departure. Now he was. He wasn't very happy about it. "I liked talking to Terrance, Mom," he told her one night before bed. "He really listened to me. Some grown-ups only pretend to. Terrance didn't pretend. It won't be the same now without him, will it, Mom?''

Danny was right, nothing was the same. For the time being, life seemed to have lost some of its luster. Rachel couldn't work up a great deal of enthusiasm over her new projects for the museum's fall and winter season. She had done virtually nothing but make airline reservations for her upcoming buying trip to San Francisco. A large estate was liquidating and she really needed to make advance inquiries about some of the major art pieces being auctioned off. And even her enjoyment of autumn, her favorite time of year, had diminished. She only felt regret at seeing the trees gradually turning gold and red with the cooler weather. They served as just another reminder of how much time had passed since she had last seen Terrance.

During the last week in September, however, the last warm spell of Indian summer befell the Boston area. One balmy morning, the doorbell rang just after Rachel had managed to get Danny dressed in school clothes comfortable enough for the sudden spurt of warmer temperatures. As Danny dashed off to answer the door, Rachel wondered who it could be. The guard at the front gate usually phoned to advise her of unexpected visitors.

''Kerry!'' Danny squealed with delight.

By the time Rachel reached the door, she found Kerry playfully roughhousing with a giggling Danny. But he stopped as soon as he noticed her. ''Hi Rachel,'' he greeted. ''I'm sorry to show up so early in the morning but I really need to talk with you.''

He looked so tired and bedraggled, as if he hadn't slept in days. The urgent tone in his voice alarmed her. Something was wrong.

Chapter Thirteen

Her first thought was of Terrance.

"Are you here about your father? Is there something wrong?"

"Oh no, Dad's okay, really," Kerry hastened to reassure her. "But this does have something to do with him—in a way." He glanced awkwardly at Danny. "Don't you have a school bus to catch or something, pal?"

Danny balked at the idea of leaving when Kerry had just arrived. But Kerry promised to come back to see him after school. Appeased, Danny ran off in plenty of time to make his bus.

Accepting her offer of coffee, Kerry sat down at the kitchen table with Rachel. She poured him a cup and then waited. He fidgeted with his teaspoon long after he had stirred sugar into his cup. She could see he was finding it difficult to talk about whatever was on his mind.

"Kerry, is it the wedding?" she gently prodded.

He looked up from his coffee. "I figured you'd understand. That's why I came. I can't go through with it, Rachel. I just can't. And I don't know who else I can talk to about it."

"You could discuss this with your father. I know he'd understand."

"Maybe about not wanting to get married. But it's more complicated than that. I also don't want to join the company. I never really did. And I don't know how to tell him," he explained, shaking his head.

"Hmm, I see what you mean." She knew Terrance would be very disappointed.

"I do love Martha, but I'm not sure I'm ready to settle down yet. I thought I was. But as the wedding gets closer, the less sure I become."

"Well, that feeling happens to a lot of people just before they get married," she offered. "It's called cold feet."

Kerry nodded. "I used to think that was the problem. But it isn't. You see, Rachel, I've finally realized what I want to do with my life. And becoming a teacher is just not going to cut it with Martha."

"A teacher? When did you decide that?"

"Probably when I was still in college tutoring the local kids. I just never allowed myself to acknowledge it," Kerry admitted. "Odd as it sounds, my becoming a teacher seemed as farfetched as my becoming a rock singer or an astronaut. It's always been assumed that I'd help Gordon run Nelson Business Machines."

"So you've never talked about this even to Martha?"

"No. I had resigned myself to the fact that I'd be joining NBM after the wedding. Only after I began working with Danny did I realize just how much I wanted to teach."

"Martha strikes me as someone who could understand that," Rachel commented.

"Or at least she'd try to understand," Kerry added. "But she's expecting the life of an executive's wife, not a teacher's. She'd be better off married to someone like Gordon."

Just like your father thinks I'd be better off with a man my own age, she recalled with some irony. Yet Kerry sounded so forlorn that her heart went out to him. She gave his hand a reassuring squeeze. "You just might be underestimating Martha. You should go see her right away. Try to straighten things out. The longer you wait, the harder it will be."

Leaning back in the chair with a weary sigh, Kerry ran a hand through his curly brown hair. "It's going to be rough. And so is telling Dad. He's been feeling pretty low since—since," Kerry glanced at her sheepishly, "well, you know."

Feeling slightly embarrassed, Rachel looked down at her hands as she spoke. "I'm sure Terrance will be there for you no matter what. He loves you and your brother very much. He may be surprised by your choice, but I think he'll support it."

"Yeah, once he gets over the shock," Kerry noted as he rose to his feet. He thanked her profusely for listening to him. "I'll admit I was skeptical about you at first, Rachel. Now I'm truly sorry that things didn't work out between you and Dad."

As she walked him to the door, Kerry promised that he would talk to both Martha and Terrance before he came back to see Danny that afternoon. Feeling like a protective mother hen, she offered Kerry a few more words of encouragement before bidding him goodbye.

Poor Kerry and Martha. They both had a rough day ahead of them. So did Terrance. Although they weren't actually a part of her life anymore, she couldn't help thinking about the three of them all day long.

"I MUST ADMIT I'm rather ashamed of myself," Terrance told Kerry. "You'd been sending me signals about not wanting to work here and I ignored them. I guess it proves that sometimes we hear only what we want to hear."

"It's my own fault, Dad. I should have just come out and said I don't want to join the business. I was afraid I'd hurt you."

"I know, son." He gazed fondly at Kerry sitting across the desk from him. His initial shock at Kerry's announcement had evolved into proud respect. His younger son had faced the truth and then dealt with its difficult repercussions like a man. Seeing these signs of maturity and decisiveness in Kerry at long last helped to soften the disappointing blow to his long held dream. But after all, it was *his* dream, not Kerry's. He truly believed that Kerry had finally taken the first step toward making his own way in the world.

"I know I hurt Martha," Kerry acknowledged, "although she took it better than I expected she would. At least she doesn't hate me."

"She couldn't hate you."

"Maybe in a couple of years we could try again. It's not as if a teacher's salary would be my only source of income."

Terrance chuckled. "No, money is one thing you'll never have to worry about. As long as you're productive and feel fulfilled, then you'll make it. If, someday, you and Martha get back together—so much the better."

Leaning forward in the chair, Kerry peered at him with intense blue eyes. "Any chance of you and Rachel getting back together? She was wonderful to me this morning."

"I'm not surprised. She's a pretty wonderful person," he remarked, feeling a tad envious that his son had seen her, had been with her just a few hours before. "As for us getting back together—I doubt it. It's been almost two months since we've last seen each other. Rachel has probably put it behind her."

As much as it rankled him to say that, Terrance believed it to be true. During the past months he had hoped that he might hear from Rachel, but of course he never did. Once or twice he had gone so far as to dial her number, only to hang up before the phone began to ring. After all, she had insisted their parting be final. And there was his promise to stay away from her, a promise he felt honor-bound to keep no matter how often and how strongly he was tempted to contact her. After the heartache he caused her, he owed her at least that much. Still, he missed her very much.

His secretary buzzed him to advise that his two o'clock appointment had arrived.

"That's okay, Dad," Kerry said when Terrance told him he had to leave. "I've got to get back to the Bonner's. I promised Danny a game of catch after school. But how about dinner tonight? I want to talk to you about graduate school."

"Sure. Come back about six." Terrance walked with Kerry into the outer office. "And say hello to Danny for me."

Terrance was glad there was someone waiting to see him right away because he needed the distraction. In mentioning Rachel, Kerry had reawakened his longing for her. Wasn't that always the way? Terrance mused wryly. Whenever he thought he had the desire and the memories under control, something would happen to set them off again.

Hell, he should be over her by now. What had happened was really for the best, he would remind himself again and again. Yet, he would sometimes stray from that conviction, worrying if perhaps he had made a terrible mistake. He couldn't stop himself from remembering her soft embraces, or her tender charm, or her warm smile. He had been and still was so in love with her.

His meeting did distract him for a few hours. Then later in the afternoon, he attempted to call Martha several times. He never reached her. He did contact her parents, however, and offered them his assistance in cancelling the myriad wedding arrangements. He thought about phoning Rachel—to thank her for her kindness to his son—but he held back. He didn't think it would be a wise thing to do.

When Kerry returned at six, the two of them stopped by Gordon's office to invite him to join them at Locke-Ober for dinner. His secretary informed them that Gordon had suddenly dashed out of the office after receiving a call from a young lady at around one o'clock. "He told me he wasn't sure he'd be back today and to cancel all his afternoon appointments. That's all," Mrs. Payne revealed.

Running out of the office like that was a rather curious thing for his elder son to do. It must have been some special young lady who called. Eventually though, thoughts of Gordon were overshadowed by his dinner conversation with Kerry. He was particularly interested in Kerry's description of his afternoon visit with Danny Bonner. Sipping a gin and tonic, Terrance listened to his son intently for some mention of Rachel. Unfortunately, Kerry had very little to say about her.

Why couldn't he get his mind off Rachel today? Even as Kerry changed the subject from Danny to education courses at Boston University, Terrance was still besieged with questions about her.

It only got worse when he returned home. The place was just too quiet. Too solitary. Since he and Rachel had split up, the condo had again become just a place to hang his clothes and sleep. The emptiness he'd been feeling for almost two months had become oppressive. He was glad now that he had arranged to take some time off to get away by himself. He wasn't sure where he was going yet, perhaps up the Maine Coast or maybe visiting friends on Long Island. It didn't really matter. In a couple of days he'd be getting out of Boston, away from all that haunted him. Now that Kerry's wedding was off, he might even extend the trip by a few weeks. He had no reason to rush home now.

Yet the prospect of a vacation did not curb the restlessness plaguing his soul that night, nor keep him from thinking of Rachel. "To hell with that ridiculous promise," he muttered aloud, finally reaching for the telephone on his night table.

Driven by the overwhelming need to know how she was, Terrance quickly tapped out the number that was etched in his memory. She answered after the third ring.

"Rachel," he barely managed to murmur. The sound of her voice had made him pause as images of her lovely face flashed through his mind.

"Hello, Terrance."

"I hope I'm not calling at a bad time."

"No, I was just reading."

Relieved to hear she was alone, he breathed a little easier. "I want to thank you for helping out Kerry."

"No need to thank me. I'm just glad he cleared things up."

"Well, I am grateful." It pained him deeply to hear her voice sounding cool and unrelenting. It was so unlike her.

"Thanks for taking the time to tell me so," she replied, still maintaining that vexing air of detachment.

"Damn it Rachel," he burst out in despair, "That's not why I called at all."

"Terrance," she said in a warning voice, "you promised."

"Yes, and I kept that fool promise two months longer than I should have," he declared. "I've been thinking about you—us—a lot. We should get together and talk about all this again."

When she didn't respond for several seconds, he was afraid she had hung up on him, or was at least considering it. But eventually she answered in a low, carefully measured tone. "No, that wouldn't be wise."

His frustration was rising quickly. "Rachel, I need to know if you're all right."

"I'm fine, Terrance. You shouldn't worry. I'm a survivor, remember?"

Clearly, she meant to keep her guard up with him. She had reason. Besides, she probably had moved ahead with her life, just as he had both hoped and feared she would do. Any question in his mind about the status of her feelings had been succinctly answered.

"Now that I know, I won't be bothering you again, Rachel. But I do have one last thing to say to you."

"What is that?"

He thought he heard her voice falter slightly, but he wasn't certain.

"You were wrong when you said I didn't love you enough, Rachel. Very wrong. If anything, I loved you too much, and that did indeed terrify me. Maybe I'll never be ready to take that kind of risk again."

"Then I feel very sorry for you," she said solemnly. "Goodbye, Terrance."

With tears streaming down her face, she hung up the phone. She finally let go of the sob that she'd been holding back during most of Terrance's phone call. In her dreams, she had often heard him say her name in that disarming, resonant way of his. Then to innocently pick up the phone and hear his voice for the first time in months was enough to unhinge her steely resolve. But out of a strong sense of self-preservation, she had remained calm and firm with him.

She and Terrance were just not meant to be. Rachel had been telling herself that every day for two months. Why didn't she believe it yet? He loved her, but wouldn't risk the commitment love required. Why couldn't she accept that? Living in the limbo of his ambivalence had been too painful. So why couldn't she forget Terrance and get on with her life?

She wished he had never called. In despair, she tossed the book she'd been reading onto the coffee table. She would just have to put the phone call out of her mind. Nothing had changed. Wiping her tear-stained cheeks with the back of her hand, Rachel marched into her bedroom. Sleep would rescue her from troubling thoughts. Besides, she had to get some rest. She had reservations on a morning flight to San Francisco, and then an important appointment at the auction house in the afternoon.

The day's mild temperatures had lingered on into the evening, except now there was a pleasant breeze. As she lay in bed, Rachel gazed at the open window. She watched the sheer white curtain lift and fall with that breeze. It reminded her of those glorious mornings in Terrance's bedroom in Stockbridge, when they would wake up in each other's arms and then gaze out the window at the fresh new day.

She had known such joy that weekend in Stockbridge. Now that joy just underlined her loneliness. She tossed restlessly in her big empty bed for quite some time before she finally gave up all hope of sleeping that night. Terrance weighed too heavily on her mind. She realized it was time she faced some facts.

She had been wrong when she decided nothing had changed after Terrance's call. Everything had changed. Hearing his voice again after two agonizing months made her realize she loved him more than ever—in spite of their age difference, in spite of his fears, in spite of her accusations, in spite of everything. In her heart, she knew they were meant to be together, no matter how many times she told herself the contrary.

Ilsa believed that a person could put up with a lot in the name of love. Well, maybe there was some truth in it. Because now, all the so-called problems between her and Terrance seemed paltry when compared with the great joy they had shared. She made him happy. And he truly loved her; he had admitted that tonight. Surely what they could have together was worth any risk on both their parts. She would make him see the sense in it.

When the radio alarm woke Rachel at seven the next morning, she felt refreshed, but also nervous and excited. One way or another, this was going to be a fateful day. It was already a beautiful one. She stood at her bedroom window, letting the gentle glow of the September sun warm her face. The sky was a deep, cloudless blue, and the air felt slightly more brisk than it had the day before. Pulling on her bathrobe, she headed directly for the phone in the kitchen. Butterflies were running rampant in her stomach as she dialed Terrance's number. She took several deep breaths to relax herself. Then she waited while his line rang countless times, until it was obvious that Terrance wasn't there to answer his phone.

She hadn't expected to be thwarted before she'd even begun. She was so anxious to talk to him, she couldn't stand the thought of waiting one more minute. That's when she decided to go directly to his office. Why waste time with phone calls?

Rachel was brought back to reality when she heard Danny rummaging around in his room. She couldn't leave until he was dressed, fed and picked up by the school bus at eight o'clock. Thankfully, Danny was in a cooperative frame of mind this morning. He got going with relatively little fuss, leaving her time to get ready herself. She showered and changed quickly into the beige shaker knit sweater and brown paisley skirt she had planned to wear that day.

Rachel was beginning to think the heavens were on her side when the taxi she had ordered arrived right after the school bus had pulled away. She had figured a cab driver could make faster headway through the morning rush hour traffic than she could on her own. Yet, amazingly enough, traffic was lighter than usual this morning, and the cab made it downtown in excellent time. As she walked through the glass door of Terrance's office building, overnight bag and briefcase in hand for her trip to San Francisco, Rachel couldn't help but feel that everything was going her way.

Chapter Fourteen

When she reached the receptionist's desk on the penthouse floor, Rachel didn't recognize the young woman sitting there nibbling on an English muffin. The blonde looked slightly befuddled when Rachel asked if Terrance was in his office.

"Mr. Terrance Nelson?" the receptionist mumbled while trying to swallow a morsel of her muffin. "I don't think he's here yet. In fact, I believe I'm the only one here now." She took a brief sip of coffee from a Styrofoam cup. "Wait a second, I heard Mr. Nelson was going on vacation."

Rachel gasped. "Vacation?"

The receptionist nodded. "Yeah, but I can't remember if he was supposed to be leaving today or tomorrow." She thought about it a moment as she took another sip of coffee. "Gee, you know, I'm just not sure when he's leaving," she admitted, benignly shaking her head.

"Can't you find out?" Rachel asked anxiously.

"Well, I don't know how I can, Miss. I'm an office temp filling in while the regular girl is on vacation. I don't know my way around here that well. I'm sure Mr. Nelson's secretary can help you. She usually comes in at nine."

Rachel looked at her wristwatch. It was only eight-thirty.

"Well, well, well, if it isn't Mrs. Bonner."

She spun around as soon as she heard the vaguely familiar voice. It was Gordon, looking as slick and as aloof as ever in his dark pinstripe suit.

"I came to see your father," she told him.

"Oh really? Well, he's not here. He left town this morning."

"He really did go on vacation?"

"That's right. He was supposed to leave tomorrow," Gordon explained. "But for some reason, he suddenly decided he had to take off today. Who knows why. He called my house at the crack of dawn to tell me he'd be gone for a few weeks."

The receptionist slapped her hand on her desk. "I knew he was supposed to leave on vacation tomorrow," she exclaimed. "Didn't I say that?"

Gordon eyed the young woman with dismay. He clearly didn't like her listening in on his conversation. He turned to Rachel. "Why don't we step into my office?"

She followed Gordon down the corridor, her mind in a daze. She couldn't believe she had missed Terrance like that. When they entered Gordon's office, she realized she hadn't been in it since the day she had first met Terrance. Lord, that seemed like an eternity ago, she thought dolefully.

"Dad told me you persuaded Kerry to fess up to Martha yesterday," Gordon said as he put his briefcase on the desk. "That marriage would've been a farce. Kerry did the right thing."

Feeling drained, Rachel sat down in one of the chairs in front of Gordon's desk. "I hope so," she said wearily.

"And Martha will get over it," Gordon continued, leaning against the edge of his desk. "In the long run she wouldn't be happy with my brother. Although yesterday afternoon she kept wailing that she could live on Kerry's terms. But Martha a schoolteacher's wife? Once I got her to calm down, she was able to think that one through. By the end of the afternoon, she was starting to see the light. She's too smart not to."

Rachel was astonished. She gave Gordon a curious look. "You mean Martha went to cry on your shoulder after Kerry broke the engagement?"

He nodded, his mouth curving into a slight, almost self-conscious smile. "Martha and I understand each other—in a fashion. I know it seems like she and I are always at each other's throats, but that's because we know each other all too well." Gordon shrugged and folded his arms over his chest. "I know I can rely on Martha to tell me exactly what she thinks. And she can expect the same from me."

As he talked of Martha, Gordon's voice softened considerably, losing that icy brittleness that Rachel had come to associate with him. Perhaps Terrance's early instincts about Gordon and Martha had been on target after all. Even now, Rachel sensed something might exist between them, even if they weren't yet aware of it themselves. Love does work in mysterious ways.

It sure does, she thought sadly, her own failed mission to get to Terrance was proof positive. Deliberating about what she should do next, Rachel drew herself to her feet. If she was to contact Terrance soon, it would help to have

Gordon's cooperation. Although her own feelings toward him had mellowed considerably in the last ten minutes, she didn't think his attitude toward her had changed much. But she had to try anyway.

"Gordon, I want to get in touch with your father."

"I thought it was over between you months ago."

"Things have changed."

"He didn't say anything about it to me this morning. In fact, he seemed like he was in a big rush to get out of town," Gordon disclosed. "Do you know anything about that?"

Oh God, it was that wretched phone call last night, she recalled frantically. She had been such a witch to him. "Maybe. I'm not sure," she told Gordon. "All I know is that I have to talk to him and I need your help."

Gordon just looked at her, his eyes not giving a single clue as to what he was thinking.

She knew she was on the verge of tears again, but she squinted them back. "Gordon, please. No matter how you may feel about me, I beg you to consider your father's happiness. I love him very much, and I think he loves me. I know I can make him happy."

Gordon averted his gaze from her imploring eyes. She had a sinking feeling that he wasn't going to help her, making it that much harder to find Terrance. Just when she was ready to give up and walk out of his office, Gordon cleared his throat. "Rachel, I don't think you understand how much my father means to me."

"Maybe I don't."

"I admire and respect him more than any man I've met. And I care about him. It took my mother's death before I realized just how much. I was worried for him and skeptical of you. I could think of a dozen reasons why a woman as young as yourself would insinuate herself on a lonely, rich widower.''

"None of those reasons had anything to do with love and caring, did they?''

"I'm afraid not. I guess I'm just a cynic by nature.'' Gordon cast her a candid look. "But I'm not blind,'' he added. "I saw how much happier Dad was after he met you, and I saw how lonesome he was after you two broke up. And now I see how strongly you feel about him.''

"I do, Gordon,'' she said calmly. "And I need to talk to him. Please tell me where I can reach him.''

"Rachel, believe me, I can't tell you that because I just don't know.'' Gordon looked extremely apologetic. "Dad was in such an odd mood when we talked. He wasn't even sure where he was headed. He was going to hop in the car and drive. No set plans. He couldn't even say how long he'd be gone.''

"Do you think he went to Stockbridge?''

"I mentioned the cabin, and he said absolutely not. But he has to contact me eventually. I'll tell him you came by. Then I'm sure he'll try to call you.''

Rachel wasn't so certain of that. What a foolish chase she had led all morning long. It had been hopeless from the start. Here she stood in Gordon's office, both emotionally and physically drained, feeling like a fool.

She knew she could somehow contact Terrance later in the week, but her faith in her plan had diminished greatly. What had she hoped to accomplish by throwing herself at him anyway? Did she really believe she could change his mind? No, it was just a stupid, crazy, desperate move to get him back. Calling him would be just as fruitless. Although she felt like she had aged twenty years in the last few hours, Terrance would still say she was too young, and he would still be afraid to commit to her.

She realized Gordon was staring at her. "Rachel?" he finally said.

"Forget about telling your Dad, Gordon," she told him, shaking her head. "I've got a flight to San Francisco to catch. Maybe I'll give you a call when I get back."

Gordon glanced at his watch. "What time is your flight? Will you have time to make it?"

"Oh sure. It's a United flight at ten-fifteen. I've got plenty of time to get to Logan."

"I'm sorry you missed him, Rachel. Really."

"Perhaps it's better this way after all." Feeling more dejected than she ever had in her life, Rachel slung the strap of her overnight bag over her shoulder and headed out the door.

GORDON'S MOUTH FELL open in astonishment when Terrance knocked gently on his open office door. "Dad! What are you...? I thought you'd left town this morning."

"I did. And as you can see I'm not exactly dressed for work," Terrance said, gesturing to his casual tan slacks and navy blue crewneck sweater.

"But what happened?"

"I'd driven about an hour north of Boston when I changed my mind. Or rather when it finally dawned on me what a damn fool I've been. Oh never mind. I don't have time to explain. I only stopped to let you know I'm in town, and to try to call Rachel one more time. If she still doesn't answer I'm going to camp out on her door-

step. I've got to set things right with Rachel today...
this morning!''

Gordon was on his feet at once. "Rachel?"

The look of total confusion on his son's face puzzled
Terrance. "Yes, Rachel," he said, suddenly curious
about Gordon's reaction. "I've stopped at just about
every public telephone between here and the New
Hampshire border trying to reach her. But there's been
no answer at her house or at her office.''

"Well of course there wasn't."

"What? How do you know that?" he demanded
sharply. "Where is she?"

"She was here just a while ago—I told her you'd left—
I didn't know how—" Gordon sputtered anxiously,
looking more bewildered than confused now.

Terrance grasped his son's shoulder firmly. "Wait a
minute. Rachel was just here?"

Gordon nodded. "She was looking for you. And she
was very disappointed when I told her I didn't know
where you'd gone.''

"Is she on her way back to Brookline?"

"No. She's gone."

"Gone?"

"On a business trip to San Francisco. She left for the
airport from here. But you know, you probably still have
time to call her.''

"What do you mean?" Terrance asked, startled.

"Her flight isn't until ten-fifteen," explained Gordon, checking his wristwatch. "That's not for another
thirty-five minutes.''

"My God, you mean she's sitting over at Logan right
now?"

"Dad, I'm sorry. It didn't even occur to me to explain...I had no...I was just so surprised to even see you here."

Terrance was frantic. "Never mind that now. What airline is she flying?" he demanded as he was halfway out the door.

"United. But you're not thinking of going over there, are you? You'll never make it in time," Gordon warned.

"There's plenty of time," he called over his shoulder as he hurried down the hall toward the elevators. His mind was spinning. She was still here, he could get to her if he hurried. Logan Airport was only a ten minute drive from the financial district.

He caught an elevator just before its doors closed. Although he squeezed past the doors in time, they snapped shut just when he realized Gordon was calling to him. Terrance couldn't make out a word of it, and at this point he didn't care. He was like a horse with blinders on. He only wanted to reach Rachel the quickest, most direct way; he wouldn't be sidetracked.

Terrance jogged to the corner of Milk and Congress Streets to hail a cab. In his frenzy, it hadn't occurred to him that finding a cab at that time of morning might be difficult. After the third one whizzed by him without stopping, he started to panic. When he spotted the next taxi heading his way, he cursed in frustration. It was already carrying a passenger.

As it approached the intersection, however, the taxi slowed down until it stopped practically right in front of him. To Terrance's utter surprise, the passenger hopped out and reached for his wallet to pay the driver.

Struck speechless by his incredibly dumb luck, Terrance just stood there staring until the driver stretched

over to the opened passenger window and called to him,
"Cab, buddy?"

He must have sounded half-crazed when he instructed
the driver to get to Logan as fast as possible. But Terrance didn't care. The driver took him at his word and
wove his cab through the maze of streets at breakneck
speed. By the time they entered the Callahan Tunnel, the
only direct route from town to Logan, Terrance was
feeling confident that he'd arrive with time to spare.

As the cab cruised through the cool, dimly lit tunnel,
Terrance was finally able to relax. Thank God he had realized in time that leaving town now was the worst mistake he could make. What did he think he was doing,
running away from the one thing—the one woman—he
wanted most? So what if their phone conversation last
night was a disaster? He certainly could drum up the
courage to have it out with Rachel face-to-face. No matter what the outcome. She was worth that, and much
much more.

He closed his eyes and imagined what Rachel would
say to him when he found her. He could practically hear
her surprised and—he hoped—pleased voice. Just the
thought was enough to make him smile. Yet as he was
foolishly grinning, he realized the cab had come to a
complete halt.

His eyes abruptly opened. He could see they were still
in the tiled bowels of the two lane tunnel. "What's the
matter?"

The driver looked back over his shoulder at him. "I'm
not sure, Mister. Traffic just stopped. Must be a break-
down up ahead."

His stomach felt as if it were being twisted into excru-
ciating knots as precious minutes ticked away. Being

stuck in the middle of a tunnel was about as stuck as you could get, he said to himself dismally.

The cab driver pulled out a newspaper and began to read. Terrance just stared ahead at the line of immobile cars before them. His head had begun to pound, and he didn't dare look at his watch.

Eventually the roar of starting cars reached his ears. The driver put down his newspaper to start his own vehicle. As the line of cars began moving in a slow trickle, the cabbie glanced at his wristwatch. "Hey, twenty minutes. That's not so bad. I've been jammed under this tunnel for hours."

Twenty minutes lost! He'd never make it now. He urged the driver to hurry anyway. There was always the chance the flight had been delayed. That always happened to him when he traveled.

When they finally reached the United terminal, he flung a twenty dollar bill at the driver and ran inside the building. Making a beeline for the ticket counter, Terrance prayed that Rachel's flight had been delayed. But the ticket agent informed him the flight had left on time, just five minutes before.

"Damn." Terrance slapped the counter with his hand. Then he immediately asked for a reservation on the next flight to San Francisco. He was disappointed, but his resolve to get to Rachel remained strong. He would call Ilsa Baird to find out what hotel Rachel was booked in. He'd catch up with her there.

While the ticket agent was tapping out flight reservations on the computer, Terrance thought he'd heard Rachel's voice. "You're in great shape," he muttered under his breath. "Now you're hearing voices."

"Terrance!"

That was not his imagination. He immediately turned toward the voice. She was about twenty yards away, but he would recognize her from any distance. Yet he still couldn't believe his eyes.

Rachel felt frozen to the spot, unsure of what to do next. There Terrance stood, so handsome and elegant, smiling warmly. Then he started toward her. With her heart beating frantically, Rachel slowly made her way through the crowded terminal. By the time they met, she was breathless. She could only stare at his sexy gray-blue eyes.

His gaze never wavering, he looked at her as if she were the only woman alive. "Rachel Bonner," he murmured, his voice deep and low. "You are a sight for sore eyes."

The next thing Rachel knew, she was wrapped securely in his arms, clinging to him with all the love in her heart. Pressed snugly against his chest, hearing his pounding heart and feeling his hand caressing her back, she lost all sense of time. They just held each other without saying a word.

Finally, Terrance brushed gentle kisses on her hair, her forehead, her lips. "It's been so long," he whispered in her ear, tightening his embrace.

She peered up at him. "Too long."

"Rachel, what about your flight?"

"It's gone."

"I know, but you're not on it."

She gave him a wry smile. "When I heard you were coming, I decided to stick around."

"You knew?"

She nodded. "Gordon had me paged. He told me you were on the way. He also said he tried to get you to wait and call me yourself. But apparently you ran out of the office like—"

"Like a madman," he finished for her.

"Well, those weren't his exact words." She shook her head in amazement. "I still can't believe Gordon called here. He reached me just as we were about to board the plane."

"I told you there was more to him than met the eye."

"There's more of his father in him that I thought."

"And you didn't get on that plane. You waited," he exclaimed, hugging her exuberantly.

That was when she noticed that something of a crowd had gathered around them. "My God, Terrance, people are staring at us."

Terrance took a look about. Then placing a protective arm around her shoulder, he steered her toward a secluded corner of the terminal.

"Do you think I'd hop on that plane knowing you were on your way here?" she continued as soon as they were free of prying eyes.

They found a vacant waiting area where they could be alone. Holding his hand as they sat down, Rachel marveled that she was actually at Terrance's side, touching him, kissing him. She couldn't take her eyes off him; it had been so long since they were together. Now it felt like a beautiful dream. She reached up to stroke his dark brown hair. "I love you Terrance. Very much."

He lifted her free hand to his lips and kissed it. "I know that now," he said, still cradling her hand between his two larger ones.

"But you're going to have to trust that this love is going to last for a very long time. Our pasts can't rule our futures, Terrance. We have to make our own choices and our own happiness, no matter what the cost.'' Rachel paused to see his reaction to what she had said.

He was gazing at her with rapt attention. "Go on," he urged gently.

"My sterility is part of who I am now, I admit that. But it has nothing to do with why I love you," she claimed. "Your fear of loving again still didn't prevent you from falling in love with me."

"No, it didn't," Terrance agreed.

"And as far as I'm concerned, the difference in our ages will only be a problem if we allow it to become one." She looked him straight in the eye. "I don't care a whit about your age. I love the man that you are—all forty-nine years of you."

"Oh Rachel, you've grown quite wise in these last two months," Terrance observed, his approval apparent in his eyes. "Not that you weren't terribly astute before," he added with a wry grin.

"I've had a lot of time to think about us. Believe me, I've thought of little else," she told him.

"On the other hand, I was trying my damnedest not to think about us at all. With very little success, I might add."

"Nice to know I'm hard to forget," she said lightly.

"Impossible." His tone was serious now, the look on his face earnest. "I know I've been selfish, allowing my own concerns to overrule everything else. And in trying to protect myself—and you—I almost lost you for good. But I didn't want to trap you into something you might regret later on."

"Trap? I'd never let myself be trapped into anything," Rachel declared. "Commitment is a choice, Terrance. It's my choice to make."

His gaze was still solemn. "Have you made your choice, Rachel?"

She smiled at him knowingly, her heart bursting with love. "I'm here aren't I?" Leaning toward him, she kissed his lips. "I love you."

He cupped her cheek with his hand. "Thank heavens for that," he murmured.

"And you? Have you made your choice?"

"I made it the minute Gordon told me you had come to the office looking for me." Holding her hand firmly, he gazed into her eyes. "I love you Rachel. We may have some rough times ahead, but there's no one else I'd rather face them with. Will you marry me?"

His smoky gaze set her pulse racing. "Yes," she murmured huskily.

"Soon?"

"Very soon."

He kissed her again, long and hard. "I've wasted a lot of precious time," he whispered against her cheek. "I promise I'll make it up to you."

She pulled back a bit, slyly smiling. "After the merry little chase you led me on this morning—you'd better." She planted a playful kiss on his cheek, before adding a little more soberly, "Just let yourself love me, Terrance. That's all I ask."

"I promise." Glancing around the crowded terminal, he stood up, pulling Rachel to her feet. "Let's go home."

"We have a lot to talk about," she added, resting her head on his shoulder as he curved his arm around her. Her heart felt at peace for the first time in years.

Arm in arm, they slowly strolled toward a side exit. Before they passed through the doors, Rachel paused to take a last wistful look at the crowded room. She'd never forget this place.

Terrance gave her shoulder an affectionate squeeze. "We'll be back, sweetheart. After all, we will have a honeymoon to take. And that's one flight I won't allow you to miss."

With that, Rachel proceeded through the doors into the golden September day, knowing without a doubt that she had made the right choice.

Make Your Christmas Special

TIPS FROM JUDITH YODER

1. Make a few handmade gifts, which are always special to give and to receive.

2. Be on the lookout for Christmas ornaments whenever you're traveling. My family and I enjoy being reminded of the places we've been when we decorate our tree.

3. Find a sing-along *Messiah* at a concert hall or church and sing your heart out.

4. Reserve a baby-sitter for holiday parties—especially New Year's Eve—way in advance.

5. Have an annual Christmas cookie baking party early in the season. It's a great way to get your baking done and also fun to do with a group of friends—but share the clean-up!

6. Remember those less fortunate with gifts. Visit shut-ins. Bring some kids and sing Christmas carols.

7. Spread the family celebration throughout the holiday season so that the Christmas fun won't abruptly end after December 25.

8. Play Christmas music, which will keep you in the holiday spirit even when you're house cleaning for all that company.

9. Share the holidays and your family with friends who must be separated from their loved ones.

10. Keep the Christmas wish of peace and goodwill in your heart throughout the year. Teach your kids to do the same.

AR228-1

Harlequin American Romance

COMING NEXT MONTH

#229 NOTHING IN COMMON by Elda Minger

Burt Thomson shared his home with his two sons, an enormous sheepdog, Wadsworth, and total chaos. When Wadsworth redesigned the neighbor's garden—for the third time—Burt knew he had to get help. Into his home came Sandy Hensley, dog trainer *extraordinaire*. She breezed into his life, too, with the force of a small tornado—and in no time worked her own special magic on the entire Thomson clan.

#230 NOBODY'S BABY by Barbara Bretton

Jill knew she had chosen the wrong man as her driver for the month's trek into the Nevada desert. But was Tony also the wrong man to love? She needed to know, because something wonderful happened, something that gave meaning to all her tomorrows. Despite the medical experts' opinion, Jill had become pregnant.

#231 WHERE THERE'S SMOKE... by Margaret St. George

Sammy had finally mustered her courage and joined a quit-smoking program, but then she found herself seated next to her old flame. But how could she renege on a promise to her kids? She barely had the willpower to kick the habit; how could she possibly overcome those other cravings, the ones that came straight from the heart?

#232 GOLDEN DREAMS by Leigh Anne Williams

Melissa Lane had never wanted to see her Ohio hometown again after she had left it years ago to make a new life for herself. But a speaking tour had brought her back for a one-day visit and then fate stepped in to lengthen her stay. When Melissa looked into the eyes of the boy—now a man—she had left behind, her homecoming became filled with interesting surprises.

ATTRACTIVE, SPACE SAVING BOOK RACK

Display your most prized novels on this handsome and sturdy book rack. The hand-rubbed walnut finish will blend into your library decor with quiet elegance, providing a practical organizer for your favorite hard-or soft-covered books.

Only $9.95

Approximately 16" x 8" when assembled

Assembles in seconds!

To order, rush your name, address and zip code, along with a check or money order for $10.70* ($9.95 plus 75¢ postage and handling) payable to *Harlequin Reader Service*:

Harlequin Reader Service
Book Rack Offer
901 Fuhrmann Blvd.
P.O. Box 1396
Buffalo, NY 14269-1396

Offer not available in Canada.

BKR-1A

*New York and Iowa residents add appropriate sales tax.

**For the millions who can't read
Give the Gift of Literacy**

One out of five adults in North America
cannot read or write well enough
to fill out a job application
or understand the directions on a bottle of medicine.

**You can change all this by joining the fight
against illiteracy.**

For more information write to:
Contact, Box 81826, Lincoln, Neb. 68501
In the United States, call toll free: 1-800-228-8813

**The only degree you need
is a degree of caring**